Searching for Gatsby

A Ronnie Lake Murder Mystery

By

Niki Danforth

Publisher: Pancora Press
Book Design: www.polgarusstudio.com
Cover Design: KT Design, LLC www.kristaft.com

As always, for Dan

INTRODUCTION

The beat-up sedan brakes quickly on the winding back road, its headlights beaming on a wooden sign, *Willowbrook Natural Lands Trust Hiking Trails*. A shrill canine yawn lets loose from the back seat as the vehicle turns into the small gravel parking area. It rolls to a stop in the corner farthest from the road.

Another yawn squeaks from the back seat, and the old man reaches behind him to scratch the sleepy Jack Russell terrier nestled on a pile of sweaters. "Good girl." His voice is gruff, but kind. He shakes his head as if getting rid of the cobwebs, blinks several times, and massages his eye lids. "Peach, wait here."

Clicking open the trunk, the wiry man steps out of the old Honda Accord. A car speeds by and he almost ducks down. "Get with it, old man," he chides himself. "It's just folks heading home."

He stretches his stiff limbs and rubs his gray-whiskered face while scanning the vegetation surrounding the lot. Glancing at the road, he assesses whether the brush will block the view of his car to the few vehicles passing by. He slams shut the driver's door as if deciding that it does. Another car drives by, and this time he ignores it.

A slight breeze blows through and the man shivers, reminded that fall is on its way. He peers inside at the disorderly back seat. Several cardboard boxes and paper bags of books surround the sweaters that serve as Peach's bed. The man reaches for an olive-colored jacket and a felt fedora tossed among the clutter. As he puts them on, the dog's big dark eyes stare at him adoringly.

Then he pushes open the lid of the car's trunk, removes a small black canvas pack, and drops it on the ground. He searches the bag and pulls out lightweight black gloves and a small beat-up paperback missing its cover. He slips it into the back of his black jeans, the skinny volume peeking out above the top edge of the pocket.

The man clips a leash to the collar of his terrier. "Okay, girl. You're my cover." Peach jumps out of the car, and the old guy bumps the door shut with his hip as he puts the gloves into his jacket pocket. Tossing the light pack over his shoulder, he's good to go.

The little man and the little dog leave the parking area and stroll down the road masquerading as any other neighbor out for an evening walk.

~~~~~

Fifteen minutes later, the man and dog come around a bend on the narrow road. A Porsche pulls into a driveway up ahead, so he and his dog turn down a small trail that leads into the woods.

He carefully picks his way along the narrow deer path, taking care not to dirty his suede moccasins. With his eyes on the path, the man walks right into a deer fence on the property, and the impact knocks the hat off his head. "Damn," he grouses in a rough voice as Peach jumps back with a small bark.

"Quiet, girl," he orders, and Peach obeys. He leans against a fence post to catch his breath and dust off the fedora. A *Private Property, No Hunting* sign with a *W. Watson* signature posted on a nearby tree catches his attention, and he sees several more in the woods.

"Pay attention and watch where you're going, old man," he grumbles to himself as he swings left to walk along the fence.

The old guy stops when he comes to a huge bush with strong, spread-apart branches. The terrier dances around with excitement, as if she's been through this drill before. "Settle, Peach," her master orders, and she does.

First the man places his fedora on one of the branches as if it's a hat stand. He opens his small pack, pulls out a pair of black sneakers, and changes into them. He carefully brushes any trace of dirt off the suede moccasins and places them on a sturdy lower branch of the big bush.

Slipping off his jacket, the guy hangs it on another branch. He tugs from the pack a black vest covered with pockets and slips it on. Next he pulls a thin, black ski mask over his head that reveals only his tired eyes.

He takes the old paperback from his jeans, kisses it through his mask as if it's a cherished family bible, and then slips it back in.

He slides on the pair of gloves and removes wire cutters from the pack. It doesn't take long to snip an opening in the deer fence large enough to crawl through. Peach dances around in anticipation, making small yipping sounds.

"Shhhhhhh." He kneels down and loops the Jack Russell's leash loosely around a lower branch of the bush. "Sit," he says in a low, gentle croak. "Peach, you be a good girl, and I'll be back soon." He rubs her head affectionately. Then he shifts to a firm tone, as he commands, "Wait." The terrier curls up quietly next to the pack and watches her bristly boss.

The old man slips through the fence into the rapidly darkening evening.

~~~~~

The mysterious stranger, who moments ago looked like any other property owner in the area, has transformed completely, dressed now in black from head to toe. He furtively darts through the woods inside the deer fence until the guests milling about the terrace of the mansion come into view. He waits behind a thick cluster of boxwoods, listening to the cocktail conversation of the first guests to have arrived.

As the sky darkens, the man makes his way to a quiet

side of the house that is some distance from the party. Turning a corner, he sees a metal trellis attached to the far wall of what could be a guest wing. Gnarly wisteria branches weave every which way through the trellis.

The man tugs on the framework to make sure it's secure, then he steps onto its lower rungs. He quickly and nimbly climbs up and quietly groans as he pulls himself onto a slate roof.

Remaining in a crouch, the cat burglar carefully tests the grip of his soles against the shingles. The traction is good. He slowly stands up and makes his way across the roof to the wall of the second floor. There are two windows, and he finds the second one unlocked. He opens it and quietly slips inside.

"Oh-kay." The black-masked man tiptoes through the mansion's second floor, scanning the walls, book cases, and elegant old furniture as if calculating where to begin. He mutters a string of continuous appraisals. "Not bad... Easy money... Hard to unload... Got the perfect buyer for that..."

Finally arriving at the edge of steps leading down to the foyer, he stays glued to a wall and takes a moment to listen to the background chatter of guests that drifts up the grand stairway.

He continues to the antique-filled master bedroom suite, and walks through a luxurious dressing room. Crossing to a delicate table lit by a small lamp, he carefully opens the drawers.

"Well, what do you know?" He removes a diamond-encrusted necklace from the third drawer. "This should be easy to fence." Pulling a jeweler's loupe out of one of his many vest pockets, he puts it up to his eye and examines the strand closely. "Got to be three-hundred-K of stones in this baby. Wait until Sam sees this. He'll have a client lined up."

The intruder walks into a neighboring room that looks like a small plush library and combined dressing room—definitely the husband's. As he takes in all the books, his lips, protruding through the mask covering his face, change from neutral to a smile, as if he's arrived at his destination.

Even though there's also a small lamp on, he pulls out a mini-flashlight and drugstore reading glasses from his other vest pockets. He starts at the top of a built-in bookcase at one end of a wall. Shining the light on the spines of the books, he sweeps the beam slowly along the row. As he takes in the titles, he gives a low whistle of appreciation.

Then he shifts the light down and repeats the move along the book spines on the next shelf. He covers the entire bookcase this way and moves on to another, adjusting his glasses at one point, and slowly reciting the names of the authors under his breath. "...Cather...dos Passos...Emerson...Dickinson...Faulkner..." He stops and beams his flashlight down to a lower row of volumes, continuing, "...Frost...Hawthorne...Hemingway..."

He slows down again, looking carefully at the Ernest Hemingway titles. He says their names in a hushed tone, almost with reverence. "*The Sun Also Rises...A Farewell to Arms...To Have and Have Not...For Whom the Bell Tolls...The Old Man and the Sea...*" His voice cracks on the last title.

He carefully slides the book from its slot on the shelf and quickly goes to the copyright page. "1952. Good." He examines the photograph of Hemingway in the dust jacket. Then he slowly turns the pages of the volume. "This is a real beauty." He puts it back.

The man glances around the room and shakes his head. "What a collection." He spots an antique desk with glass cabinet doors on top and heads for that.

Opening the doors, he shines his light to take in more volumes. "These must be the best." He peruses the titles and lets out a sigh. One pops out at him, and the flashlight freezes on the spine of a small volume sitting inside a leather slipcase. "Holy shit, is that...it is." He chuckles in amazement. "*The Great Gatsby.* Damn."

The guy looks around as if he might be caught, then cautiously takes the book off the shelf. He sits in a huge wingback chair near the lamp and opens the book carefully. Flipping to page 205, he counts down the lines to read *sick in tired*, rather than *sick and tired*. He flips through the book for the other first edition mistakes, all of which he knows by heart.

He goes back to the beginning of the novel to read a long inscription, almost a letter, that F. Scott Fitzgerald had penned on a blank page. Fitzgerald had written that the first owner of this volume served as one of the models for the character of Jay Gatsby. The burglar wonders if the recipient at that time took this as a positive or something negative.

The old guy closes the book to admire the perfect dust jacket. "Man, oh man. This is gold." He sighs, realizing he's holding a giant among first editions. "Probably worth three, four, or maybe even five-hundred thousand." He stretches, his hand holding the *Gatsby* reaching for the sky. "Hey, snap out of it. This is not why I'm here."

He puts the priceless book on the table next to him and pulls the beat-up paperback out of his jeans. He takes off his glasses to scratch his eye with the back of his glove. He puts the readers back on and peers closely at the pale writing in pencil scattered in the margins of the worn pages. A smile forms underneath the black mask. "No way anyone's getting their hands on this."

He tucks the soft, shabby book back inside his jeans and looks around. "One down, two to go. It's gotta to be here somewhere."

He gets up too quickly, causing him to momentarily lose his balance, and knocks against the small table where he placed the priceless hardcover. *Gatsby* falls, bouncing against the angular legs of the table as it crashes to the floor.

He chastises himself. "Shit. You're an idiot!"

The man cautiously picks up the book and sees the perfect dust jacket now has a small tear on the back, and one corner of the back cover is smashed in. "You idiot," he repeats. He looks down at the floor. "Too bad the rug didn't cover this section…damn, just my luck."

The thief returns the book to its shelf in the glass cabinet and goes back to searching the room.

CHAPTER ONE

A couple of high-end luxury automobiles drive slowly through the imposing columned entry and past the stone gatehouse leading to what was once a nineteenth century robber-baron estate. I can see a Land Rover and a Mercedes further up the gravel drive.

Then there's my late model, bright red Mustang convertible—which pales in comparison—with its top down, of course, even though it's late September. I'm happy to have a black cashmere shawl draped over my shoulders to keep out the evening chill. Looking up at the fiery setting sun behind the historic beaux arts mansion, I drum my fingers on the dashboard to the music playing from my car's speakers.

...You can't start a fire

you can't start a fire without a spark

This gun's for hire

even if we're just dancing in the dark

I run my fingers through my shoulder-length, straw-colored hair as my left foot taps along to this classic Bruce Springsteen number. I would love nothing more than to blast the volume and sing along with Bruce at the top of my lungs while I drive, but I manage to keep a lid on it. By the end of the song, I park at the house and go inside.

One cocktail later, I'm positioned at the back of the foyer, watching my host and hostess greet their guests by the massive front door. I get a kick out of Win and Marilyn Watson. They're over-the-top rich, and they don't hide it, so, they wouldn't usually be my type. But Win and Marilyn are fun, and they give a lot to the community. Besides, I just plain like them.

Anyway, it's always special to be invited to one of their so-called intimate dinner parties, and this one's a fundraiser for our local animal rescue. Whimsical, illustrated faces of different residents at the shelter stare out from centerpieces on Marilyn's festive tables, and I find myself drawn through a huge open door into the dining room. I take my time walking among the five cozy round tables, admiring the six beautiful place settings at each. I notice my place card at one of the tables and quickly look to see who's sitting on either side of me.

"Now, Ronnie," an immediately recognizable husky voice calls out from the door to the kitchen.

"Wait a minute, I thought you were out there!" I say, grinning at my hostess and gesturing toward the foyer. "How'd you—"

"A sudden issue in the kitchen, but no catastrophes,

thank god." Raising the back of one hand against her forehead while looking at the ceiling, the woman feigns relief with a smile playing at the edges of her mouth.

"I promise I wasn't rearranging place cards." I grin sheepishly.

"The thought never crossed my mind." The petite, silver-haired Mrs. Watson swoops into the dining room, a half-filled martini glass in one hand. "Shall we head out for some cocktail chit-chat with the others?"

I zigzag between the tables to accompany my friend to her guests. "Well, it never fails that I have the best conversations during cocktails with the two people who also end up sitting next to me at dinner," I say. "And then I worry that they'd probably like a change of scenery by the time the meal is served."

"Never." Marilyn links arms with me as we walk through the French doors of the dining room onto the back terrace where others enjoy their drinks. "Any man here would be thrilled to be next to you at dinner. Don't you realize, darling, that you're a hot ticket ever since you came back on the market?"

"Hot ticket, my eye. Come on, I'm closing in on fifty-six, and that's hardly a hot ticket."

Marilyn drops into her lower vocal register. "All in the eye of the beholder." Her throaty laugh is irresistible, and I join in.

"Seriously, Ronnie, look at you," my hostess says. "Lean and blond and stylish and hip and amusing—"

"Enough." I feel a blush work its way from my neck

up to my face. "Look over there." I nod at a couple leaning against a balustrade on the outer edge of the terrace.

Lanterns flicker around them, casting them in a radiant light. He's tall and handsome with salt-and-pepper hair, in his late-fifties. Beautiful dark locks flow down the woman's back, and she stands on tiptoe to whisper something into the man's ear. He smiles and embraces her. They are oblivious to the possibility that anyone may be watching them.

"It's been more than a year since Juliana came out here from California," Marilyn says of my sister-in-law. "And she and Frank are still crazy-in-love, aren't they?"

"It's been quite a while since I've seen my brother so happy," I answer. "She's been the best thing that happened to him since Joanie died. How could I have *ever* doubted her?" I exhale slowly. "I mean, come on, she saved his life. And almost lost hers in the process."

"Quite a brave lady," Marilyn agrees. "And how's Juliana's daughter doing with Frank and his kids?"

"Francesca gets along great with all of them—Frank, Laura, Richard, and his wife Susie. Best of all, she's a happy high school freshman." I smile. "How are your two these days?"

"Katherine loves Georgetown, and Andrew's working hard at U.V.A. They'll both be home for Win's birthday next month. And how about your kids?"

"Brooke's still very happy with her job in New York, and she's got a nice boyfriend, too." I sip my wine.

"Jessica's back from Arizona and in her last year at Lafayette. She's doing well. It's hard to believe she'll be out in the world soon." My thoughts turn to my oldest, Tom, and a painful sadness washes over me like a flashflood. I quickly pull it together.

My friend watches me. She knows, and puts her arm around me. "It's about that time, isn't it?"

I shake my head. "It's hard to believe another year has gone by. The girls and I will head down to Arlington to visit in a couple of weeks." I think about our yearly trek to the cemetery on the anniversary of Tom's death in Afghanistan.

"Is your ex meeting you there?"

"He came the first year…" I shrug.

"He hasn't been back?"

"Not with us, anyway."

Marilyn gives me a squeeze, and she and I resume watching Frank and Juliana, who continue speaking in low tones, probably sharing another special secret. Suddenly they turn as if they feel our eyes on them, and all four of us laugh.

Something catches Marilyn's eye inside the house, and she stiffens slightly. "Time to be a good hostess." She goes back by way of the dining room.

I greet several friends near the back doors of the foyer. I glance into the large hallway, which is now empty except for Marilyn's husband, who still stands on the other end by the front door. Win talks to a woman with blue-black hair dressed elegantly in black pants, a black silk top, and a colorful shawl dramatically draped over one shoulder. I can only see her from behind, but her body language is tense. She holds her highball glass so tightly, I wonder if it will shatter in her hand.

I spot Marilyn listening to them from the other side of the dining room entry. Her cheery expression from moments ago has changed to anger.

The group I'm chatting with doesn't seem to notice, but I can tell that the conversation by the front door ratchets up in intensity on both sides. Win looks livid and cuts off the woman. "This is not the time or place."

"You think so? Fine." She pitches the drink in his face. "We're not finished." She tosses her hair, sweeps past him, and leaves the house. I look around and realize I'm the only guest to witness this drama. It feels as if I've stepped into the middle of a time-worn soap opera.

Clenching her hands, Marilyn hurries to a tall window to discreetly watch the woman while Win rushes upstairs to change his drink-splattered shirt and jacket. As I walk into the dining room, I also watch through the windows as the mysterious figure gets into a white car and drives away.

"Are you okay?" Then I see the shattered expression on my friend's face. "Marilyn, what can I do to help?" Almost in answer to my question, her expression changes to one of resolution, as if she's just made a decision.

"We only have a moment before dinner starts, so I have to be quick." Marilyn glances nervously toward the stairway. "Ronnie, I want to hire you."

"Hire me?"

"Yes, to do your private eye-thing and get the goods on Win and that Alessandro witch. I need to know the truth."

I'm speechless.

"So you're hired. Come for dinner on Monday, and I'll tell you all the dirty details…well, the ones I know." She turns me back toward the foyer and gives me a gentle push. "Right now put on your party face, and let's get this show on the road."

I turn back and watch Marilyn remove a place setting and chair from the table where I'll be sitting, so we'll now be five instead of six. It's too bad this woman—Katya Alessandro, according to the place card I'd read—left in such a hurry. I could have started my investigation right at my own table.

More importantly, without this woman right in her face, the evening is now nicer for Marilyn. She's quietly singing to herself and her mood appears to have lifted.

CHAPTER TWO

"Ronnie, why didn't you join Club Nucleus?" Win Watson asks, now in a fresh shirt and different blazer. We stand near the open front door. "I gave you that wonderful introduction to the manager, and she would have processed the paperwork in a New York-minute."

Laughing, I answer, "One club in New York is enough for me, and I can stay there when I don't want to drive home late at night."

"But that's a women's club. And Club Nucleus has some very powerful and, might I add, available men. It's time for you to get back in the game." He clinks my glass with his. "Marilyn thinks so, too."

I sidestep his matchmaking efforts. "That's so nice of you, but there's plenty of time for all of that."

Win nods at Marilyn, who stands by the pocket door signaling him to the dining room. Some of the guests are already inside taking their seats. He places our drinks on a nearby table. "It's time to sit down."

Before he can escort me in, a man I don't know walks through the front door. He's late, but he doesn't rush.

Instead, he's cool and collected.

"Hey, Win. Sorry, man. That meeting went longer than I thought when I texted you." His calm voice has a tone of authority, yet it's still relaxed.

Before Win can respond, the man's dark brown eyes shift to me. I meet his gaze, and it's crazy—neither of us moves or breaks eye contact. Perhaps it's really just a couple of seconds, but it feels much longer.

Win looks back and forth between us, and he smiles slowly. "Ronnie, darling, I don't believe you know Jamie Gordon," he purrs. "Jamie, this is Ronnie Lake. She's on everybody's A-list of fabulous women out here."

I reach out to shake his hand. "Nice to meet you, Jamie."

Our eyes reconnect like magnets, and I take in a quick, small breath as he takes my hand. "It's great to meet you, Ronnie." The tone of his voice says *you are the only one at this dinner that I want to know.*

Win is grinning like a Cheshire cat, and before anything more can transpire between Jamie and me, he leads us into the dining room. "Okay, kids. Time for supper!"

~~~~~

"So Derek's the handsome fellow sitting next to our hostess over there?" an older gentleman in a bow tie and light-weight tweed jacket asks the forty-something redhead sitting next to him.

"Mr. Johnson—" she says to the distinguished-looking man.

"Now Sandra Harper, your father and I may have been roommates in school, but don't you think it's time you call me Bill?" he asks with a chuckle. "So how did you meet?"

"Mr. Johnson—I mean, Bill—we met online two months ago." Sandra looks at me for help across our table. Our company also includes the gay and fabulously fun Jeffrey Bennett, and the recently widowed Christian Gaines.

"You met where? *Online*?" Bill's scrunched expression is one of concern. "Sandra, have you had him checked out?"

"Bill," I speak up. "Meeting online is perfectly acceptable these days. I'm sure Sandra has taken all the necessary precautions for her safety." She looks at me like I'm her supportive big sister, and then I ask quietly, "You have, haven't you?"

"Of course, Ronnie," Sandra answers. "I made sure our first meeting was in a public place and that my family knew where it was. Plus, I took a photo of his license plate and texted it to my girlfriends…"

As Sandra continues her online dating saga, I gaze at the beautiful mural adorning the walls of the room. Soft lighting from the small glass candle holders scattered on each table not only gives the painted scene of the surrounding countryside an enchanted glimmer but also flatters the guests. Win and Marilyn's dining room is magical, and it's one of my favorite rooms in all of Willowbrook.

I glance around, surveying the guests. My brother,

Frank, is sitting at Win's table and Juliana is at Marilyn's table, both lost in conversation with their dinner companions. The thought of their happy marriage does make me smile.

I look at the other people around Marilyn's table, and immediately stop when those dark brown eyes lock on mine again. I look back at Jamie Gordon almost fiercely, and I feel a slight shiver up my back. Truth be told, I could swim in those eyes. I am unable to look away from his devastatingly handsome, weathered face topped by a thick windblown mop of graying blond hair. I feel as if his eyes are sending me a message, one that my body willingly absorbs. Finally, a little flustered, I shift in my chair and break eye contact.

Juliana glances at Jamie and then back at me with a slight smile and nod. She's seen the entire exchange, and I'm a little embarrassed at being caught. I quickly refocus on Sandra.

"...so after talking until one in the morning about everything, and he was such a gentleman, we just dealt with the elephant in the room." Sandra stops.

"Need I ask, what was the elephant in the room?" Christian, the widower, smiles.

"Sex?" Jeffrey throws in and rolls his eyes.

"Nooooo," Sandra protests. "We un-Matched ourselves!"

"You, what?" I ask. "Is that like going steady or something?"

"No," Sandra answers. "Derek and I talked about our

online profiles on Match-dot-com that would continue pairing us with other people if we didn't do something. And we both decided we didn't want to stay active on Match or any other site…that we just wanted to focus on getting to know each other. It was a very sweet moment."

"Wow, this is a new world," I say.

"You should try it. You've been divorced longer than I have, Ronnie, and you'd be fabulous with some of the, um, older guys on Match-dot-com," Sandra quips with her perky voice.

"Am I slightly out of it," I ask the table, "that I prefer to meet eligible men the old-fashioned way, you know, through friends?"

"Not at all," Bill Johnson pipes up. "And Jeanie and I will be on the look-out for some nice young man…well, not too young—"

"That's okay, Bill," I interrupt.

"So will I," Christian says. "Be on the lookout, I mean."

"Me, too," Jeffrey says. "Maybe my parents know a nice available guy, someone kind of their age…"

~~~~~

We've finished dinner, and our group drifts into a large library filled with huge overstuffed furniture and a pool table off to one side.

"Oh, my, gosh, Ronnie." Jeffrey's eyes shoot skyward. "You want to be a private investigator?"

"Yes. I've been working part-time for a P.I. and taking courses."

"At your age?" Bill fusses with his bow tie. "Isn't it rather dangerous?"

"Not at all." I smile and lead the way to a young lady setting up demitasse cups on a table in the corner. Jamie Gordon already has his coffee and looks at some of Win's leather-bound volumes in a bookcase across the room.

"What happened to the TV business?" Christian asks.

"I got laid off last year, like a lot of other people." The woman offers me a coffee, which I take. "It was the perfect time to do something new. Call this my next chapter."

"Gosh, Ronnie, didn't you work in TV for a long time?" Sandra gushes. "Good luck to you."

"Just don't ignore your next-chapter personal life," Bill says. "Otherwise, you'll end up alone. I'm going to get right on this with Jeanie. We'll come up with some good candidates for you."

Jeffrey laughs. "It's much more fun to help you with your love life, Ronnie, instead of your next job!"

"That's very kind of all of you." I chuckle and make my exit from this uncomfortable conversation. As I walk over to one of the bookcases, I notice that Jamie's been observing my little dinner group plan my personal life. He has an amused look on his face, and he joins me by the bookcase.

"You didn't look too happy back there," he says.

"Have you come to rescue me?" I ask.

He leans in toward my ear and says in a low voice, "I imagine it to be a rare occasion when you need rescuing, but I would happily volunteer."

"How generous of you." I hope he hears amusement in my voice.

"Generosity has nothing to do with it," he responds. "I hear you're quite ferocious in Aikido."

"I might have taken a few classes here and there...why, what did you hear?"

"A few classes? I heard you have a black belt. I'll be sure to give you a call the next time I need rescuing." We both laugh.

"So, did you fall victim to Marilyn's penchant for bringing her friends together at these things?" I hint in a way that I hope isn't too obvious.

"You could say that," he says, hiding his grin behind a sip of scotch.

"Same here...divorced and comfortable in this town means eligible and pathetic, at least if you're a woman."

"I don't see anything pathetic here," he answers, eyeing me in a way that no one has done in a long time. I laugh, hoping to distract him from the goose bumps spreading up my arms and the fact that I'm probably blushing a little.

Before this conversation can go any further, we're interrupted by Win, Frank, and Juliana. As the men dive into sports chatter, Juliana gently tugs my arm and we find a cozy corner where we settle on a small sofa.

Jamie Gordon speaks to Win, who nods back toward the foyer. He says in a low voice, "Second door to the left of the stairs." Jamie slips out of the room.

"Well, this could be the start of something exciting,"

Juliana says in her quiet, silky voice. Her eyes twinkle as she looks at me.

"Whatever are you talking about?" I stir the milk in my cup.

"Don't act all innocent with me, Ronnie Lake. Remember, I know you." She chuckles and leans in to me. "I've been watching the way he looks at you."

"Who?"

"Ronnie. Come on. Jamie Gordon, of course."

"Funny, I've never met him or even seen him around."

"Well, I'm surprised you haven't heard the gossip floating around about him." Juliana sips her coffee and doesn't say a word.

"Okay, are you going to make me beg?" I ask. "What have you heard?"

"Well, he's definitely available." She giggles.

"Divorced?"

"Widowed." She notes my surprise and quickly adds, "That's what I heard, but I don't know anything more. I guess he's very private. Anyway, every divorcée around is trying to figure out a way to get her claws into him, and so far no one has succeeded—"

"Juliana! You are so anti-gossip, I would have never expected—"

"Hey, it's just what I've heard." She smiles sweetly.

"How about his work?" I ask. "What does he do?"

"Oh…" Juliana looks away. "A little of this, a little of that."

"Please don't hold back." I smile and drink my coffee.

"I got the sense that maybe his work is tied in with philanthropy. And at dinner, when I said his work sounded like it must be fulfilling, he said not everyone would agree with me there. What do you think that was supposed to mean?"

"Who knows?" I sip my coffee. Still, I consider what he meant. Do people actually think his work is unfulfilling? Who would even care? Maybe Juliana used the wrong adjective and he didn't bother to correct her?

I remember something else odd. "I think he's done some asking around about me. He knew about my Aikido and made some crack about the next time he needs rescuing I could help? What do you think that means?"

Juliana's eyes go wide, and she clutches my arm. "Really? Those aren't things you exactly broadcast. I wonder how he knew…anyway, how about one step at a time? You know, like a first date?"

"We'll see. I'm not a big fan of dating…" I glance around the room, curious as to where Jamie Gordon has gone. *That's a long bathroom break,* I think to myself.

"Don't look so disappointed," Juliana says to me in a gentle teasing tone. "He'll be back soon."

An explosive sound outside makes us jump.

CHAPTER THREE

Through an open window, there's the crack of breaking branches. "Come on, Juliana. Something's happening out there." We rush to the back terrace ahead of other dinner guests who do the same. We glance around, but the terrace is empty.

A splintering sound and moaning come from above. We look up at a large dogwood tree not far from the terrace just in time to see a figure in black tumble through branches that jab at his injured body. One shoves him in the abdomen, and he shrieks like a wounded animal. "Holy shit," he groans and passes out, coming to a stop two-thirds of the way down the tree.

"Over here," I call to Win, who has rushed through the French doors. The limp figure hangs upside down in the dogwood.

My brother joins us as more groaning comes from the tree. "Sounds like he's coming to," Frank says, pulling out his phone and punching in 9-1-1.

Win calls up to the figure, "Try not to move. We'll figure out a way to get you down."

Juliana looks around the terrace. "What can we grab as a canopy to catch him if falls—"

Crack! A large branch completely breaks off the tree, and as it falls it drags the rag-doll figure with it. The man cries out repeatedly during his final plummet through the rest of the tree limbs. The huge branch hits the ground first with its smaller jagged limbs poking upward like a strip of spears. The guy howls in pain as he lands on top of the branch, his leg impaled all the way through by a dagger-sharp limb.

Frank speaks with the 9-1-1 operator as Win rushes over to help the man.

"You can't move him," I caution our host. "He'll bleed out."

Jamie comes onto the terrace. "What happened?"

At the sound of Jamie's voice, the man's eyes blink open and look in his direction. His gaze freezes on Jamie, who looks back. The old man sneers in a whisper, "The book," and his head collapses back to the ground.

Jamie's face shows surprise, but no sign of recognition. "Who is he?" he mutters.

I move closer. Behind me, Marilyn nervously urges the other dinner guests to hang back to give the emergency medical technicians space once they arrive.

Win kneels down next to the man in black and listens to his ragged breathing. "It'll be easier to breathe without this over your mouth and nose." Our host carefully pulls up the black mask to reveal the grizzled old man's whiskered face. His thinning gray hair pokes out in different directions, giving him a wild look.

Win jerks back slightly, surprised. Was that recognition on his face, I wonder. Whatever it is, the moment is fleeting, interrupted by the man's continued moaning. His fluttering, panicked eyes look around. In between rattling breaths, he gasps again, "The book."

"What book?" Win's spine straightens, and he looks at the black mask on the ground as if putting two and two together. "What are you talking about?" The old guy appears to be unconscious, so Win shakes his shoulder gently.

The man's eyes snap open and wildly glance around. His breathing is growing even more labored. His eyes settle on Win, and his expression hardens with a bitter half-smile.

"I always said…if it was the last thing…I ever did…" he whispers, closing his eyes and exhaling deeply with one more hard rattle from his throat. Then he stops breathing.

Win feels for a pulse at the man's wrist, then checks the carotid artery in his neck. He shakes his head to confirm, "No pulse." He immediately begins CPR with quick chest compressions, causing the guests on the terrace to gasp.

"Oh, no. That poor man," Marilyn says anxiously as she grabs Juliana's arm to steady herself. Juliana appears somewhat frozen, her eyes startled. Somewhere, on or near the edge of the property, there's barking.

I look up at the tree and roof. "That was quite a fall

from up there. Did you hear that loud noise, maybe a gunshot?" I say to my brother as I kneel next to Win, who continues the chest compressions.

"I don't know." Frank kneels down on the other side and says to Win, "I'll take over. You go handle the rescue squad and police when they get here." Frank maintains the chest compressions. There is more barking off in the distance, along with canine whining this time.

"Why did this man choose our house for a home invasion?" Marilyn asks in a rapid-fire, shaky voice. "What did he want? Does he have a weapon?"

Win focuses on a bulge in one of the man's vest pockets below the chest compressions. He reaches toward the pocket, but I stop him.

"If this was a robbery, the police will want to investigate," I caution Win. "Maybe you should wait—"

"If this was a robbery, then I want to know what's in his pockets," Win snaps.

"Do you have a handkerchief?" I ask. "The police won't want extra fingerprints on anything connected with this man. It would confuse the scene."

Frank continues CPR. "The response time around here can't be quick…you're so far from the station." Win nods in agreement. Again, I hear the distressed barking. I don't think the Watsons have a dog.

Win takes a linen handkerchief from his pocket and shakes it loose. Carefully reaching into the man's lower vest pocket, he pulls out a lavish diamond choker.

Shocked, Marilyn asks, "Isn't that my necklace?"

"Certainly looks like it. It appears this man was robbing us." He shakes his head in disbelief. "How did he get in? I never heard him enter the house."

"Look at that wet area on his abdomen," I say. "It's hard to tell on his black clothing, but is that blood?"

Win leans in and dabs the corner of his handkerchief on the wet part of the man's clothing. He holds it up to examine the red stain. "Maybe a branch impaled him on the way down."

"How about a gunshot wound?" I repeat. "Remember the loud noise that sounded like a gun?"

"Who is he?" Juliana asks.

"I don't know," Marilyn answers. "I've never seen him before." Her tone is now steely and flat, and I find it odd.

The sirens sound closer. In a low voice, I tell Frank and Win, "Stay with him until the police get here, so that there are witnesses who can say the body has not been left unattended."

I walk over to Marilyn and Juliana and quietly ask, "Can you get everyone into the library for more coffee? Don't let anybody leave—both guests and the caterers. The police will want to speak with everyone."

I walk away from the terrace as our hostess rounds up the onlookers with a shaky but friendly, "More coffee anyone? Let's head inside and wait for the police." There's more of that unhappy barking some ways from the house.

"Ronnie, wait." Juliana comes after me. "Where are you going?"

"That dog. I want to check it out."

"Maybe I should come with you. Or better yet, why not call Will?" Juliana looks worried and nods in the direction of the robber. "What if he wasn't alone? What if he was working with an accomplice, who's still out there?"

"I'll be fine." I smile, genuinely appreciating that my sister-in-law is concerned for my safety. "Be right back." I hold up my phone. "I have my cell, and nothing's going to happen to me. I'll call Will. Promise."

CHAPTER FOUR

Guided by discreetly placed exterior spotlights, I quickly make my way around the house. As I head toward the parked cars, I look for any sign of where the thief might have approached the house to break in.

Once at my Mustang, I dig out a large flashlight and a walking stick that looks like a ski pole, in case the barking dog is aggressive. I switch from guest to sleuth-mode and head outside the walls of the mansion. The police sirens are much closer now. The mystery dog barks again, and I walk more quickly.

Along the way, I speed dial my good friend, Will Benson, a former cop turned private eye. He's also a fellow black belt at the dojo where I practice Aikido. He doesn't pick up, so I leave a message.

"Hi. There's been a break-in at Win and Marilyn Watson's place on Dutchman's Road. And it looks like the burglar fell from the roof, or he was shot, and he's dead, I'm pretty sure. Nothing like this ever happens out here—whoops." I trip on a small stump but catch myself to regain my footing. "We're waiting for the police to arrive, so in the meantime there's a mysterious barking close by, and I'm checking it out. Catch you later."

Carefully picking my way along the path, I sweep the flashlight beam back and forth from fence to path to brush, looking for a dog or any sign of where the robber entered through the fencing.

Then I hear a whining sound up ahead—it's got to be a dog, or some other small animal. I hurry along the path until maybe thirty yards later I finally see the creature in the beam of my flashlight.

A small Jack Russell Terrier waits in a sit-position next to a small pack, but that changes to lots of jumping when it sees me. The whining also switches to barking. "Quiet." I put a finger to my lips as I approach. "Shhh! Sit." As the dog half-sits, I can see it's a female.

"Hey, little one." I keep my voice soft as I slowly draw near the animal. The dog stares up at me with dark eyes, her tail wagging enthusiastically like a windshield wiper on the ground.

I kneel down and reach the top of my hand out for her to sniff, which she does eagerly. "What are you doing out here all by yourself?"

The leash attached to her collar loops around a lower branch on a bush. "This is odd." Using my flashlight, I read the tag attached to the collar around the terrier's neck. "Peach." The dog barks once. "Okay, Peach it is." I scratch her head and she nuzzles my hand.

Looking around, I shine my light on a nearby bush. A classic Barbour jacket and fedora hang from two of the limbs, and a pair of soft leather moccasins is propped on a lower branch. I quickly snap a few pictures with my phone.

My light shifts to the brand name on the insole of the shoe. "Hmm…expensive." I glance up at the jacket and hat. "These are, too."

I reach for one of the moccasins, and the terrier lunges for it and grabs it from my hand, even though she's restrained by the leash.

"Whoa, Peach." I take the other moccasin, hold it up, and say in a firm voice, "No. Now, sit."

Instead of minding me, she growls and maintains her grip on the shoe, bouncing around me as far as her leash will allow. She finally approaches, drops the moccasin, and nuzzles her head against my arm for attention, and I rub it. "Hey, Peachie."

Standing up, I speed dial Frank's cell. "The police will want to see all of this."

As I wait for Frank to pick up, Peachie growls and dances around nervously. "What is it, girl? Another animal out there making you jumpy?" My brother's cell continues to ring. "Come on, Frank, pick up."

Sticks snap on the path behind me, and Peach's growling turns aggressive. It quickly escalates to loud barking and snarling.

"Will, Frank, is that you? I'm trying to call—"

I don't even completely turn toward the direction of the sound when something hard and heavy crashes down on me, and my world goes black.

~~~~~

"Ronnie, Ronnie, wake up!" The voice is far away and hard to hear because of the yapping, noisy barking. Someone shakes me gently by the shoulders.

"Come on. Wake up!" It's my brother's voice. I open my eyes and turn to look at him. My head hurts and I try to sit up but Frank, who is crouched next to me, holds me down.

"Take it easy for a moment, sis. We found you unconscious." A police officer stands on my other side, watching Frank and me.

The Jack Russell terrier, still tied to the bush nearby, prances, growls, and barks ferociously at a cell phone on the ground close to the policeman.

"Officer, can you please grab that phone?" Frank asks while pulling the noisy terrier by the leash away from the mobile device. "That could be my sister's. It would explain the barking that I heard when I answered mine back at the house."

Using a glove, the man grabs the phone right before the ferocious little dog lunges at him, trying to bite. Frank holds the terrier back. "Quiet down," he orders Peach, who ignores him.

The officer looks at the screen on the phone and asks over the canine racket, "A call to Frank Rutherfurd?"

My brother nods. "From my sister. It's hers."

The man reaches my phone down to me as Frank helps me slowly sit up. "Sis, this is Officer Philman."

"Glad you're here," I say, almost yelling over the

noisy dog. I look at her. "Shhh! Quiet." I command, my head pounding even more. "Sit." Miraculously, she finally does both.

"We found you unconscious here just moments ago," the policeman says. "We heard this dog barking when we were at the house. And your open phone line with your brother had the same barking in the background, so that led us to you." He keeps plenty of space between himself and the Jack Russell. "Maybe you hit your head on the way down?"

"It's possible." I rub my temples.

Philman nods, walks a few steps down the path, and clicks his walkie-talkie. While he requests a medic, Frank asks, keeping his voice low, "What happened?"

The dog, now calm, nestles in right next to me. "Hey, Peach."

"How do you know this dog's name?" Frank asks. The dog growls again.

"Quiet, Peach." I rub her head and hook my finger through her collar. "It's on her tag."

Both my brother and the officer stare at me, then look at each other. Frank asks, "So how'd you end up out here?"

"Right after that man fell from the tree at the house, I heard a faint barking off in the distance, so I decided to check the outside perimeter. It was just a guess, and I don't have Warrior with me. Warrior could have found this sweet girl in seconds—"

"Who's Warrior?" Philman asks.

"Her German shepherd," Frank answers.

"Not just any German shepherd," I emphasize. "He's a war dog—"

Frank interrupts, "So you're checking the perimeter, and what happened next?"

"Okay. I heard this whining sound, and that led me to Peach here, who could be waiting for her master, that dead guy who won't ever come back to her, poor little thing," I ramble, unable to organize my thoughts through the fog of being attacked. "Or maybe someone just didn't want her anymore—"

"Ronnie!"

"Okay." I gesture toward the bush, trying to piece it together. "So I saw the hat, the jacket, and those moccasins. This guy's got expensive taste. Frank, even you won't spend this much on a pair of shoes."

"Mrs. Lake, how did you fall and knock yourself out?" the policeman asks.

"Did you trip while you were calling me and hit your head on a rock or something?" Frank asks.

"Hold it, both of you." I cautiously touch the bump on the back of my head. "It's coming back to me. I didn't trip. Someone hit me over the head."

"Are you sure?" Philman asks. "Did you get a look at him?"

"No. Frank, I was calling you to bring the police when I heard something behind me. Peach was growling up a storm, so I turned to look. I saw a quick flash of someone before everything went black. I guess that's when he clobbered me." I feel the back of my head. "I've got the bump to prove it. Feel here." I guide my brother's hand to my bump. "Ouch!"

"Mrs. Lake, are you feeling well enough to walk back to the house with your brother's assistance?" Philman asks. "The other officers are busy with the body."

"I'm fine." I crouch next to Peach and free the leash from the bush. "We'll take her with us."

"I don't know, ma'am—"

"If we leave without Peach, it will stress her to be left behind, and she'll trample the scene and make it more difficult to—"

"Okay, okay," he answers, a touch of annoyance in his voice. "Mr. Rutherfurd, would you please escort your sister back to the house while I stay to secure the scene?"

"Will do," Frank says. "Come on, Ronnie. Can you manage that dog, or should I carry her?" My brother extends his arms.

Peach barks aggressively at Frank and then looks at me with big, sad eyes, as if she knows something has gone very wrong.

"I've got her." I scoop her up and stand up with Frank's help. I retrieve my walking stick and give it to Frank. Shining my light on the path, we leave Officer Philman to do his work.

We pick our way carefully along the trail, taking the shortest way back to the house. As Frank and I walk up the drive, we wave at a few of the other dinner guests leaving, who look curiously at the dog now walking on her leash beside me.

We circle around the mansion, and Peach's barking and growling start up again the closer we get to the back terrace. Juliana and Marilyn spot us as we approach.

"There you are, you two," Marilyn says. "And who is this little guy, Ronnie?" Peach repeatedly tries to jump on Marilyn, while I attempt to control her with the leash.

"We think *she* belongs to…" I nod my head toward the body on the ground, now surrounded by police and the rescue squad. Peach's loud yapping does nothing for my pounding head. I crouch down and fold my hand around the terrier's snout to keep her mouth closed, look her in the eye, and command, "Quiet." She looks toward the body and whines, now circling me in worried nervousness.

A strong, good-looking, forty-something man—not in uniform—stands off to the side, speaking with Win and a woman in jeans and a jacket. It's my friend, Will, and we wave to each other. The woman glances my way and turns back to Will, who says something. I overhear her say, "Just keep her out of our way."

Will and Win walk away from the group, still talking. The woman eyes me suspiciously as I pick up the little dog to comfort her. I see something shiny on the woman's belt, and I realize it's a badge.

"They're waiting for the coroner," Marilyn says, "before they can remove the body."

"Will's here, Ronnie," Juliana says. "Did you call him? I mean, he's not on the police force."

"I did while I was looking around."

Peach wiggles out of my arms, jumps down, the leash slipping from my hand, and runs over to the dead thief. She whines and prods the body with her nose.

"Hey, somebody grab the mutt," the policewoman yells. "He'll mess up the scene."

Another policeman makes a move toward the dog, who explodes toward him in shrill barks and fierce growls to keep him away from the body. She darts in and out pushing at the body.

"Wait." I say. "Don't grab her. This is probably her master, and she's upset."

Peach closes in on the thief's face and barks. When there's no response, she whines and nudges at the old guy. Finally, the little dog plops down next to the body's head and shoulder and quietly buries her face in the crook of the man's neck.

It's heartbreaking, and my eyes tear up. I glance at Marilyn and Juliana, who seem to have a similar reaction, and Frank puts a consoling arm around his wife. I step in and carefully scoop up the terrier, who responds with the saddest little whine.

Will heads in my direction, and we give each other a quick hug. I catch a glimpse of Jamie as he returns to the terrace. Out of the corner of my eye, I'm aware that he watches Will and me sit down off to the side, away from what's left of the crowd.

"Did Win hire you?" I ask. Will looks surprised, and I continue, "I saw you two talking over there, so I figured he hired you to work on the case."

"He brought it up, but I'm pretty busy. I'm here because I wanted to make sure you were alright." Will's expression is one of concern. "Ronnie, what were you thinking, poking around the place in the dark while you waited for the police? I thought I taught you better than that."

"You know me," I answer, softly rubbing Peachie's head, "too curious for my own good."

My private eye friend gestures toward the body. "This man was robbing the place, and he could have had help close by. And who knows, an accomplice could still be out there. Maybe that's who knocked you out."

Surprise must register on my face because he shakes his head and sighs. "I heard the chatter on the walkie-talkies."

The woman in jeans squats down close to the body. She appears to be looking at the intruder's abdominal area. Her chin-length chestnut-brown hair falls into her face, and she pushes it back. "Who's the woman with the badge on her belt?"

"That's Detective Sofia Rossi. She's in charge of the scene. Let's stay focused. Once again, you put yourself in harm's way." Will brushes a strand of hair from my face, and his eyes convey the affection he still has for me. His eyes are not dark brown like Jamie Gordon's, but a beautiful blue; Will is a first-class hunk.

"Now start at the beginning, and tell me everything," he says. And I do, still holding the dog as Peachie's eyes dart nervously around the scene.

CHAPTER FIVE

It's early Friday morning, still dark outside. I sip my steaming cup of coffee. Warrior, curled up next to me on the rug, quietly snores while I sit cross-legged, leaning against the bottom of an overstuffed chair in my kitchen. I gently scratch the top of his head.

It's been more than three years since my son Tommy died. My heart aches for him every day, especially when I look at Warrior, who'd been Tommy's K9 partner. I fought to bring Warrior home after he was too shell-shocked to continue his service, and it's a comfort to know that Warrior's sweet face was probably the last thing my son saw.

I lean over and kiss the top of his head and rub his neck. Warrior's eyes crack open, but a moment later, he's back asleep.

I switch my focus and scroll online to learn what the local press is reporting about last night's death at the Watson dinner party. There doesn't appear to be much on the internet that I don't already know, having been a witness to most of what happened. I do learn that there will be an autopsy, but so far, the police have not identified the robber. His fingerprints aren't in the system for any past crimes, so the investigation is ongoing.

It's strange that this guy chose to break in during Marilyn and Win's busy fundraiser. Why wouldn't he pick a better time, when no one was at home? I do come across articles about a burglar who specialized in stealing silver and often broke in while the residents were at home. There was speculation that he got an adrenaline rush from the possibility of being discovered, and maybe it was the same for the thief last night.

I sip my coffee and continue to speculate about that grizzled old burglar with expensive shoes who tried to snatch Marilyn's diamond necklace. I can still hear his last words before he died—*I always said if it's the last thing I do...*

And what was that about a book? How odd.

~~~~~

Warrior sits on the front seat of my Mustang, his canine seat belt holding him firmly in place as I drive along the twisty roads not far from where the Watsons live. In the back seat, Peachie also sits quietly inside a canvas dog carrier that I borrowed from my brother on my way to pick her up at the police station. The carrier is also strapped in with a seat belt. She watches my every move through the windows of the small crate, emitting a steady stream of squeaks, yips, and barks.

Last night, I offered to provide Peachie with a

temporary home. And even though Will vouched for me, Detective Rossi turned me down flat and hauled the terrier off to animal control. She wanted to find out ASAP if the "mutt" had an ID chip that could help them identify the dead thief. Animal control confirmed there was no chip and returned the dog to Rossi, saying their kennel and the shelter they use were both full.

After a night at her house of listening to Peach whine and bark, Rossi had her fill of the dog and took me up on my offer. Forget any friendly chit-chat when she called this morning. Just a clipped, "Come get the dog."

And when I arrived, there was no cheerful *good morning, how are you* greeting. All I got as I lifted Peachie into my arms was a grouchy command. "Don't let her out of your sight. That dog is my only lead right now...so don't screw this up."

Rossi's winning personality cannot bring me down. I sing along to Joni Mitchell's "Free Man in Paris" as my convertible whizzes along the narrow road and its many blind corners. Even though it's late September, it's not so chilly that I can't have the top down and enjoy the scenery.

Suddenly, a low growl comes from the back seat. As we pass a sign that reads *Willowbrook Natural Lands Trust Hiking Trails*, Peach lets loose barking for what feels like an eternity, but is probably only thirty seconds.

I pull over and look into the carrier. "You okay, girl?" Peachie, now quiet, is stretched out with her head resting on her paws. The terrier looks at me with deep sad eyes.

"I wish you could tell me what you're thinking." I look around. "Was it an animal that you saw?"

I shift into drive and continue down the road, but I don't get far. I'm still thinking about Peach barking near the hiking trails sign, and my inner P.I. gets the better of me. I slow down as I approach a small dirt triangle where the road splits for a left or right. I drive around the triangle instead and backtrack. "Peach, you've got me curious."

A mile or so later, the low growl again comes from the carrier, and it picks up volume as we get close to the same spot on the road. Then Peachie shifts into full out barking as I brake at the *Willowbrook Natural Lands Trust Hiking Trails* sign.

I turn into what appears to be an overgrown, empty parking area, and Peachie goes ballistic. Deep growls next to me tell me that Peachie's racket in the back seat agitates Warrior, too. His posture stiffens slightly, and I know he's on alert.

"What is with you two? It's just an empty parking—" I glimpse the back end of a car. "Hey, what do we have over there?" I drive slowly toward the parked vehicle, tucked in behind a stand of bushes, and stop.

The barking continues. "Peachie, Warrior, quiet. I can't hear myself think." Both dogs settle down.

"That's better." With the top down, it's easy to look around the entire parking area. There's no one here from what I can see, but I'm also on alert. Peachie alternates between whimpering and sharp barking.

I reposition my car so that the front end points toward the road and keep the engine running—just in case I need to make a sudden getaway. I stare closely at the thick brush that surrounds the parking area. You never know who might be lurking nearby.

I unsnap Warrior's seat belt. "Stay," I command as I step out, leaving the driver's door open. On the other side of the car, I reach in to open Peachie's carrier, snap on her leash, and lift her out of the back seat.

We walk toward a tired-looking old Honda Accord. The Jack Russell makes happy yipping sounds and dances around my feet.

"You seem to know this car." Together, we circle the vehicle. I photograph the Honda's license plate and its VIN number, which is visible through the front windshield. I peer inside the other car windows, where there are several boxes and paper bags of books and other stuff surrounding a pile of sweaters. The sweaters have an indentation in the middle, as if they served as a nest. Warrior, still calmly sitting in the Mustang, stares at us.

"Is it possible that this car belonged to your master?" Peach pees next to a tire and then puts her paws up on its side, as if claiming the vehicle as her own. I pick her up, and we look inside the back windows. She goes nuts when she sees the pile of sweaters in the back, almost wiggling out of my arms to get closer.

I hurry back to the Mustang, despite Peach wanting to stay close to the Honda and tugging on the leash. I call

Will to let him know that it looks like I've found the robber's car.

"Why don't you call the police?" he asks.

"Well, I thought you'd want to see it first, since you may end up investigating for Win Watson—"

"Investigating for Watson is a different matter than checking out a car that may belong to a murder victim. You were right, by the way. The guy was shot before he fell, so at the very least it's a suspicious death. Anyway, call Detective Rossi." He pauses and then adds, "And don't touch anything. I'm tied up at the moment, but I'll come as soon as I'm finished here."

~~~~~

"...so you see, it was really Peach who found the car. I was driving along, minding my own business, when she started acting up. So I decided to stop and take a look..." Why do I feel a need to make small talk with this unfriendly woman?

Detective Sofia Rossi glances toward Warrior, holding a slim metal tool. "Do I need to worry about that dog?"

"No. He's exceptionally well-trained."

In silence, the cop slowly circles the car, looking inside and out. I stand close by with Peachie in my arms, her leash hanging loosely around my wrist.

"Will should be here soon," I say.

"And why do I care?" She continues moving around the Honda.

"Well, I guess not," I answer. "Forget it."

Rossi uses the slim jim to unlock the driver's door, and the exact second it opens, Peach squirms from my arms and lunges toward the car, tearing the leash from my wrist. She hops into the vehicle.

"Now, wait a minute," Rossi hollers as the terrier scurries around the inside of the car, happily yipping away. "Get that dog out of there. It's ruining the scene."

As Peachie paces back and forth across the rear seat, I throw open the door and try to make a grab for the leash. But the little dog jumps into the rear footwell between some bags and under the front passenger seat.

"Peachie, what are you doing?" There's a lot of scurrying and growling. Then the Jack Russell's hind end pokes out from the front of the driver's seat, her little tail wagging furiously. It appears the dog is pulling on something.

Detective Rossi tries to grab her, but Peach is too quick and slides back under the driver's seat. "Damn! I'm going to wring your neck..."

More growling, sniffing, and tugging noises come from the floor under the seat. *Squeak! Squeak!*

"Peach, what did you find?" I run around to the driver's side, open the back door, and lean down in the footwell to try to see underneath. It's too dark.

Peachie dislodges the item, but she's stuck because the leash is caught on something. So I unclick it, and she jumps onto the sweater-nest on the back seat with something fuzzy in her mouth. She plops down and curls up contentedly with a well-loved toy chipmunk in her mouth.

"Peachie, what is it?" I ask. "Is that your favorite toy?"

Rossi reaches toward the stuffed animal, and the dog snarls ferociously, dropping the toy. Her paws clamp down over it as she snaps at the woman.

Peachie's mouth immediately grabs the toy chipmunk as the detective jumps back. "Get that annoying excuse for a dog out of here—"

"Don't you want the stuffed animal—"

"I don't give a flying-F about that ratty toy," she shrieks. "Get them both out of here. That mongrel is ruining my scene."

All the commotion is upsetting Warrior, who barks and jumps out of the car.

"Warrior! It's okay. Stay," I command, and he returns to the car. I turn my attention back to the terrier and cautiously reach inside the car toward Peachie. "Come on, girl. I won't try to take it from you, but it's time to go back into your house." I scoop her up, but she wiggles and whines and wants to stay put.

"Let's go." I carry her toward the Mustang, and the terrier stares at the Honda, maintaining a death-grip on the toy chipmunk as I scoot her into the carrier.

I look back to see Rossi still glaring at us as Warrior, Peachie, and I drive onto the road.

CHAPTER SIX

I take the dog carrier inside the house as Warrior and Peach dance around my heels. After I place it on the kitchen floor, Peach darts inside the little khaki crate. She dashes right back out and races around the kitchen, her jaws once again clamped on the toy chipmunk.

"Oh, right. Let's not separate you from that toy."

I go back outside to bring in a bag of groceries from a quick trip to the supermarket. As I unpack it, my cell rings. I click on the speaker and continue putting things away.

"Hi, Will. Are you at the scene?"

"Yes, and they're towing away the car with everything in it," he says.

A fierce growling sound comes from the little dog as Peach dances around Warrior with her toy, taunting the bigger dog.

"What's that racket?" Will asks.

"Peach! No!" I command, and the terrier stops and looks at me. "In your house! Right now!" The little dog hides behind a large upholstered chair, peeking out defiantly and growling.

"Peach, that's enough." I point toward the khaki carrier. We're at a stand-off, staring at each other. "Peach, now," I repeat and drop my voice an octave. She looks at me, surprised by my new pitch and trots inside the crate with the chipmunk. Resigned, Warrior lies down, his eyes moving back and forth between the carrier and me.

"What's going on?" Will asks again.

"That's just Peachie teasing Warrior with her beat-up toy. Oh, I meant to tell you, when Peachie jumped into the Honda, she dug that old thing out from under the front passenger seat. I haven't been able to get it from her…when I do, should I take it to the police station."

"I'm sure that toy is so full of dog slobber that it's useless. Don't worry about it." Will tells me he's off to meet a client and will not be reachable.

The two dogs play tug-of-war with the terrier's chipmunk. Their escalating growls cause me to look up from my newspaper and cup of coffee at the kitchen island.

Without letting go, Warrior changes strategy and now stands calmly as Peach dances around his front, tugging on her beloved chipmunk. Maintaining a death grip on the toy, she shakes her head furiously, trying to loosen Warrior's hold. No such luck.

I head for the mudroom and reach into a drawer where I store dog paraphernalia. I select a squirrel and a duck that are approximately the same size as Peach's chipmunk.

Back in the kitchen, I hold up the toys. "OK, you two. Take a look at these."

Warrior and Peach stop tugging to stare at the new prizes I offer. But neither lets go of the chipmunk.

"Warrior, drop it." He lets go. "Sit." This time both dogs sit obediently, Peach still hanging on to the old toy.

"Warrior, come." He does, and I give him the duck, whereupon the German shepherd walks over to his nest and happily curls up with the toy tucked beneath his chin.

I squat down, offering the squirrel in exchange for the chipmunk. Peach eyes the new toy with interest. I toss it into one corner of the kitchen, and the terrier immediately drops the chipmunk in her haste to retrieve the squirrel.

I snatch the old toy, ready to toss it aside in the mud room, when I feel a protrusion from its furry underbelly. I move my thumb over it. It's long, kind of snake-like.

I flip it over. "What do we have here? Peach, did you injure your chipmunk?" Contentedly curled up next to Warrior, Peach mimics the German shepherd and has the new toy squirrel tucked under her chin, too.

I examine the chipmunk with its matted fur more closely and discover a narrow Velcro flap. Carefully pulling apart the Velcro, I find a zipper that was sewn in by hand. I gently unzip it to reveal a pocket. My fingers feel around inside and touch a small paper roll. "What do we have here, Peachie?"

I put on some thin cotton gloves, remove the paper

tube from the toy, and unroll it. There are two small notepad-sized pages taped together and filled with writing. I stretch out the roll, placing a salt shaker and pepper mill on the top corners and two small juice glasses on the bottom corners.

The first thing I see at the top of the page is an elegant logo and the name *Alessandro Rare Books*.

That name echoes in my head. And then I remember the place card with Katya Alessandro's name and also Marilyn's voice telling me...*do your private eye-thing and get the goods on Win and that Alessandro witch. I need to know the truth.*

I don't believe in coincidences, and Alessandro is not a name you hear every day. That woman who left their dinner must be somehow connected to this rare book business. At the bottom of the first page I read a Summit address, website, hours of operation and phone number, and this repeats on the bottom of the next page, too. I quickly go to the website, but it's all about the rare books, and there are no bios about the owner and staff. I Google Katya Alessandro, but there's not much about her except for social events that she's attended.

So I shift back to the unrolled pages. I study what I can only describe as nondescript printing in black ink. The heading is odd—

The Great Gatsby (ASE)

What is *ASE*? Someone's name? It's followed by a list of dates and initials.

1944 J.W., L.A., M.G.
W. 8/8
S.,J. 10/12

I take off my gloves and, with my camera phone, snap close-ups of the mysterious rolled-out paper.

Then I call Will, but his voice mail tells me that he's out of the office, as he told me he would be, and to leave a message. I hang up instead. I don't want to bother him.

My mind jumps to the detective with the choppy haircut from last night, but I make an immediate decision to not call the hot-tempered Sofia Rossi. I'm already on her shit-list. No, this is the perfect opportunity to take some initiative.

I look back at the paper. If I learn more about the dead home invader, then perhaps this list will make sense. Did he just happen to pick up one of their memo pads to write this list, or is he also connected to this Alessandro Rare Books? I glance at my watch. They ought to be opening soon.

CHAPTER SEVEN

First, I load up my car with the dogs and head for Meadow Farm. There, I switch my bright red Mustang for an old beat-up compact that is part of a small fleet of cast-off, nondescript work vehicles at my brother's farm. It's best to have a car that doesn't attract attention during an investigation. I spend a few minutes transferring Warrior's canine seat belt to the Toyota, as well as Peachie's carrier, and strap them both in.

We arrive in downtown Summit a half hour later and drive through the town's shopping district. There are endless chic boutiques, restaurants and cafés, art galleries, antiques shops, and home design businesses. It certainly would be easy to blow through a lot of cash around here.

I roll past an elegant hunter green-lacquered storefront that surrounds a large multi-paned bay window. Carved into the lacquer above the window and painted black with gold edging is the name *Alessandro Rare Books*. Peering through the glass, I make out a couple of people browsing among multiple floor-to-ceiling bookcases. Once I've turned the corner, I park on a side street and crack open the windows for the dogs.

Upon entering the shop, I discover that it's larger than it appears from the street. I walk around a table piled with hefty volumes, their intriguing covers face up. These appear to be newer publications, many of them art, travel, or garden books—perfect gifts to place on a coffee table.

I wander up and down the aisles until I spot a young woman with red hair twisted up in a messy knot, filing books down at one end of a row. She's petite and up on the balls of her feet, trying to rearrange a shelf that I could easily reach. I'm five-foot-seven, so maybe she's around five-two. She grabs the step-ladder nearby to climb up to finish her task.

The girl could be a college student maybe in her early twenties, and she's completely engrossed in her work and unaware that anybody's watching her. She spots a book on her way down the ladder, pulls it from the shelf, and sits on one of steps. She flips through its pages and reads, probably one of the benefits of working in a shop like this.

I walk over and say in my friendliest voice, "Excuse me, do you have a moment?"

Caught in the act, the girl snaps the book shut and quickly puts it back on the shelf, trying to cover her guilty expression. "Absolutely. Uh, hi." She replaces the guilt on her face with a sheepish grin. "How can I help you?

"Well, actually, I'm looking for this very nice man who helped me here a week or so ago." I smile at the girl, who's now all eager attention as I make up a story. "He was rather elderly, maybe in his seventies. I wanted to find out about two books I ordered, and I also had another question for him. He's a small, wiry guy, kind of grizzled and gray—"

"Oh, you mean Casey." She breaks out in a huge grin. "Casey Whitmore. He works here. Has for a long time. He knows a lot about books. I can't believe you actually met him."

"Why is that?"

"Because he's not really a salesperson," she says, reaching toward a different shelf and switching two books around. "Ninety-nine-point-ninety-nine-percent of the time, if you need to ask Casey a question, you find him in his teeny-tiny office in the very back of the building with Peachie."

"Peachie?" I ask.

"Yeah, that's his cute, little dog. He's always got her with him, you know, talking to her, but he almost never ever talks to customers 'cause he's very private." She puts another book on a lower shelf. "Well, he talks to me, but that's because we're good friends."

"I guess I got lucky and caught him when he had to come out front for some reason or another." I'd love to see that office of his. "What does he do in the back all day long? Special projects? Research?"

"Yeah," she says. "Casey checks out all the valuable first editions that come into the shop, because, like I said, he knows *everything* about books, especially old ones.

He writes up descriptions and also decides which ones to post online on AbeBooks.com. Things like that for Ms. Alessandro, the owner."

"So he's the resident expert on old books."

"He's definitely the resident expert." The redhead laughs. "Resident because it seems like he lives at the shop. Casey comes in first to open up, and he's usually the last to leave, too."

"If he's the one, then he's trying to locate two Edith Wharton first editions for me. *Ethan Frome* and *The House of Mirth*," I say. "I hope he's the right one—this Casey—because—"

"Follow me," the girl says.

We walk toward the area of the store with the customer desk and cash register, passing another salesman I glimpsed when I first entered the shop. He says he's making a coffee run and will return in fifteen minutes.

We stop in front of a large bulletin board filled with community notices. There, pinned to the top of the board, are photographs of all the store's employees and their picks of favorite books in the shop.

I look at the photograph of the young woman helping me. "So you're Sally Richards."

She nods and points to a photograph of an older man holding a Jack Russell terrier. "Is this the guy who helped you?"

I step up and look at the photograph closely. The man is elderly, but clean-shaven, unlike the old burglar, who had a heavy five-o'clock shadow on his face. The picture also shows him with little round tortoise-shell specs and a dark brimmed cap—it's like he's got a John Lennon-thing going on from the 1960s. At first glance he looks too clean-cut, but I do recognize him as the old thief who broke in during the Watson dinner. And I do recognize his companion, Peachie, of course, who is sitting in my car with Warrior outside the shop.

"Yes, Casey Whitmore was definitely the nice man who helped me." I think the now *dead* Casey Whitmore, but they don't seem to know that here at the shop. "Is he in today?"

"Not yet," Sally answers. "I know his car was in the shop, but I think he borrowed one from a friend and took a couple of days off. Anyway, he's due back after lunch."

I note Casey's pick-of-the-week, *The Great Gatsby*, a rare first edition recently acquired from a private collector. It makes me even more curious about his office in the back.

"Do you know if he found the two Edith Wharton first editions I'd like to purchase? *Ethan Frome* and *The House of Mirth*?" I repeat. "I need them soon. They're a gift for my daughter." Do I feel guilty weaving my daughter into this fabrication…well, yes…

Sally flips through a stack of papers on the desk. "Let's see." She stops on one page and reads through it. "Here's a list that Casey wrote out before he left of books we should expect to arrive at the shop. I don't see any by Wharton, but why don't you take a look while I check his office?" She heads down the hall.

The list is signed *Casey Whitmore*, and, once Sally's out of sight, I whip out my phone and snap some pictures to get a sample of his handwriting, including his signature. This could prove useful, and I compare it with my photograph of the list that came out of the chipmunk toy. They look like a match.

I finish just as Sally sticks her head into the hallway. "No luck so far." She chuckles. "It's small but very cluttered. I'll continue looking if you aren't in a hurry."

"Take your time," I answer, and she disappears again.

I glance to the right of the hall through a picture window that offers its inhabitant a view of the store. This office looks spacious compared to Casey's probably closet-sized room. It must belong to the boss. Mid-twentieth century furniture decorates this elegant, sparse room.

Sitting on a small table as if it's a priceless sculpture, under a painting that also looks mid-twentieth century, is a red leather Birkin bag. With at least a ten-to-twenty-thousand-dollar price tag, this purse may as well be a priceless sculpture. If the owner of this bag is the temperamental woman that Marilyn wants me to investigate, then she certainly has expensive taste. My mind drifts to Win Watson. Was this a gift, or could she afford to buy it for herself?

A moment later, Sally reappears at the desk. "Any luck?" I ask.

"No, I don't see them," she says. "But I'll keep looking, see what I can find, and call you."

"Thank you. Hey, I have to ask, because I melt at the sight of a beautiful handbag." I nod toward the big picture window showing the glamorous office. "Is that the owner's Birkin bag?"

We both glance at it sitting on the small table. Sally looks nervous. "She helps other people collect books, but she collects purses."

"I have a couple of friends who are clients of Ms… or is it *Mrs.* Alessandro?"

"Oh, she's not married," Sally says, almost too quickly. "I don't get it, because she's soooo beautiful and has some very hot guys who like her." Something about her enthusiasm sounds slightly forced, but I try not to show that I've noticed.

"Win Watson may be a client here," I say conspiratorially, as if he could be on the hot guy list. Sally nods with a knowing smile, and I go on. "He and his wife are friends, and I'd like to find a small gift for them—it's a surprise, so please don't tell him I was here."

"Got it."

"Thank you, Sally." I glance at my watch and feign surprise. "But I'll have to do that another day. I'm late and due for an appointment."

I hand Sally a card. "Here's my phone number. If the Wharton books come in, please call me. See you next time."

The young woman smiles. "Glad to help."

CHAPTER EIGHT

I drive to the corner to turn onto Summit's main street and I spot a chic woman in huge shades with her dark hair twisted up. Even from three blocks away, it's not hard to make out her mile-high heels and the expensive coat worn over her shoulders. She's walking in the direction of the shop and towards me.

Rather than make the turn, I cross through the light and pull into an empty parking space right at the corner. I open the window and slide lower in the seat, then tilt the rearview mirror so that I can discreetly watch her. This splendid woman strides down the street as if she owns the entire town.

Then from the opposite direction, a silver Jaguar races through the intersection and past the shop. The sports car suddenly screeches to a halt and makes a U-turn on the main drag in the middle of light traffic. I turn in my seat to look through my side window. Who in the world…

The Jag's window rolls down, and sure enough, Win Watson hollers, "Katya, we need to talk." He doesn't use the friendliest tone of voice, and the woman stiffens slightly, glancing around quickly. There aren't many people around, and no one appears to have noticed anything more than a driver pulling his Jag into a parking space and hopping out to greet a beautiful friend.

With an unobstructed view of the scene, I watch the woman continue walking briskly, her head now low as if she wants to avoid a confrontation. But Win marches up quickly and demands, "You stop when I call out to you." He grabs her arm roughly. This is a side of him I've never seen before.

"Please don't make a scene out here." She shakes him loose.

They're in front of the shop, and he roughly backs her up against the entryway with its glass windows and points his finger right in her face. "Don't you dare ignore my calls..." Her oversized shades create an extra barrier of protection for her, and it's hard to make out the details of her face. Is this really the same woman who threw a drink in his face last night? Where did all that audacity go?

I can't understand any more of the conversation, so I study the body language between them. Katya has her arms crossed high on her torso and her chin tucked down, as if she's trying to put space between herself and Win, which is difficult to do since she's right up against the glass.

Suddenly she slaps him hard across the face. He steps back, stunned. Speechless, he can't believe it, and his hand goes to his face, lightly massaging it.

Unexpectedly, Katya throws her head back and laughs, angering Win. "Don't you dare play me," he hisses. At least that's what I think he says. This is unbelievable. She sells books; he collects books. This is unlike any business disagreement I've ever witnessed.

I glance toward the shop window and notice that Sally stands transfixed near a book case. She's probably also watched the entire scene unfold. When Katya and Win turn to enter, Sally quickly scoots down an aisle where she'll be hidden.

I glance at the dogs, both looking very relaxed as they half-snooze while cracking one eye open every now and then. I take several slow, deep breaths. This would be a good moment to *not* jump to conclusions.

~~~~~

Now that I know his name and have looked up his contact information, I dial Casey Whitmore's phone number and hit *send*. An older, gruff male voice picks up after three rings. "This is 973-376-5521. Leave a message, and I'll call once I'm back. Thanks."

Over a long beeping sound, I wonder if this is the same voice I heard coming from the thief at the Watson party. All I ever heard him say was "the book..." and "I always said if it's the last thing I do..." At those moments, his voice sounded pretty ragged since it was right before he died. Then a digital voice cuts off the long beep, announcing that the voice mailbox is full, and ends the call.

I turn on my GPS and enter Casey's address. I switch on another Joni Mitchell song. This time it's "Raised on Robbery," and I laugh a little at the irony. I drum my finger nails on the steering wheel to the beat while I drive.

Ten minutes later, I find myself outside of Summit in a neighborhood of modest houses and apartment buildings. Squeaky noises come from the carrier in the back seat. I figure Peachie is perking up because she knows she's close to home.

I pass a light brick apartment tower on my left. Beyond that building's parking lot, I drive by a row of small Tudor-style wood and stucco houses until I spot number twenty in this post-World-War-II mini-development.

Cruising around the block, my car passes the parking lot for the second time. I pull over so that I have a clear view of the half-dozen bungalows across the street. It's quiet at the moment, since most people are probably at work.

A woman attending to a squirmy young child locks her front door and leaves number twenty-two. They walk in my direction on the other side of the street. Peachie gives a couple of quick barks. "Shhh, girl." I wonder if Peach and the woman know each other and quickly hide behind my newspaper instead of staring out the window like someone casing the neighborhood.

All the other houses on both sides of number twenty appear to be quiet. Whining sounds come from the back seat. "Shhh."

After ten minutes, I've had enough waiting around, so I grab a baseball cap off the back seat, twist up my hair, and put it on. I crack open the Toyota's windows and rub Warrior's neck. "You're going to stay right here and guard the car." I give him a kiss on his forehead.

As I get out, I slide on my sunglasses and reach for a small shopping bag in the back seat. I open the back door and clip on Peachie's leash. My plan is to make like I'm walking the dog and dropping off a package. Warrior watches us intently. I give him one last scratch on his head. "I'll be right back."

Crossing the street, I discreetly try to look into the large front windows of numbers sixteen and eighteen as I stroll down the sidewalk, but I'm too far away to see much. I walk up to Casey Whitmore's front door at number twenty, and Peachie perks up, excited to be home and bouncing like a little ball on the end of the leash.

I knock on the door but, of course, no one answers. Without any commands from me, the dog sits quietly and politely, as if she's just returned from obedience school. While I wait, I look in the right front window of Casey's house. The furniture is basic—a sofa with two end tables and lamps, a couple of upholstered chairs, and a coffee table.

Over on one wall and hanging over the sofa, there's an oil painting of a very large house in a village. It's hard to see the details from where I'm standing, but it doesn't look like anything special, more like something you'd buy at a garage sale. Still, I take out my phone, discreetly zoom in as much as possible, and take some pictures.

There is something remarkable about this otherwise unremarkable room: the endless stacks of books everywhere. On the tables, on the sofa, on the chairs and on the floor. Some of the books lean precariously like the Leaning Tower of Pisa. Others have tipped over, and the volumes lie toppled and scattered. This room telegraphs loud and clear that books not only comprise Casey Whitmore's professional life but also his life in this house.

I lightly knock again and look into the picture window to the left of the front door. In the middle sits an inexpensive dining table and six matching chairs. They look like cheap motel furniture. The theme of book clutter repeats itself in this room, only this time there are no pictures on the walls.

Looking around and seeing no one, I inconspicuously pull one latex glove from my jacket pocket. There's no need to leave my fingerprints around here. I try the door knob. Locked. There's no flower pot or some other obvious hiding place for a key. I reach above the door. Nothing. I'm not sure what I would do even if there was a key, since I don't want to be picked up for breaking and entering.

Next, I head around the house and open a small gate. A six-foot hedge lines the fence behind the house, and there's a feeling of privacy back here. Peach bounces around, excited to be home, and pulls me toward a small enclosed pen with a little dog house inside. I open the gate and the terrier runs inside the house and stretches out with her head peeking through the opening. She settles down, and I leave her there.

I try the back door, and it, too, is locked. I peek into the window of a vintage 1960s-style kitchen. Books, books, and more books everywhere—they appear to be his major personal possession.

Slow down, Ronnie. Take your time and really look at the room. A pen and legal pad with a lot of writing sit on the kitchen table, which is also filled with books. There's a coffee cup next to the pad. He must have been working on something before he left to go the Watsons'. It looks like he expected to come home and pick up where he left off...as if he obviously didn't anticipate the evening would take such a fatal turn.

I jiggle the door knob again. Out where I live, people leave their doors unlocked all the time, but I guess not around here. Even Whitmore's neighbor, who left earlier with the squirmy child, took great care to lock her front door.

I wish I could gain access to this house and check out that pad of paper. Thank god, I snapped the picture of his handwriting at the book store.

I glance around the kitchen one more time and note something odd. There's an orange shopping bag with two brown leather handles—possibly part of a designer purse—poking out the top. The paper bag could be from Hermès, and it sits so hidden among piles of books that it's easy to miss. I mentally flash to the red Birkin bag I saw earlier. Two of these in one morning would be unusually coincidental.

I shift left to what turns out to be the bedroom window and scan the room slowly. Again, there are stacks of books everywhere, but I also notice a six-by-eight-inch framed photograph on a bureau against a wall close to the window.

It appears to be four men in fatigues at a military facility, maybe World War II or Korea. For a moment my mind goes back to the year 1944 at the top of the mystery list I found inside Peachie's worn-out chipmunk toy.

I pull out my phone and click off a few shots of the photograph through the window. I wish I were inside the room where I could get a really good picture of those four men, but I settle for zooming in as close as possible and snapping off a couple more.

As I scroll through to check the pictures, splinters suddenly fly off the kitchen window sill. A fraction of a second later I hear a loud *Boom!* More splinters fly off the bedroom window sill, followed by another equally loud *Boom!*

Someone's shooting at me. I throw myself down on the ground as Warrior barks from the car on the other side of the house, knowing I'm in trouble. I reach up with a shaky hand and try the back door again, regretting that I don't have my own set of skeleton keys to open it and take cover. A third shot explodes off the top of the door frame, and I drop like dead weight, using my arms to cover my head as little pieces of wood shower down on me.

Thank god, someone out there is a terrible shot. Still, I'm terrified and almost hyperventilating.

And then it's quiet. I wait for an eternal five minutes, then grab a bucket near the door and slowly raise it to see if the shooter fires again. Nothing. I stay low and, with my heart pounding, sprint for the dog pen. Still no more shots. Maybe that's the end of it. I snatch Peach and we get the hell out of there.

~~~~~

On my way home, Will and I finally connect by phone. I'm still so shaken up that I can barely get it out that someone was shooting at me. After establishing that I'm fine, he makes me start at the beginning.

I tell him about the mysterious note I found in Peachie's toy and how that led me to *Alessandro Rare Books*, where I learned the thief's identity. I finish up with details about my visit to Casey Whitmore's house and someone shooting at me. It really hits me that this wasn't some Hollywood shoot-em-up with fake bullets. No one's ever shot at me before, and the entire episode leaves me unsteady. I pull over to calm down and also email him the pictures of the note inside the toy.

Will plans to call everything in to the police. He tells me the towed Honda Accord may have been borrowed or stolen, slowing down the process of identifying the thief, so my information may help. We agree that I won't share what I've learned with anyone until the police have a) talked to me and b) decided to release the victim's ID to the public.

After we hang up, I continue replaying the gunshots at Casey's house. One to the right of me. One to the left. And one above me. Maybe the shooter wasn't a bad aim after all. Maybe he was warning me away from Casey's house.

And then I think back to the guy who hit me over the head when I found Peachie. Was that also a warning to stay away?

Could both of these warnings have come from the same guy who killed Casey?

CHAPTER NINE

As I pull into my driveway, Sofia Rossi gets out of a gray SUV parked in front of my house. I groan. This cannot be good. Why couldn't a different officer come to the house to talk to me?

Still, I put on a smile. "Hi, Detective. How can I help you?"

There's no smile from her, just a clipped, "I'm here for the dog toy and the rolled up paper. And to get your side of the story on the shots fired over in Summit."

"Of course," I answer, still maintaining a welcoming tone. Peachie chooses that exact moment to begin an obnoxious yapping that I haven't heard from her since she arrived this morning. She minds me for less than ten seconds, and starts up again. I sigh.

"Give me a sec to get her settled down." I take Peach from her crate, then open the front passenger door and unclip my big dog's seat belt. "Warrior, come."

He hops out, takes one look at Rossi, and responds with a low growl. Rossi stiffens, and her hand flies to her holstered weapon. "Stay," I say to my shepherd as I step between him and the detective. "Do not even think about shooting Warrior," I say in a low, firm voice.

"As long as you can keep your animals under control, we won't have a problem," Rossi says.

"Warrior will not be a problem."

She drops her hand to her side. "What the hell kind of name is Warrior for a dog?"

"As a matter of fact, I didn't name him. He's a retired war dog, a veteran of Afghanistan, and if anyone has earned the name, it's him. That's all I'm going to say about that. Wait here. I'll be back as soon as I put them in their pen." I head for the side of the house, carrying Peach, with Warrior following us.

In a moment, I return. "Come on in." I walk inside, and she follows. "How about a cup of coffee, and I'll fill you in on what I know—"

"This isn't a social call, Mrs. Lake—"

"Please, call me Ronnie. And may I call you Sofia?"

"Mrs. Lake, let's get to the details about the shots fired."

Okay, so no friendly chatting with Detective Rossi. I recount what happened. I even finish up with my theory that the shooter was trying to warn me away. "I didn't stick around. You'll probably be able to recover at least one of the bullets, since the shooter fired three times."

She gives me a look of impatience. But it's when her eyes close and she shakes her head slightly that I feel her dismissal, as if I'm an interfering amateur. I stare back, unwilling to be cowed by her.

"I'll take the toy and the paper, and then I'll be on my way." Now she's all business.

"Sure." I reach down to open a cupboard.

"You should never have removed it from the scene in the first place." Rossi cannot resist lecturing me and continues in her scolding tone, "…and then you should have called us the minute you realized there was something inside that toy."

"Hold it." I stand back up. "Have you forgotten that I offered to give you that slobbery chipmunk at the scene where *I* discovered the car?" I hold firm. "You were very clear that I should get out of there with Peach ASAP, so that she would not mess up the scene."

We stare at each other like two gunslingers ready to draw.

"Furthermore, how could I know if the roll of paper inside the toy was important enough to make the call to you unless I checked it out first? Had it been insignificant, you would have barked at me not to waste your time, just like you're doing now." Her head jerks back just a little as if she's surprised someone would challenge her. I reach back into the cupboard and almost slap the paper bag with the toy and the ziplock with the list of mystery initials on the counter. "There."

Rossi looks at me as if she's sizing me up, and then she looks inside the paper bag at the toy and picks up the ziplock. "Did you handle this roll of paper without gloves?"

"I'm a licensed P.I.—what do you think?" I fire back at her. "Of course I put on gloves."

She heads for the door.

"Wait," I say. "Don't you want to hear the rest of what I learned today?"

"Will's told me everything I need to know, and I've got my team at the bookstore and the house."

"Please note that I did not enter the cat burglar's house, although I tried in order to get cover from the shots."

"So what? I don't care if you are licensed. It doesn't guarantee that you're a professional. Stay out of this investigation."

For once, I have nothing to say, and anyway, Rossi wouldn't give me a chance to speak up if I did, because she jumps back in. "FYI, why do you insist on calling Whitmore a cat burglar? Mrs. Lake, that term is so out-of-date," she says as if she's telling me I'm out-of-date. "Stealing one necklace doesn't make him a cat burglar. And at this point, we don't have his history. It sounds like you're romanticizing him." Her tone is condescending and annoys me.

"FYI, Detective. I read about an actual New Jersey cat burglar who often robbed while his victims were at home and even entertaining guests in their houses. I will text you the links—"

"Don't bother." Detective Rossi leaves with the chipmunk toy and the mystery list.

As far as I'm concerned, *good riddance, Rossi*!

~~~~~

I definitely need a distraction from the unpleasant Rossi, and the Aikido dojo is the perfect escape. So I catch a

Friday afternoon class, where I also connect with Will.

Isabella Sensei watches her students practice a sequence of techniques using the *morotetori* attack. In this Japanese martial art, *morotetori* is a two-handed grab of the opponent's arm. A dozen of us, all clad in off-white, two-piece outfits called *gis,* have been practicing four variations of techniques to blend with and then reverse this attack.

Our petite brunette teacher claps her hands to signal the end of running through the *morotetori* techniques and also the end of class. All the students, some of us with black belts and skirt-like pants called *hakamas,* kneel on the mat facing Isabella, a sixth-degree black belt. We kneel in the respectful *seiza* posture, and we bow to conclude today's practice.

After class, I meet up with Will, who stands by his car. He's a *Sandan,* or third degree black belt in Aikido, whereas I'm a humble first degree black belt, or *Shodan.* Not only have I benefitted from his vast knowledge as a private investigator, but I also benefit from his physical fighting experience when we practice this Japanese martial art together.

"Are you okay?" he asks, looking concerned.

I shrug, trying to act tough and not wanting to make too big a deal out of it. But deep down, I kind of wouldn't mind if he made a big deal because it did scare the shit out me.

"Have you ever been shot at before?"

I shake my head just as my cell phone rings. "It's

Sally Richards from the book store." Sally gives me an update on the Wharton books I had asked about, and that she's sorry, but she can't find any paper trail about my pretend order. She sounds distracted and upset.

"Are you alright?" I hear some kind of commotion in the background over the phone.

"Please, I'll move those books for you," an anxious Sally says to someone at the store. "They're valuable, and you might damage them."

"What's going on?"

"It's the police—" Another voice interrupts Sally, but I can't make out what he's saying. She responds with a tremor in her voice. "Please, I'm happy to move any of those for you." A pause. "Excuse me a moment."

"What's going on with the police?" I ask her, but look at Will as I speak.

"I'm outside Casey's office." Sally's voice sounds a little muffled, as if she has her hand covering her mouth and the phone. "They have a search warrant, so I'm trying to help."

"Where is Mr. Whitmore?" I look at Will when I ask Sally the question, knowing full well that Casey's body is in the morgue.

"I don't know. He never came in."

"What do the police say?"

"They're not telling us anything." Sally's voice is shaky.

"So they're not saying anything," I repeat for Will's benefit, and he shakes his head at me and makes a zipper motion over his lips. I get the message to not tell her what we already know about Whitmore, that he's dead.

"I hear how upset you are. Can't Ms. Alessandro help you?" I ask.

"She's not here…she's in and out all the time…" Sally sniffles and her voice cracks. "I'm sorry, Mrs. Lake." She tries to pull herself together. "I'm worried about Casey, that maybe something bad happened to him."

"Of course you're worried…" I feel for the girl and wish I could be honest with her, but Will has made it clear that's not for me to do at this time.

"He's my friend, and I don't know where he is or how to help…" Sally starts to cry. Between sobs, she manages to say, "I've gotta go," and clicks off.

"Well, it feels crummy to hold out on her," I say to Will.

"You did the right thing, until the police rule her out as a suspect."

"Suspect? No way."

"How do you know?"

"She's a kid, maybe still in school, who works in a bookstore. She was very emotional on the phone, very worried about Whitmore's well-being. Maybe he was a mentor to her…you know, like a father-figure."

"You're probably right," Will says, "but the police still need to rule her out."

CHAPTER TEN

"Parishioners baked these early this morning, and one of the volunteers dropped them off fifteen minutes ago." I place the fresh-baked fruit pie in a box and hand it and some coins to the woman. "Here's your change. Gosh, I can smell the rhubarb and strawberries. This should be delicious. Thanks for supporting the food bank, Mrs. Daly." I stand behind the display table for the booth manned by the ladies committee at our church. The sun has erased the earlier chill in the air.

The local Saturday morning farmer's market with its two dozen booths filled with fresh produce, flowers, and baked goods is my weekly ritual as a shopper and a volunteer. Sadly, in a couple of weeks, it will shut down through the winter.

I feel jumpy and somewhat hyper-vigilant ever since someone took shots at me yesterday at Casey's house. The shooter's still out there somewhere. But coming here is as good as going to the local post office. You get to see everyone and catch up on all the friendly gossip. And you never know—I may even pick up some helpful info regarding the shooting two nights ago at the Watsons'.

But not from the elderly woman I observe two booths over who's dressed in worn jeans, an old green checkered shirt, and a blue sweater tied around her neck. Sheila Johnson pays for three jars of Warwick Farm Honey from local beekeeper Dave Reynolds. They wave at me. Since there are two of us manning our booth and it's quiet for the moment, I stroll over.

"Well, hello there, Sheila." I love the way she sweeps up her beautiful silver hair into a classic French twist.

"How are you, young lady?" Sheila's work clothes cannot hide the refined old-school sound of her voice.

"I'm fine, thank you." I've always had a soft spot for Mrs. Johnson, because she was one of Mom's best friends and so caring and thoughtful after my mother died.

"Dave, how's business today?" I ask, shifting my attention to the man behind the small Warwick Farm Honey stand.

"Excellent," the tall, gangly beekeeper answers. "I'm down to my last case."

"Do you still have two jars for me?"

"Absolutely." He pulls them out of a medium-sized box.

I take several bills from my wallet. "One will make a nice gift for a friend, and the other...well, that one's for me. My jar at home is nearly empty."

I glance at Sheila's muddy muck boots. "Have you been working in your garden this morning?" I smile. "Or grooming your favorite horse?"

"Why, how'd you know?" She catches me looking at her boots, and laughs. "I just finished up in the garden. It's what keeps me young."

"I'm sure it does!" I agree.

The beekeeper hands me a bag with my jars. "Thanks for the honey, Dave. Good to see you both."

I return to the church booth and relieve the other volunteer. My eyes dart over the crowd milling about the market, looking for anyone who might fit my idea of a shooter...as if I even know. And why would he be here? There are much better opportunities to take me out.

I scold myself for being overly dramatic when I catch sight of two friends who also attended the Watson dinner. The men stand a little to the side of the White's Family Orchard cider stand, apart from the half-dozen customers who purchase bottles from owner Stan White.

They appear to be in the middle of an intense discussion while sipping cider. A couple of other customers shift slightly in order to pay, revealing a third person who's part of their conversation but rushes off. I'm sure it's Katya Alessandro. What I wouldn't give to abandon my post and walk over there to get a good look, but I lose sight of her in the crowd.

I wave, and my friends see me and wave back. One of them, the tall gray-haired Josh Brown, husband of a close friend, takes a glass and pours more cider. He holds it out to me, I nod, and he pays. The two men continue talking as they walk over to my booth.

"...I'm trying to talk Win into selling it," says George

Smithson, the other man in the conversation. He's a barrel-chested, professorial type and a rare book dealer who lives in Willowbrook with his family but has his business in the city. "I think I have a client who would pay almost five hundred for it."

"Five hundred?" Josh repeats. "Really?"

I take the glass from Josh. "Five hundred what? Dollars?" I ask. "For one of your rare books, George?" The two men say nothing, but have amused expressions on their faces.

I finally get it. "You don't mean five hundred *thousand*?" They nod at me as if saying, *But of course.* My eyes pop open, and Josh and George laugh. "What book could possibly be worth five hundred thousand dollars?"

"In this case, it's Win's very special first edition of *The Great Gatsby*," George answers. "But his copy was slightly damaged during that attempted robbery. It appears that intruder had a thing for rare books and may have dropped it when he was snooping around upstairs." George looks at me. "Don't look so shocked, Ronnie."

"I thought he wanted Marilyn's diamond necklace...at least that's what was on his body when he fell. So, what...he also went after Win's priceless first edition but didn't take it?" Because I promised Will, I do not tell them that I have discovered the identity of the intruder, and that he also happens to be a rare book expert.

"That book is worth more than the necklace," George

adds. "So, I take it back, maybe he doesn't know much about old books."

"Go figure," I say.

"Plus *Gatsby* is small in size," Josh adds. "He could have easily slipped it inside the vest he was wearing."

"Well, that prize is already at my New Jersey warehouse, ready for some restoration work," the book dealer says.

I jump in. "One of these days I'd love to see the warehouse. Is it close by?"

"It is. Come over any time. How about tomorrow?"

"You work on Sundays?" I ask.

"I work all the time, and I'll be there," he says. "I'd be happy to show it to you. You too, Josh, and bring Susan."

"I'll see if she can come," he says.

"Sounds great." I smile and nod as two prospective customers walk up. One orders a box of cookies and the other four pastries. We settle up, and I turn back to George and Josh.

"Not to change the subject, but tell me about that glamorous woman you were talking to at the cider stand before you came over here." I try to keep my voice kidding and light.

Josh jumps in. "Ah, she happens to be a competitor of George's."

"You mean Katya?" George asks, then harrumphs. "Well, I guess you're right."

"Ooh, tell me more," I say, wanting not to sound too curious.

"Katya Alessandro owns *Alessandro Rare Books*, a half block from my shop in the city. She's got another store in Summit," George answers. "Why do you ask?"

"I thought I saw her at the Watsons' party, but she left early."

"I half-expected she'd be there," Josh says. "But then again, Marilyn might not be crazy about that idea."

"Oh?" I ask, hoping Josh will offer more.

"Probably just rumors," George cuts in, ending the topic.

"Okay, okay, let's not gossip." But I'm a tad disappointed. "Next topic. Is there a lot of rare book theft out here in New Jersey?"

"Hardly ever," George says, and then corrects himself. "Well, except for some twentieth century American fiction disappearing from a few collections in the state lately. The strange thing is they turned up again right back on those same shelves. Do those count as thefts? I don't know."

"Hold that thought while I help this nice customer over here." I assist a young girl who eagerly chooses an apple pie with her mother, while George and Josh look over the cookies and pastries.

After the mother and daughter leave, I ask, "Josh, you're a book collector. Are there a lot of you in the Garden State?"

"You'd be surprised how many people collect books," he answers. "Getting the really good editions of *The Great Gatsby* can be expensive—so that's a smaller group."

"Any other collectors out here?" I continue, with a twinkle in my eye. "Important ones like you two?"

"Well, you met a third one at the Watsons'," George points out. "Jamie Gordon's a serious collector. He's been a client of mine for a while, even before he moved to New Jersey when he was still on the West Coast."

I respond, probably a bit too enthusiastically. "I did notice him looking at some of Win's books after dinner."

"We noticed you noticing him at Win's dinner," Josh says and chuckles along with George.

"Was I that obvious?" I can't hide a small smile.

"Only to us." George smiles, too. "Anyway, he grew up in California, and early on, all he wanted was forgeries of famous first editions or real first editions with forged author signatures or inscriptions."

I look at him quizzically. "What? Forgeries?"

"Believe it or not, there's a market for them," Josh adds. "Hey, anything can become collectible if it's rare and hard to find. Of course, the category of forgeries is nothing compared to the price a book like Win's could fetch. That's where the serious investment is."

I smile. "I guess there's something for every taste in the world of books."

"There sure is. Like a sexual fetish, there's something for everyone," George says with a wilting smile.

"Isn't that a little twisted, or at the very least, cynical?" I laugh nervously at his joke.

"Some might say that, but the money's spot on," George adds. "Jamie did broaden his focus, and he's built a fine collection—" George stops mid-sentence when he sees someone. "Excuse me, Ronnie. We'll be right back. Josh, come on. I want you to meet that guy." He gestures toward a man in khakis who's leaving the market. "See him? I'll explain later. Hurry." And they rush off.

As I tidy up the display of pie tins and other baked goods on the table, an explosive noise from behind startles me and hurts my ears. Dropping to the ground, I seek cover under the table. *Did the shooter find me here?*

I hear the crash of something falling down and people yelling. *Not again.* I look behind me. Nothing.

I stand up very slowly, keeping cover behind my booth, and look around. The flower stand behind me is fine, with its owner also cautiously looking around.

Katya rushes by. She looks me straight in the eye, and the stare sends shivers up my spine. Then she's gone.

I look further down the row of booths behind the one I'm manning, and I see that a vegetable stand has collapsed completely. There are already people helping the farmer pick up his produce.

I look back in the direction that Katya was heading. What is her story? Was she somehow responsible for that stand falling down? And if so, why?

CHAPTER ELEVEN

"Of course. I'm on my way! Well, actually right after I drop off Peachie at the groomer's," I say to Juliana over the speaker phone in my Mustang. I don't tell her about the stand collapsing at the farmer's market earlier this morning. I've calmed down since then. "Yes, of course I'm bringing Warrior. Didn't Frank say it's okay to bring dogs to this fundraiser as long as they're well-behaved?"

After I drop off Peachie, Warrior and I drive into Willowbrook and the post office parking lot where we pull in right behind my brother's Porsche. Frank and Juliana turn to look back, and we wave to each other and then take off as I turn on "Good Vibrations" by the Beach Boys. It's an upbeat song for a beautiful day. My hair whips in the wind as Warrior and I drive with the top down in my convertible.

Fifteen minutes later, we drive through an entrance and cruise up a tree-lined road. Teenage boys walk in small groups across grassy lawns and past clusters of tall sycamore trees, some beginning to display autumn colors. A sprawling two-story clapboard building with black shutters comes into view, perhaps the original farmhouse on the property.

We pass several institutional-looking buildings—most likely classrooms and dorms—and arrive at a gigantic open meadow. It's surrounded by cars and SUVs. I wonder how many football fields would fit inside the lines marking this playing field. Eight riders on horses, swinging mallets, gallop toward the goal at the other end of the meadow.

Frank and I park our cars toward the center of the field and near the Watsons. We all greet each other.

"Ronnie, you decided to come after all!" Marilyn hugs me and then continues fussing around a table filled with baskets of sandwiches, fruit, and cookies.

"I was supposed to finish something for Will," I say, "but the bottom line is I had to get out of the house."

As Marilyn places pitchers of iced tea and lemonade on the table, Win gives her a quick squeeze. Things seem normal between them. She gives no sign of how upset she was two nights ago when we talked about her husband and Katya. Either she's gotten over her suspicions, or she's a great actress.

The polo match is well underway, and I climb onto the top of the back seat of my car for a better view of the field. Warrior crawls onto the back seat, too, in order to sit next to me.

With the sun in my eyes, the players are almost silhouetted against the blue sky. It's a beautiful site—the strong polo ponies galloping across the field, their helmeted riders deftly swinging mallets to move the ball down the field toward the goal. The sound of the thundering hooves only adds to the drama.

For a moment I think I recognize one of the riders even though I don't personally know any polo players. His dark brown pony is being shoved to the side by another player's white horse, and he hurls obscenities at the offending rider. The umpire fouls the aggressive rider and tries to calm the angry player, who definitely has a bad temper.

Still, it's hard to ignore the beautiful physicality of the sport as the angry player settles down and resumes playing, guiding his brown pony with his sculpted thighs. The muscles in his shoulders and arms ripple through his shirt as he twists and turns in the saddle, then smoothly swings the mallet backhand to strike the ball, passing it back to a teammate. I can't see his face against the sun and contemplate if it's as beautiful as his body, or is it still angry?

The riders stop for a moment, and the player I've been watching looks down at his stirrup, his helmet blocking his face. I glimpse his firmly set jaw, and I catch my breath. No, it can't be… I raise my binoculars and adjust the focus slightly. As the man comes more clearly into view, he looks up and straight at me with those penetrating dark eyes.

Where a moment ago there was anger, now a slight smile plays at the corners of his mouth, and Jamie Gordon mouths the word, *Hey.*

I slowly lower the binoculars, never breaking Jamie's gaze and mouth a greeting back to him. How is it that a simple word can feel so intimate when quietly tossed between two people who barely know each other?

The moment passes as he gallops away to join his teammates. What is it about this man? My days of schoolgirl-crushes are long gone. I've been divorced a couple of years, and there's been no one during that time.

Well, except for almost Will Benson a year ago, when I hired him to investigate a family matter. Our friendship grew into a strong attraction, but ultimately the fifteen-year age difference bothered me. When push came to shove, I didn't want the man in my life to be that much younger. So we agreed to be best friends, and that's worked out fine.

I glance over at Juliana and Marilyn, who are smiling at me. "You go, girl," Marilyn says quietly. Suddenly my face feels flush, realizing they've seen the quiet exchange between Jamie and me.

"That's some temper he's got," I say to Marilyn. "Did you see Jamie and the other rider shoving their ponies at each other?" I wonder if he always flies off the handle so easily.

Marilyn pours an iced tea and hands the glass to me. "Ronnie, Jamie's a nice man, and he's been asking Win about you." She refills her own.

"Well, well, Mrs. Watson. Are you playing matchmaker at a benefit to raise money? Shouldn't we be focusing on the students and this wonderful school instead of romance?"

"We can do both." Marilyn clinks my glass with hers

and glances toward Jamie on the playing field.

"For god's sake, don't look at him." I stare into my iced tea glass.

"You like him, don't you?"

"I've exchanged a handful of words with the man…I hardly know him."

"You do like him, I knew it," Marilyn interrupts and laughs. "Okay, here's what I know. He's a self-made guy just like Win—those are the best kind, and I should know. No offense to inherited money—you turned out great and worked all those years as if you didn't have a dime." All of a sudden she narrows her dark eyes, looking past me, and her husky voice gets raspier. "Son of a bitch!"

I look around to see what she's talking about. Further down the field, where a dozen horse trailers are parked, I see Win with two pretty women and another man. He's refilling their glasses from his bottle of wine. Then Win dips his head toward one of the women as if he's telling her a secret. She bursts out laughing.

"Damn him." Marilyn glares in his direction, seething. Will she ever realize that Win really only loves her, no matter how much he may flirt…at least I think he does.

Marilyn pulls it together pretty quickly. "Now let's get back to the very sexy Jamie Gordon. I'm pretty sure you'll be hearing from him. Soon."

I shrug. "We'll see."

"None of that we'll see." Marilyn smiles. "Darling,

it's time for some fun." She lets loose with her signature throaty laugh, and my German shepherd emits an enthusiastic *woof.* "See, even Warrior approves."

Frank, Juliana, and Win join us just as Jamie scores a goal. The crowd erupts into cheers, and the first half of the match ends.

~~~~~

Forty-five minutes later, after Jamie's team wins, the school's principal awards the trophy, thanks the crowd for their support, and reiterates the important work they do for the boys. She invites the audience to meet some of the teachers.

I walk along the sidelines with Warrior on his leash and chat with friends. As I stride in the direction of my car, a steady masculine voice comes from behind.

"Well, well, Mrs. Veronica Rutherfurd Lake." I turn to find Jamie Gordon leading the gray pony he rode at the end of the match. His eyes twinkle.

Mine twinkle back at him. "It's a mouthful, I know, but if I dropped Rutherfurd, I'd be Veronica Lake, and I hardly fit the role of a movie femme fatale." I laugh. "Anyway, everybody has always called me Ronnie as far back as I can remember."

"Done," he says.

"How about you? Is Jamie an old childhood nickname?"

"No, it's always been Jamie."

"And how about your pony?" I stroke the animal's forehead.

"How about my pony what?" Again, that slow smile emerges as the corners of his eyes crinkle.

"Does your pony have an interesting name?" I could drown in those brown eyes of his.

"Persia," he answers.

"Why Persia?"

"Polo is thought to be the first team sport, and the Persians were among the earliest polo players around 600 BC. So I named her in honor of the sport's proud history."

"It's the perfect name for this gray beauty," I say.

"I have a soft spot for Persia. She's been with me for six years." Jamie rubs the top of the pony's nose affectionately. "This one I trained myself. She and I have a close relationship."

Warrior, sitting quietly by my side, finally can't stand it anymore and whines. We look down at him as his tail revs up to supersonic speed, and we laugh.

"He and I also have a close relationship." I lean over to rub Warrior's neck. "Jamie, this is Warrior, and I'm happy to see how calm he is this close to your pony."

"Animals have an infallible instinct about their fellow creatures," he says as we walk toward his horse trailers.

The thought crosses my mind that Jamie's really talking about people instead of animals. I also can't help but think of his family's tragedy.

"If you're not busy tomorrow..." Jamie's voice startles me from my thoughts. "Well, once a month I host a party, an open house, if you will."

"An open house?" I ask.

"I never know who will turn up, because I tell people to bring their friends." He grins.

"That's awfully brave of you," I say, and he breaks out in a wonderful deep laugh.

"Please come and bring some of your friends."

"Thank you, I will."

We arrive at the trailers, where Jamie hands off Persia to one of the grooms. "Let me walk you to your car."

"How long have you been at Sheffield Hall? Has it been about a year?" I ask. "Word has it—" I stop, not wanting to sound like a gossip. "Didn't you do a lot of work on the place?"

"Yes, I did." We continue strolling. "Word has it? Is that so?" He pauses for just a beat and then smiles. "I brought in a first-rate architect and contractor. They started two years before I moved out here, because the house needed a lot of work, and now the outside is fully restored. Six months ago, we finished the inside. I guess the word is out, and people are curious, so sometimes they come from all over. Let me give you the address—"

"Oh, Jamie, everybody knows where it is. It's the most famous house around here!" We both laugh.

"See you Sunday at six-thirty?"

I nod. "See you then." He leaves with a wave.

I've never heard anything about the parties at Sheffield Hall, not even from Win and Marilyn, and they know everything about everybody around here. After Frank and Juliana, they'll be my second call to go with me to Jamie's party on Sunday.

CHAPTER TWELVE

"Where is it?" Josh Brown laughs. We drive around a huge loop in a business park filled with warehouses.

"George said it's number four-A." I search for numbers on the buildings. "Look that's number fifteen-B, so we passed it. I bet this road will circle back, and we'll find it."

We drive on. "It looks nice in the day time, but it would be kind of spooky if you were here alone working late," I comment. "Wonder how often George does that?"

"He's in the city most days, so probably not a lot." Josh slows down and parks. "That's George's car over there." He refers to the only other parked vehicle on this late Sunday morning.

We press the bell at four-A several times, as well as knock. Finally, we just go ahead and open the unlocked door, entering a front office with several chairs and a desk covered with disorganized piles of papers.

"George," Josh calls out in a booming voice. No answer, except banging sounds coming from the back of the building. "Come on."

We head down a short hallway leading to a cavernous warehouse with a fifty foot ceiling. Row after row of towering book cases fill the vast space. The sound of boxes being pushed and tossed comes from somewhere toward the other end of the building.

"George!" Josh calls again.

We hear a sudden crashing sound of what could be books falling to the floor, and then, "Damn! Damn! Shit!" That's followed by some loud huffing and the sound of boxes being pushed across a floor. Then a loud noise of something knocking into a bookcase. "Damn! Mother Mary…"

"George," I call out. "Are you alright?"

"Ronnie, is that you?" he calls back, making a racket as he moves through the stacks.

"Yes, and Josh, too." I walk down the long center aisle asking, "What on earth are you doing?"

George peers around a corner looking a bit flustered. "I was on a ladder and lost my balance trying to lift a few stacks of books onto an empty shelf. The books crashed down, and I almost fell off the ladder." He's out of breath. "Close call."

"I didn't know a rare book warehouse could be such a dangerous place." Josh cracks up.

Eager to change the subject, George turns down another aisle and signals us to follow. "Hey, you two, come see Win's damaged prize!"

"Thought you'd never ask," Josh says.

Once we reach an open area in the warehouse,

George leads us to a desk and several large tables piled with books and files. Behind the desk is an open wall safe. He reaches in and pulls out a small green Moroccan leather slipcase. The container leaves one side open to reveal the hardcover's binding with its title. He carries it to a table, where he pushes things aside to make space for the container. Josh and I move closer. Even I, who knows almost nothing about book collecting, can hardly wait to see what he has.

George carefully removes the book from its case, and I ask, "Is that really Win's book?" He holds it up to show us the mint-condition front of the dust jacket covering the little book. The jacket itself is encased in its own protective clear Mylar cover.

"Here it is." He holds it up.

"What in the world makes this book worth almost half a million dollars?" I ask. "It's unbelievable that someone would pay that much."

"Well, the fact that it probably has the most famous dust jacket of all time goes a long way," Josh says. "This cover with the woman's eyes staring out of a dark cobalt sky is iconic. The illustrator Francis Cugat created it…the brother of the drummer, by the way." He looks at the small volume, his eyes filled with yearning. "And it looks like this book's in perfect condition."

"Well, it was." George flips the book to the back side to show us an ugly gash torn through the plastic cover and the paper dust jacket. "And check out this bruised corner." He points to one of the book's hard cover corners that looks crushed. "The thief may have dropped it, and on its way down it could have slammed up against a sharp object or edge and then bounced on the floor."

"What a shame," I say. "Can it be repaired?"

"We'll see. It's going to my restoration guy later in the week."

All of us look quietly at the no-longer-as-priceless volume until the phone rings. George almost jumps when he grabs it. "Give me a sec." He looks at the display. "I've got to take this."

He turns his back on us and nervously walks down an aisle. All we can hear when he picks up is a tense, "Why are you calling me here?" and then his voice turns into mumbles.

"Ronnie, take a look at the back of the dust jacket." Josh points to the blurb on the back. "See, line fourteen has a lower case *j* in the name *jay Gatsby*, and it's been corrected by hand with a capital *J* in ink."

"Wait a minute," I interrupt. "How do you know all of this?"

"I've been collecting twentieth century American lit since college, and you learn along the way," he says.

"Do you own this particular book?"

"I have a first edition of *The Great Gatsby* that I bought right after law school, thirty years ago when the prices were much lower. And mine has no dust jacket." Josh smiles. "If I were starting out today, I could not afford a first edition *Gatsby*."

"Oh, come on, Josh." George chuckles as he returns

to us, more relaxed than when he took the call.

"Okay, back to this once-perfect dust jacket," I say. "How does that make this book worth almost five-hundred-thousand?"

"It's one part of the total equation." George carefully opens it to the title page. "And the book itself is in perfect condition. It contains all the verifiable first edition errors in the text."

"Such as?"

"Well, Josh described the mistake on the back of the dust jacket," George answers, and then he quickly checks off the others verbally.

"There's got to be more to this exorbitant price than those mistakes," I say. "I mean, come on, this isn't the Gutenberg Bible." I look at my two friends. "Right?"

"Many experts consider it *the* great American novel." George turns back to a flyleaf. "What takes this volume over the top is a handwritten inscription inside the book from F. Scott Fitzgerald himself. He wrote it to the recipient, and stated that he served as a partial model for Jay Gatsby. Take a look at it."

"Given the way Fitzgerald wrote that character," I add as I study his precise and looping handwriting, "I'm not sure I'd take that as a compliment."

"Nonetheless, it makes the book unique and very special," Josh answers.

"Does Win hope to sell the book at a profit—so it has to be perfect—or does he own it for sentimental reasons?" I ask.

"Win inherited some old books from his father," Josh says. "That's what got him started collecting. That, and he's a voracious reader."

"Whatever the reason, I've been trying to talk him into selling for some time." George puts the book back in its slipcase. "I've got someone who's been looking to fill in an excellent F. Scott Fitzgerald collection with a *Gatsby* volume of this quality and importance."

Josh and I stare at George as he quietly places the box inside the open safe without saying another word.

"Come on, George," I plead. "You can't leave us hanging. Who is it? Do we know him or her?"

"That must stay confidential, my dear!" the dealer answers, an air of mystery in his voice. "Now take a look at this."

George picks up an old leather-bound book from a pile on his desk and turns it every which-way. "At first glance, this looks like?"

"A very old book?" I offer.

"A beautiful, well-preserved old book," Josh adds. "With gilt edged pages."

The book dealer's face lights up, and he uses his fingers to separate the hard cover from the gilt pages. He holds the book up like a tray, and Josh and I stand next to him as he slightly bends the entire body of interior pages. That bending causes them to fan slightly. The solid gold edges turn into a beautiful painted landscape of buildings along the water. He lets go of the pages, causing the scene to disappear.

"That is magical," I say. "I've never seen anything like it."

George closes the book. "It's called fore-edge painting. This picture is not actually on the surface of the book's edge when you see it closed." He gives the book to Josh, who repeats the slight bending of the gilt pages to reveal the scene once again.

"What's the process to create the painting?" I ask, amazed.

"Well, the artist starts with a book that already has all edges gilt," George says. "Then he puts the book in a vice that fans out the pages so that he can paint the scene. Unless you fan the pages, you don't see the painting, as with this book."

Josh gives the book back to George, who continues, "This one is going to a college library with a substantial collection of these fore-edge painted books."

"Do you have any more of these?" I ask. "This is much more fun that looking at *The Great Gatsby*."

CHAPTER THIRTEEN

As I zip up my dress, I almost trip over a small, furry ball of energy spinning around my feet, carrying one of my shoes in her mouth. "No, Peach." The terrier freezes and stares at me.

I lean down to encourage her to release the shoe. "Not these. They're a gift from Juliana." She lets go, and I slip that shoe and its nearby mate onto my feet.

"How do I look, Warrior?" I twirl once in my black cocktail dress. Warrior, in his attentive sit-position, woofs twice, and I laugh. It's part of our regular routine before I go out for the evening. Peach, sitting next to the German shepherd and now holding onto her squirrel-toy, eyes me as I check my outfit one final time in the full-length mirror inside my closet.

The closet is the size of a small bedroom, because that's what it was before I remodeled. It was my big splurge when I renovated my guest cottage almost two years ago. After all, I'm a downsizing-empty-nester.

It's not that I own a boatload of clothes—I gave most of them away when I was laid off from my corporate job at a cable network a couple of years ago. But I like being able to actually see the clothes I've kept, instead of having them stuffed inside a small closet where they hang forgotten most of the time. This bedroom-into-closet redo was my answer to the eternal complaint of almost all women—not enough closet space!

I've had this dress for years. It's a classic form-fitting, but not too tight, sleeveless sheath. I check the modest off-center slit at the hem. It's just enough to show off the lovely sheer black stockings leading down to the even lovelier black pumps on my feet.

I turn profile to the mirror to get a look at the iconic red soles of these Christian Louboutin shoes. Even though I'm a confirmed admirer of Juliana's out-of-sight shoe wardrobe, I would never have indulged in a pair myself, always joking about my achy fifty-something feet. Then my wonderful sister-in-law took me shoe shopping for my most recent birthday.

I remember a moment of disappointment upon first entering the Madison Avenue store in Manhattan, reminding myself that my feet would never tolerate the mile-high heels usually associated with Louboutins. Juliana saved the day when she spotted just the right pair at a more realistic, almost kitten-heel height. The sling-backs were love at first sight.

Channeling the elegant Audrey Hepburn in her classic black *Breakfast at Tiffany's* cocktail dress, I grab my black cashmere shawl, a small clutch, and head out the door.

~~~~~~

On the way to Jamie's party, I pick up Juliana since Frank is out of town. During the drive over, I click on "Smooth Operator" by Sade, a favorite of mine from the 1980s.

Juliana and I sing along with Sade's smoky voice as we cross a small bridge and the view opens up. There above the treetops, we glimpse the silhouette of an imposing mansion at the top of the hill. A Gilded Age financier constructed the stately home at the beginning of the twentieth century.

The jazzy sound of Sade accompanies us as the Mustang drives up to Sheffield Hall.

As my car approaches the hilltop, I feel unfamiliar butterflies at the thought of seeing *him*. It's been a long time since I've felt goose bumps on my arms because of a man. I laugh.

"What?" Juliana asks.

"Oh, nothing." It's nice to be my age and still feel like a twenty-something over a man.

I turn the car into the long u-shaped entrance with a pool running up the middle. Spotlights feature water splashing from six fountains in the pool. Even if this were considered a McMansion back in its day, a century later this beautiful entry is definitely working its magic on me.

I give the car to valet parking while Juliana hands over our shawls. "You're expecting a big crowd?" I ask, distractedly, putting my valet ticket in a small pocket.

"Yes, ma'am," the girl with our shawls answers. When I look up, I first notice long hair the same shade of red as my niece, Laura, and just as wild, too. I do a double-take as she rotates back to me.

"I know you," I exclaim to the petite, young woman. "Sally from *Alessandro Rare Books*, right?"

We both smile, and Sally gives me a ticket for my shawl. "Good to see you, Mrs. Lake." There's a twinge of sadness in her voice, and I detect circles under her eyes that I didn't see the other day.

"Are you alright?" I ask in a quiet voice. I suppose she could be a student working multiple jobs to pay her way through college.

"Yeah, I'm fine," she answers. "I'm just reeeeally worried about Casey. I still don't know what's happened to him." Her voice quivers. "I don't know what to do."

"Of course you're worried," I say. "He's your friend. I'm sure you'll hear something soon." Juliana looks on sympathetically, and she and I turn to walk away.

"What was that about?" she whispers.

"Tell you later," I whisper back.

We walk down an enormous grand hall leading to equally enormous rooms where other guests float in and out, many visibly gawking at the elegant surroundings. On the walls, ancient tapestries alternate with massive paintings, some showing bloody battle scenes and others populated with mythical figures. Massive porcelain animals and vases sit on oversized tables placed against the walls.

The loud sound of voices coming from the end of the hall draws Juliana and me toward the largest room of all.

We look through colossal double doors at what was perhaps once a gigantic ballroom. We step inside and find ourselves on a landing at the top of a grand stairway that swoops down both left and right to a crowd of perhaps a hundred-and-fifty people. I scan the lengthy room and imagine myself waltzing its entire length.

We walk down the long marble steps and at the bottom a waiter offers us either a glass of champagne or bubbly water. We both opt for the water.

Juliana nudges my arm. "I hear some wonderful jazz. Come on, let's find it."

As we walk down the length of the room toward the music, both of us scan the crowd. "Do you see anyone you know?" my sister-in-law asks.

"Not a soul."

"But you grew up here. You and Frank know everyone in town."

"Not anymore. A lot of people have moved into the area, and Jamie told me that he encourages the people he invites to bring friends. He's the host, but even he may not know all of these people."

"How odd." Juliana links her arm in mine and guides me toward the musicians playing in one corner of the room. We manage to politely work our way close to the trio and enjoy an up-tempo number played by a keyboardist, bass player, and guitarist. Soon, more people drift over to listen and watch. The music features each of the musicians' improvisational solos, and we can't help but catch snippets of conversation coming from several people further back in the crowd.

"Where'd he get all the dough to buy this place?" a gravelly voice asks.

"I heard he made it in tech," a nasally female voice answers.

Juliana and I give each other a sideways glance. I mouth, *Don't look.* We stare straight ahead, smiling.

"Must cost a lot of dough to run this joint," the gravelly voice says. "What do you figure his overhead is?" His long, deep smoker's cough jars us, and we grimace in unison.

The woman answers, "I betcha it's a million bucks a year to take care of this place, pay for all the parties, hire all these people. Think about what we spend, Vito. Our house is huge, but not this huge."

A different female voice, this one husky, pipes up. "Russians."

"Russians what?" Vito asks.

"Freddy says Jamie Gordon went into business with some Russians," the husky voice answers.

"Mob-type guys?"

"Maybe," she says. "Anyway, that's where he made his dough."

"Have you met him?"

"No, but Freddy knows him a little, I think," the woman says. "Hey, enough with this music. I need a smoke."

"Yeah," Vito agrees. "Let's find a place."

Juliana and I watch the trio leave. We do the same, but in a different direction.

"Don't pay attention to them," Juliana says as we cross the room.

"What do you mean?"

"What those people were saying about how Jamie Gordon made his money. You know, the Russian mob and all that."

"Any time someone has made a lot of money and lives like this…" I sweep my arm around the room, "…the stories are bound to swirl. Most of the time it's all rumors."

"I'm glad you see it that way," Juliana says as we walk through an immense arched doorway into a banquet-sized dining room.

We stare at an old, mammoth, dark wood table that anchors the center of the room and is laden with food. "Perfect to seat thirty," Juliana quips.

A line forms at one corner of the antique table where people pick up forks, napkins, and small plates, before they make their way around to choose from endless platters of hors d'oevres. We walk up to the line and stand behind three non-stop chattering women who are about Juliana's age.

"…and he's handsome, too," says a sparkly voiced, brown-haired beauty with a petite, tight body.

"He's kinda old," a tall, leggy blonde responds.

"He's kinda rich," the beauty answers back.

Juliana and I look at each other, stifle grins, and quickly focus on the food.

"How come he's not married?" the third girlfriend asks the other two. "You know what they say, that the good ones are always married. Must be something weird about him that he's not."

I close my eyes and shake my head slightly.

"Shhh!" one of them hushes her friends. "Just tell the whole world." She glances at Juliana and me.

"Jamie Gordon *was* married," the blonde says, her voice more of a stage whisper this time. I do my best to focus on the array of finger foods. Endive spears filled with an avocado mousse topped with smoked trout, figs wrapped in prosciutto and stuffed with blue cheese and pecans, plump red radishes with butter and flavored salts. It's too much to take in, and I find myself listening to the women's chatter again.

"What happened? Messy divorce?" one friend asks, her tone broadcasting that she's ready for juicy gossip. I study a platter of tiny blinis with crème fraîche topped with caviar. I reach for a silver pasty server to scoop up a couple of the blinis.

"Noooo," the tall, leggy one answers, and then drops her voice again, as if it's just between the three of them. "His wife and kids are dead. Didn't you hear?"

Even though I already know Jamie is a widower, I didn't know he had children who'd also died. For a split second, I freeze, my arm midway in the air with the pastry server between the platter and my plate. The gossipy women don't notice, but Juliana does. She whispers, "Are you okay?"

My heart is pounding, but I nod. I deposit the blinis on my plate, but all of a sudden I've lost my appetite.

Sadness washes over me at the thought of Jamie losing his entire family.

"Dead? I hadn't heard that," the brown-haired woman comments. "What happened?"

Now on automatic, I help myself to one of this and one of that, quietly following the women. Juliana looks on with concern.

"Heard it was a car accident a long time ago," the tall blonde says. "His wife and two children died."

"How sad," the other two say, almost in unison.

"But I'm not sure," the blonde continues. "There have been some other stories floating around. All kind of strange. So you may want to set your sights on some other rich guy."

"Why?" The brown-haired beauty asks. "Does he have a girlfriend?"

"I don't know about that, but I heard he loves 'em and leaves 'em," the blonde answers. "Could be just a rumor, you know…"

I leave the table immediately, and Juliana follows me to the bar where we both get a glass of wine. We find a small empty table and sit with our food and drinks.

"Well, you're getting some of your color back," Juliana says, still worried about me.

"How do you even begin to pick up the pieces of your life when you've lost your entire family?" I stare at my food. "I can't even imagine." But my thoughts immediately turn to my Tommy, and I have to blink quickly to force back the tears.

Juliana sees this and places her hand on my arm gently. We sit quietly for a moment.

Finally, I pick up my glass. "Anyway, I just couldn't listen to any more of that." I sip my drink.

Juliana delicately pops a small salted radish into her mouth. "Mmmm. These are delicious. Well, there are probably a lot of curiosity-seekers here, people he's never met before."

"Who will drink his wine and eat his food and then say gossipy things about him."

"By the way, where is our host?" Juliana asks.

A waiter takes our empty plates, and I stand up. "Let's find out."

We finally spot some friendly faces in the ballroom. Win and George are sipping martinis when Juliana and I join them.

"This was a great idea," Win says to me. "Thanks for including us in your posse tonight."

Suddenly, all four of us stop our conversation as we discern a buzz spreading through the crowd. Everyone seems to look up at the same time at the top of the grand stairway.

CHAPTER FOURTEEN

There on the landing, with her back to us, stands a tall, curvaceous woman. Her shiny blue-black hair cascades past her broad shoulders in loose waves on her back. She and Jamie Gordon embrace for a long moment.

She turns, and it's the first time I get a really good look at Katya's face with its exotic high cheekbones, piercing dark eyes, and lush mouth painted deep red. Her simple black dress skims a well-toned body and leaves one shoulder and arm bare, the other covered in a long black sleeve. She defines the concept of pure elegance.

She looks out at the room with a slight, closed smile playing on her face. I'm surprised when she makes eye contact with me. Is it my imagination, or does her look linger a moment too long? Then her eyes continue sweeping the ballroom, and the effect is one of confidence; this woman knows how to make an entrance.

Jamie walks the raven-haired beauty down the grand stairway. All eyes in the ballroom remain fixed on her. I glance at Win, and he looks stone-faced. My thoughts jump straight to my friend Marilyn, who also couldn't come this evening.

I look back, but Jamie and Katya are now lost in the crowd. Given the long embrace, just how friendly are things really between the two of them? Does Win wonder the same? He certainly doesn't look happy.

I quietly slip away from my circle and lose myself in the crush of partiers. I spot Katya through a throng and try to follow her, which takes me upstairs and back to the foyer. I think I see her for a moment at the top of the steps leading to the second floor. Is she that familiar with Jamie's house that she freely moves wherever she wants?

I pause for a powder room visit. When I come out, I see Win heading up the same stairs. I look around, and when the coast is relatively clear, I dart up the stairs, too. After all, Marilyn wants me to find out what's going on between these two, and opportunity has presented itself.

I take the last few steps slowly, listening for their voices. It's totally quiet as I arrive on the second floor. There are open doors to mostly empty rooms that I glance into on both sides of a large hallway. I head toward the far end of the hall, passing a back stairway, where it's possible Win and Katya could have descended.

I arrive at massive double doors that probably lead to the master suite. Even though I'm tempted to peek inside, I resist. I can't believe they would engage in a tryst in Jamie's bedroom, and when I put my ear up to the door, I hear nothing.

I turn around to go back and almost reach the

stairway when the sound of the valets returning vehicles to the guests stops me. Could Win and Katya be leaving together? I enter a small room and walk to the window to watch for them as a few of the guests wait for their cars. I lean against one of the floor-to-ceiling bookcases to angle my view down the driveway.

"Well, what do we have here?" a deep voice behind me asks a moment later.

Gasping, I turn quickly toward the door. Arms crossed, the man leans casually against the door frame, almost in silhouette. I know immediately that it's Jamie Gordon.

Feeling a flush come over my face, I'm grateful for the dark that hides my embarrassment. I've been caught snooping upstairs in the house of a man I barely know, and there's no escape. I'm no better than some of the unattractive people I overheard gossiping earlier downstairs.

His confident stance seems so calm, cool, and collected, and I feel anything but that. I look down, sigh, and move to exit as quickly as I can.

Before I can cross the room, he orders in a firm voice, "Stop. Don't move." I freeze, startled. "Now step back to exactly where you were."

"Excuse me?" I ask. "I know I should have—"

"It's the moonlight from the window on your hair."

"What?"

"Just humor me, Ronnie. Stand in the exact same spot by the window. Please."

"Why?"

"Please." He chuckles. I walk back and look out the window. Again. "Now turn slowly. Not so fast as before."

I do as he asks, feeling somewhat awkward, but defiant at the same time.

"There," he says. "Stop." He pauses a moment, before he says, "Perfect."

"Perfect what?" I demand, impatiently.

He strides across the room until he's so close we almost touch. "The moonlight on your hair. Like gold." He pushes a wisp out of my face.

I pick up the amusement in his tone. "Don't be silly—"

"Mrs. Lake, are you always this stubborn?" he asks in a quiet voice, almost a whisper next to my ear.

"Always," I answer him back, equally quiet.

Even though we don't touch, I feel the heat coming off his body. He's so close. Close enough to…

Then I remember the spectacular Katya Alessandro making her entrance at the top of Jamie's grand stairway, and how he welcomed her with a huge hug and escorted her down the stairs. It's enough to break the spell, and I push past him to leave the room. "You have a lot of empty rooms in this house, Mr. Gordon."

He follows me. "And how is it you know that, Mrs. Lake? And by the way, what exactly are you doing upstairs in my house?"

Thinking quickly, I respond, "The powder rooms downstairs were busy, so I came upstairs to find one. That's how I know you have a lot of empty rooms, Mr. Gordon."

He laughs heartily. It's that deep laugh, and I love the sound of it. In the light of the spacious upstairs hall, we unconsciously seem to simultaneously circle each other, simply taking each other in.

"I love design and seeing how people build their nests," I say with a twinkle in my eye.

"And what conclusions have you drawn from my nest?" He laughs again.

"Well, the public rooms downstairs are more formal than how I like to live, but they're beautiful," I answer. "Really, it's the private rooms that tell you a lot about the owners."

"And?" he asks.

"And you have a lot of empty rooms upstairs, so I don't know what to make of you." I go for a carefree delivery.

"Guess I'll have to remain a mystery." Now it is he who has the twinkle in his eye as he walks to the end of the hall and dramatically swings open one of the large double doors to the master bedroom, as if he were a real estate agent showing the house. "Unless you'd like to see my bedroom?"

"Is that what you say to all the ladies when you show them Sheffield Hall?" I smile.

"No," he responds, smiling too. "Because usually I don't find them roaming around upstairs at Sheffield Hall."

I say nothing. He says nothing. It's a stand-off that feels interminable, although it's probably only ten seconds long. I turn on my heel. "Time to go back downstairs." I hope my tone sounds blithe.

His deep steady voice cuts through me. "I never took you for a coward, Mrs. Lake."

That stops me. That, and when I turn back, the amused expression I find on his face. I respond in what I hope is an equally steady and amused tone.

"Cowardice has nothing to do with it, Mr. Gordon. Thank you for inviting me to your lovely party. Good night." I smile and make my exit.

CHAPTER FIFTEEN

The three attackers move quickly down the mat toward Steven. He freezes for just a nano-moment at the sight of three strong *ukes* rushing toward him, so his attempts to deflect their assaults are late, half-hearted, and somewhat confused. They finally trap him and overwhelm him.

Isabella Sensei claps. The rest of the Monday noontime Aikido class claps, too, as the four students disband with quick bows, friendly smiles, and a few slight slaps on the back before heading to the side of the mat with fellow students.

"Steven, remember, do not wait for the *ukes* to run toward you. Be aware of all of your attackers, but choose the one you wish to engage with first and move toward that person. You need to blend and change direction, either sending him past you or away from you. It depends on where the other attackers are located and who you will be dealing with next. You need to have control of all your attackers." She pauses. "Okay. Ronnie, now it's your turn."

She looks at the other students. "I need four *ukes* this time."

Will is the first to jump up. He is the largest and strongest of my attackers. I feel my pulse speed up even more as I walk to my end of the mat. I kneel, take in the entire dojo, and inhale several deep breaths to calm myself. I remind myself that *randori*, the rapid freestyle technique where multiple students attack one classmate simultaneously, is about focus and not muscling or forcing the attackers.

I bow to the floor, look up, and spring to my feet, eager to meet my opponents. First I head for a brunette named Allison, pretending she's Katya Alessandro in Jamie's embrace, and slam her into the ground.

I deflect each of my four attackers at least twice, and my focus remains razor-sharp throughout. As I throw Ben, who's so young and with the energy to match, I realize I'm tired. That's when Will surprises me, coming in from the side.

I have a sudden spark of déjà vu.

I still see Will, but a figure is now behind him off to the side, tucked back in the woods and difficult to make out. Just as suddenly, whoever it is disappears. The moment passes quickly, but throws me off in the middle of *randori*, causing me to step back numerous times.

I'm still off-balance and unable to move to the side as Will steps in to grab my *gi* from the front. I know that in a split second we will collide straight on.

In desperation, I take the heel of my palm and punch upward toward Will's chin, which causes his head to move back in order to avoid the blow. The momentum throws him to the rear, and he takes a backward roll.

Isabella claps, and the action stops. My four *ukes* and I find our places on the mat, and we bow to each other.

"Excellent, Ronnie, especially the finish with that reliable punch underneath the chin when you felt yourself losing control of the attack."

That déjà vu image of that guy behind Will, the reason that I lost control of the attack, feels familiar to me but just out of reach. I struggle to retrieve it from my memory, but I can't.

I glance toward Will, who gives me a small smile and quick wink. I feel myself blush. The old spark is still there. For a moment, I give in to the attraction and wonder if I should just go for it with him.

To be honest, I feel like a pressure-cooker ready to explode. It's been several years since I last had sex, what with my divorce and all. But with Jamie Gordon on my mind at the moment, that most definitely wouldn't be fair to Will. If we were to have sex, I think Will would want more of a relationship, as would I, and I'm not prepared to take it there. He's too good a friend and mentor to me to risk ruining that with sex.

So, get a grip, I remind myself. And what about Katya? Why do I find her so threatening that I have a fantasy in the middle of Aikido class that has me throwing her around like a rag doll? Something about her nudges at me, and it's not just that Jamie gave her a huge, long hug at his party.

CHAPTER SIXTEEN

Marilyn and I sit on her terrace, each of us with a glass of wine, on one of the last warm evenings before the fall chill permanently sets in. We're finally getting down to business since she first talked to me about investigating Katya and Win.

"I... I'm worried he's having an affair with her." Marilyn says the words as if she can't quite believe it.

"No way. He's crazy about you." I hope I sound convincing, but after watching his behavior toward Katya in front of the book store and at Jamie's party, I'm not sure. Should I tell Marilyn what I saw, or stay quiet until I know more?

Marilyn bursts into tears. I quickly decide on the latter, take her hand to console her, and give her a moment to let it all out. Finally, her tears die down and she blows her nose and dabs her eyes.

"Why do you think he's having an affair?" I ask.

"Ronnie, I've never told anyone this..." Marilyn closes her eyes. She seems to be struggling to gather her thoughts, then pushes forward with extreme inflections and hesitations. "Back when we lived in Summit years ago, Win had an affair—"

"Noooo," I protest. Is this for real? I've never seen Marilyn like this, so dramatic. "Who was the other woman?"

"Her name was Sydney Ballantine." She shudders as if it's all too painful to remember. "It almost ended our marriage."

Sydney Ballantine, I repeat to myself. *Why does that name ring a bell?* I can feel my furrowed brows, my default expression for confusion, and I try to relax.

Marilyn continues. "I don't want to talk about it, but I will say this: the situation corrected itself, and Win understood he'd better not try it again. We've been fine for a long time. Until now, although Win doesn't know that I suspect him of cheating."

"Tell me what you know about Katya."

She takes a deep breath. "She's a book dealer over in Summit…" Her voice drifts off, and she gazes at the ground, lost in another world.

"I saw her at your dinner the other night, but she didn't stick around." I try to use a gentle tone. "It looked like she and Win had a disagreement over something."

"Good riddance, as far as I'm concerned. Win included her because she's good for a decent donation to the animal rescue. Not my choice, and I have to admit, only to you, that I had a delicious revenge dream about her last night that included finishing her off."

Whoa, girl. Let's take it easy, I think to myself. This

is not a side I've ever seen in Marilyn, but then it's clear she's hurting. *Sydney Ballantine, Sydney Ballantine—I know that name. Ronnie, forget Sydney. Stay focused on Katya.*

"If Katya went away in real life or went *poof* and disappeared, I wouldn't be sad for a second. I detest that woman." Marilyn's voice has a bitter edge to it.

"What do you mean, went away?" I ask. "Do you mean moved out of this area?"

"That would work for me, but she has those two shops, so that's not going to happen. Oh Ronnie, use your imagination."

"Went away…as in went away to *prison*?" I ask. "Isn't that a far-fetched fantasy?"

"Well, stealing someone's husband is really criminal—"

"It sounds like wishful thinking, my friend." I'm still distracted by the idea of Win's old affair. *Sydney Ballantine! I do know that name. She was the socialite over near Summit, the one who went missing some years back*, I think to myself. I try to hide my shock by plastering a half-smile on my face. *She never turned up, and there was talk she may have been murdered. But the police never recovered a body. Wait a minute…*

"Earth to Ronnie," Marilyn says. "Hello, have you not heard a single word I've said?" She stares at me as if I'm an imbecile. "I have something to show you, and everything will make more sense." She stands up. "I'll be right back." She disappears into the house.

I take another sip of wine. I still find this possibility of an affair hard to believe. Marilyn and Win have always appeared to be one of the more rock-solid couples out here, and they did look like they were having fun at the polo fundraiser the other day. But appearances can be deceiving.

Marilyn returns with a piece of paper and a volume that looks like a diary. She sits down and hands me the paper. "Take a look at this. I think *she* sent it to my husband."

I read a note that is written in blue ink.

Dear Win,   *August 8*
You've got what I want, and I'm coming to get it. Nothing can stop me. I've waited so long...

The message has no signature. Was the writer interrupted? Or was she confident the recipient would recognize the small, tight script and know who penned this? I look up at my friend.

"Are you sure this is Katya's handwriting?"

"No, but who else would write him this note? I found it among some papers when I was picking up around his desk in his upstairs library." Her voice cracks as she begins to cry again.

I put my arm around her to try to calm her. "This note could be interpreted several ways."

"I'm not a fool, Ronnie. You said you saw them yourself at our party. Even if they were arguing, it looked too cozy, more like a lovers' quarrel."

"Have you spoken to Win about this?"

"No, because there's something else that has me nervous. I looked in his diary, and there've been a number of meetings with his lawyer." Marilyn shows me several entries in Win's book.

"Doesn't Win use the calendar on his phone?"

"Yes, but this diary was a special gift from one of his friends, and he keeps it upstairs in his library."

I close the calendar and touch the marbled chestnut brown cover.

"Is he—" Her voice cracks as she speaks. "Is he looking to trade me in?" Marilyn breaks down sobbing and puts her face in her hands, her body shaking this time.

"What makes you think that?" I ask. "Maybe you're jumping to conclusions too quickly."

"No!" Her voice is sharp, and she sits up ramrod straight. "Win and I always tell each other everything about our schedules. We do it at breakfast, and now I've discovered he's left out all these appointments over the last several weeks. Something's going on. Is he changing his will with all these meetings at the lawyer's? What does that mean for our children?"

She pauses, rubbing her temples as if she feels a headache coming on. I'm speechless.

"Here." She lays out the two items. "Do you have your phone handy?" I nod, and she asks, "Can you snap some pictures? I need to have these in a safe place, you know, in case the originals disappear."

"Why in the world would they disappear?" I click my

phone over the letter.

As I do so, Marilyn scoffs, "Because I think this is all somehow tied to that bitch Katya, who may be his lover."

I'm astonished by this turn of events about one of the most solid and generous couples in the community. I move on to the diary pages and carefully snap pictures of those.

"First, I don't buy that femme fatale act of hers." Marilyn takes a drink from her rapidly disappearing glass of wine. "It's straight out of a bad 1940s Rita Hayworth movie. And I've heard too many stories."

"What stories?"

"That she uses her high-end book business to sink her claws into very rich, very successful, very *married* men."

"Is Katya a home-wrecker?"

"She's broken up her fair share of marriages over the years, according to the local gossip. You know Susie Davis?" I nod yes, and Marilyn continues, "Well, from what I've heard, she got the Katya Alessandro treatment when Bud left her two years ago."

"But Katya's not married, is she?"

"I heard there used to be a marriage, and then a divorce." Marilyn pours more wine into my glass.

"Maybe that's why she goes after other women's husbands?"

"I don't think so. It doesn't seem to be her end-game."

"What is?"

"I suppose receiving lots of very expensive, important

gifts and going on extravagant trips, you know, lovers' getaways." Marilyn's voice drips with sarcasm. "And finally, motivating men to leave their wives. And when she's finished with her games, she dumps them in some grand, overly-dramatic way straight out of a bad soap opera."

"Wow, so it's not about the wives. It's the husbands she's out to get. Is that what you think?" I ask. "And the wives are collateral damage?"

Marilyn doesn't answer but slowly inhales the crisp evening air, and we both sit quietly looking out at the garden. It's early enough that the light is still good, and we watch a red fox peek out from a perennial bed and dart across the wide lawn to a hedge of boxwoods. He turns to stare at us and then dives between two shrubs, his bushy tail the last thing we see before he disappears. It's a welcomed intrusion into this conversation, and we are transfixed by the moment.

"What a healthy-looking fox," I tell my friend.

Marilyn pulls it together, and a stillness washes over her demeanor. "I'm not really sure what any of this means," she says finally as she sweeps her hand over the diary and letter. "And that's why I want to hire you to investigate my husband and get to the bottom of things." The tone of her voice is determined and fierce.

Dead silence. We stare at each other for what feels like an eternity. It's probably less than ten seconds.

"Cat got your tongue?" Marilyn gives me a sly smile. For the moment, she's back to her old charming self.

"You're serious. You really do want to hire me? Why?"

"Because this is what you do now. Didn't you just get your license as a private investigator?"

"Yes, but I'm still pretty green."

"I don't care. You'll get more experience working on this case for me. And Ronnie, you're my friend, the only one I can trust with this, and you understand, because you know Win and me."

"And that's exactly why I'm not so sure that's a good idea. I may be too close to see things objectively. I could call Will Benson, who's the best—"

"No. It has to be you."

Before I can answer, we're interrupted by a masculine voice calling out, "Hello. Anybody home?"

I recognize it and turn to my friend, stunned. "Marilyn, you didn't..."

CHAPTER SEVENTEEN

"Enough of my sad story. Now it's time for some fun and darling, remember, I'm looking out for you." My friend grabs the diary and note, then dashes into the foyer.

"This way, Jamie." I hear her call out. "Please excuse my allergies—they're killing me today," she says to him with a faux sneeze, an excuse for her slightly puffy face from her earlier tears.

I hear a rapid, tense conversation that I can't make out. Jamie's pitching a fit and his voice grows louder and sharper, but with a sudden command Marilyn hushes him up. I guess she's successful, because the next thing I know is they're laughing. How odd. "We're on the back terrace," she says. "Head out and please make yourself a drink while I finish up a couple of things in the kitchen." The last thing I hear her say as she moves through the dining room is, "Win's running a little late."

Jamie steps onto the terrace and beams a huge smile my way, probably remembering that he caught me upstairs in his house last night. I'm so glad he's amused.

"Did you know about this?" I ask as I point my finger

back and forth between him and me.

"Absolutely. I'm the one who planted the idea with Marilyn." He struts over, amused by my surprised expression. "Can I freshen up your drink?"

I smile sweetly. "Only if you take that smug look off your face."

We walk to the cart that serves as a mini-bar, where he pours wine for each of us.

We lightly clink our glasses, and I say, "It's hard to believe what happened here last week." We look up at the gigantic dogwood tree through which the burglar tumbled to his death.

I glance around the garden, and then stop and go back to a large boxwood. "Hey, what's that?" I put my glass on the cart.

He automatically does the same with his. "What?"

"Over there, on the ground by that huge boxwood." I take off toward whatever it is that's near the bush. "Come on."

"I don't see it…but okay." He follows me.

We pass the massive tree and walk toward a cluster of bushes. Sure enough, there's something underneath the largest of the shrubs but toward the back, so I can't make out what it is. Maybe a pamphlet of some kind?

I circle around the rear of the bushes for an easier approach and see a flimsy, thin paperback lying in the dirt. It looks like something for the trash until I see the word *Gatsby* in the text on the first page.

"Whoa!" I shake out my wadded up paper cocktail

napkin. "I don't know what this is, but I think it's important." I use the napkin to pick it up and reach it to Jamie. "Careful. This may have something to do with the guy who fell off the roof."

"It looks like some torn up old book..." Jamie takes it with the napkin and turns it every which way. "But it's not."

"How so?"

"I can't believe it," Jamie mutters to himself, almost in a trance. He carefully looks at both the front and back of the bound pages.

"Jamie!" At the sound of my voice, he snaps out of it and looks at me with a somewhat strange expression. I bushwhack through several branches; then, he grabs my hand and pulls me back to the terrace.

"Give me a sec," I say. "I have a box of gloves in my car." I call back to him, "Please don't handle it, you know, flip through the pages, until I give you a pair."

When I return, the book sits on a chair next to the table. He's retrieved our glasses from the bar and holds mine out to me.

Marilyn reappears carrying a tray laden with a small platter and several smaller bowls of food. "We're almost set." She nods her head in the direction of the French doors. "I've got the rest on the dining room table."

We help her set up outside and then sit down to enjoy a cold supper of poached salmon and grilled vegetables. I'm famished, and it looks delicious.

More importantly, I'm dying to show Marilyn what

we found under the boxwood, but a door slams in the house. At the same time I receive a text from Will. He says the police have released the identity of the dead thief to the press. He also sends me the press release with more details.

A gray-haired woman peeks out a door from the dining room. "Excuse me, Mrs. Watson, if you don't need anything else, I'm leaving." She starts to go, but catches herself and says under her breath, "Oh, and...he's home."

Marilyn says quietly, "Thanks, Ginny. See you tomorrow."

An aggravated voice booms from the front hall. "Marilyn, where are you?"

Both Ginny and Marilyn flinch slightly, and the housekeeper rushes away.

"Out here, darling." Marilyn stands up as Win walks onto the terrace. "Just in time for supper," she says, and he nods and gives her a kiss.

"First, I need a stiff one." On the way to the drinks cart he leans over and gives me a quick hug. "Hey, Jamie!" he says, and they nod at each other.

"Hard day at work?" I ask.

"Not at all. But you'll never believe where I've been since four o'clock," he says to Marilyn as he makes his drink—vodka over a few ice cubes in a tall glass. His tone of voice broadcasts that at the moment he's not a happy man.

"It sounds like a meeting that didn't go well?" she asks, as she fixes her husband a plate of food. I hear a slight tone of suspicion in her voice.

"I've been at George Smithson's warehouse, talking to him and the police." He comes back to the table with his drink.

"What on earth—" she responds.

"Some son-of-a bitch stole my first edition *Great Gatsby*!"

"What?" Marilyn and I say in unison.

"It's true." He plops into the chair and takes a long drink from his glass. "That dead thief must have dropped it when he was snooping around upstairs, so I sent it over to George for repairs. It was at the warehouse, and a different intruder stole it from him. George was even knocked unconscious. He was in a daze when he came to and doesn't remember much about the break-in." Win takes another drink.

"Is George alright?" Jamie asks.

"Yes, he's fine. When he woke up, he called the police. He's okay. He got checked out."

"What a relief," Marilyn says.

"It's got me thinking." Win puts his glass down on the table. "What are the odds of two thefts happening to us?"

"Pretty remote," Jamie says.

"Unless the two are somehow related?" I offer. Everyone looks at me.

"Nah, I don't buy that." But Win pauses as if he's considering my theory and then continues, "The book is insured, of course, but that's not the point. It's priceless, and a cornerstone of my collection."

Win digs into his salmon, and I announce, "Well, hot off the presses, I just found out that the police have released the name of the dead thief."

All three stop eating. "Well, come on, Ronnie," Marilyn says. "Don't keep us in suspense."

"His name is Casey Whitmore, age seventy-two, and he lived over in Summit." No one says anything. I hesitate, and they notice.

"What else do they know?" Win asks.

"Well, let's see what's in the press release." I tap and scroll down on my phone and read. "Okay...longtime employee at Alessandro Rare Books in Summit, New Jersey—"

"I never saw this man at Alessandro's," Win interrupts.

"Me, either," Jamie adds. "I never saw him there."

I'm taken aback, remembering Whitmore's response to both of them right before his death. "That's because Whitmore didn't work in sales out front." I pause a moment to continue reading. "It sounds like he was the resident expert on old books, but more behind-the-scenes, according to..." I look up for their reaction. "...Ms. Katya Alessandro, the owner." They all stare at me for the longest moment, but none of their expressions telegraph anything.

I look back at the screen. "At this time, the police are calling it a suspicious death." All three of them continue to stare at me.

Then Win notices the paperback on the chair. "What's that?" he asks, changing the subject.

"First, put on some gloves in case this is tied to the shooting." I remove two pairs, give Jamie one, and push the cardboard container towards Marilyn.

She takes a pair, and then she pushes the box to Win. With her now gloved hands, she looks at the book. "Darling, our dinner party thief may not have taken your first edition, but he could have been planning to take this, along with my necklace."

"Jamie and I found it in the bushes over there," I remark, pulling on the gloves.

Once Win puts on a pair, Marilyn hands the little book to her husband, and continues, "Isn't this part of that book your father left you?"

Rather than answer, he just stares at the paperback, and his face registers a range of emotions, everything from surprise to anger to sentimentality, and Win is not a sentimental man.

CHAPTER EIGHTEEN

"I guess the old guy dropped it when he fell off your roof," I say, trying to fill the awkward silence. Marilyn lights candles for the table as dusk dims the sky.

Win finally nods thoughtfully and then looks eerily calm. "This is a piece of an old World War II Armed Services Edition of *The Great Gatsby.*"

He slowly pages through the paperback. Puzzled, Marilyn and I watch him.

Finally he hands it back to me. "But this isn't my copy. My father left me the front of the book, not the middle."

This news surprises both Marilyn and me, and we take a closer look. Captivated by the small paperback printed on flimsy paper, I carefully rotate the four-by-six-inch squat-looking book to examine it from different angles. "A World War II-what? And why is it bound on the short side instead of the long side like most novels?"

"That beat-up little paperback is part of what has been described as the most successful book publishing project ever. These novels were sent to our soldiers during World

War II." We're all transfixed as if it's a priceless first edition *Gatsby* like Win's, and he tells us more. "The titles were printed two at a time per page and then cut horizontally in half. That made it small enough so that a soldier could slip one of these into the pocket of his fatigues."

I look at the front. "But where's the cover and beginning of the book?" I flip it over. "And the end and back cover?" I carefully turn the pages. "This appears to be just the middle."

"Well, these books were so popular among our troops—everything from mysteries and Westerns to literary books like this one—that soldiers would often tear them apart, allowing one guy to finish a novel while his buddy had just started to read it."

"Isn't it strange that this one looks like it was torn into thirds?" I ask. "Especially since *Gatsby* isn't a long novel. This section starts with chapter four."

Win hesitates. "I can't answer that. But I can tell you that the Armed Services Edition, or *ASE*, of *The Great Gatsby* renewed an interest in F. Scott Fitzgerald. It's hard to imagine now, but this was an almost forgotten novel at that time. Some scholars say that the ASE edition launched this little book on its path to becoming the great American novel, and that's because they sent so many copies to our soldiers."

"Amazing. Hey, check this out." I show Jamie one of the pages and point to some penciled writing in the right-hand margin. I know immediately that the penmanship is different from the note that Marilyn showed me moments before.

—ville, NJ

"Isn't this odd?" I ask. "It's missing the first part of the word? How many places in New Jersey end with 'ville'? Probably a lot."

Jamie doesn't look like he's paying much attention, as if his thoughts are elsewhere as he stares at the page, so I continue slowly flipping through the paperback.

"Here's another one." I tilt the book so that the group gets a look.

LPLDM

"What in blazes is LPLDM—sounds like the initials of a law firm?" Jamie mutters, more to himself than me.

I continue looking through the pages.

Olivie secretary

"Olivie, probably Olivia, somebody's assistant. Do you think these notes were written by the last soldier who read this part of the book?"

"Can't say," Jamie answers.

I glance at Win, who adds quickly, "Don't look to me for help on the scribbles."

I continue paging through this piece of the novel, and I'm near the end. "Wait. Here's one more." I show it to the group.

2nd floor

I flip through the final few pages. "There's nothing else."

Jamie just stares at the book, and I give it to him. "Hey, I've got it...humor me for a second, and let's imagine what happened. The guy who wrote these notes was taking down the address of a cute secretary named Olivia, a woman he met in Germany. The general's gorgeous young secretary, maybe?"

Jamie and Marilyn laugh, and I go on, pointing back at the page. "Do you think the second floor was where her office was? Or maybe even her living quarters?"

Jamie looks up, and his dark eyes crinkle with amusement as they look straight into mine. "Hey Sherlock, that's quite a theory you've developed."

"Hey yourself, look at the edge of the pages. Did someone try to write something on them?" I ask.

He gently flips the pages. "It's probably just the wear and tear of carrying it around during the war."

"Maybe," I say, as Jamie passes back the book.

Marilyn beams that her matchmaking may be working. "So, Win, this copy isn't yours?" She holds out a wooden bowl with salad for second helpings, and Win shakes his head. "Is it the thief's, you know, Whitmore's?" she asks. "Although, just because he may have had it doesn't mean it belonged to him. He could have stolen it, too."

"Wait a minute. I remember writing my paper on *The Great Gatsby* for school, but I don't remember ever hearing about these ASE editions until this evening, and now I find out that two of you have pieces of an ASE *Great Gatsby*? This cannot be a coincidence." I pour myself some coffee. "Win, when you're finished with supper, may I see your copy?"

"I'm finished. Let's go upstairs."

This is when Jamie calls it a night, but not before he invites me to shoot with him at his skeet and trap course the next day. Win waves good-bye and bounds up the steps to the second floor.

On our way upstairs, Marilyn mentions that Jamie's good pal Katya will also be there shooting.

"How do you know that?" I ask.

"Oh, you know, you just learn these things." Marilyn smiles knowingly. At the very least, skeet shooting could be a good opportunity to learn more about Ms. Alessandro.

Moments later, the three of us enter Win's small library off their master bedroom. He gestures, and Marilyn and I sit on the sofa. He pushes a small table out of the way and squats down to a bottom shelf in a corner of the room, an area that would be easy to overlook. He pulls out a thin book similar to the one that Whitmore probably dropped during his fall.

"Let's take a look." He sits in his big chair and puts the two pieces side-by-side on a table between us.

Win's book has a front cover. He flips through the first pages. "This is the one my father left me. One of his Army buddies tore it up, I guess, so they could all read it when they had a little downtime from the battlefield." He stares at the cover. "My dad's piece of the book was special to him because it reminded him of his time serving with those guys, but I don't remember the name Whitmore."

Win picks up the one that Jamie and I found under the boxwood. He looks at the last page of his father's piece and the first page of the section the burglar had. He slowly puts them together and gently pages from one section to the other. It's a perfect fit, and we're all amazed.

"That's not possible. It's just too coincidental that they're from the same book," I say.

"Did Casey Whitmore know your father?" Marilyn asks.

"Not that I know of," he insists, but then he hesitates slightly. "Oh, hell, I really don't know."

I remember Win's surprised reaction after pulling back the black mask from the old thief's face as he lay on the ground dying. "Win, had you ever seen that thief before? Anywhere? Even just for a moment? Think hard."

"I don't believe so." His voice is firm and final. "I value my father's ASE edition for sentimental reasons, but it's not worth much...unlike my first edition *Gatsby*, which is gone."

He hands me the two parts, and I note there are also marks on the edges of the pages of Win's section. They appear to line up with the section I found on the ground, but I can't make any sense of them. It probably is just wear and tear, and I put down the pieces of the paperback.

Then I pick them up again and hold them together.

"Marilyn, please humor me," I say to my friend. "Take my phone and snap some pictures of me holding this a certain way." I slightly bend the pages of the two sections, which causes them to fan somewhat. Now the marks extend into lines that don't make much sense, except they look like a three-sided enclosure, maybe part of a box. "Okay, take the pictures now."

Marilyn snaps a few plus some video, and then I let go of the pages, causing the lines to turn back into marks. "What was that all about?" she asks.

"Probably nothing." I check the shots, and they look clear.

Win isn't interested in my discovery and heads straight for the glass cabinet, filled with other valuable books. "When I came up here after the police left, the hardcover was on this shelf where it always is." He opens the cabinet and points at an empty space where the volume once stood. "I was so unsettled by the evening that I came here to have a drink and do a little reading before bed."

He gestures toward the large chair. "I was sitting there when I glanced at the cabinet. I noticed that the book was not pushed into its slot evenly with the others on the shelf."

"So the spine stuck out?" I ask.

"Exactly. I pulled it out to look at it, and I saw it was damaged—one of the corners mashed, and it had a scratch on the back cover." He shakes his head. "That's when I knew the old man had been looking through my books. If he had just left things alone, he wouldn't have dropped it and, well, the rest is history—"

"Why don't you keep a priceless book like that locked in a safe?" I ask.

"Exactly my sentiments," Marilyn says.

"What's the point of that? They're beautiful, and I like to see them while I unwind from a busy day." He sits back down in his favorite chair.

We're all quiet for the moment. I gaze around Win's cozy literary man cave filled with first editions of his favorite books. Something nags at me.

"The fact that Casey Whitmore went straight for your cabinet and chose the most expensive book in this room…" I look at Win, and continue. "Well, he's either stupid or brilliant."

CHAPTER NINETEEN

"Come on, Ronnie, it's been a long day. What are you getting at?" Win asks wearily.

"Well, Whitmore really knows his books."

"That appears to be the case," Marilyn agrees.

I stand up and pace the room. "So, what's really curious is that he passed up stealing a book that's probably worth a lot more than the necklace. *Gatsby* is thin, and he could have easily slipped it into one of his other vest pockets. Why did he leave such easy pickings behind?"

I pick up the two pieces of the flimsy paperback and hold them together. I put down the thief's middle section, and hold up Win's father's front section. "Unless *this* is what Whitmore was looking for."

"What?" Win asks. "Why?"

"That doesn't make sense," Marilyn says.

"Humor me," I respond as I slowly leaf through Win's first third of the ASE *Gatsby*. On page eighteen, I hit pay dirt. There in the outside margin I see what appears to be the same cryptic handwriting in pencil that's in the middle section.

Liberty Head Nickel

Win and Marilyn peer at the writing. "Funny," he says. "I've never noticed that, but then I never really looked."

They hold the paperback open as flat as possible, and I snap a few pictures of the page. Then I carefully turn more pages. After I've flipped through twenty or so, we see the next entry.

Twenty-dollar Double Eagle

I snap more pictures.

Win pages further through his father's section of the book. "Here's one more."

Wheat Penny

"What is it about these coins?" I snap a wide shot of the entire page and then zoom in as close as possible to the writing in pencil.

Win continues turning pages until he gets to the next to the last page.

Lambert—

Again, I take more pictures with my camera phone.

"Of course that's not a coin," Marilyn says. "And see that dash after the word?"

While she talks, I take the burglar's section of the book and flip to the page near the beginning where they read—

—ville, NJ

We put the sections next to each other and say in unison, "Lambertville." Marilyn laughs and holds them flat so I can take more pictures, while she and Win look back and forth between the two sections.

"So, you think these coins are maybe in Lambertville somewhere?" she asks.

"Well, I suspect they may have been there around the time of World War II." I check my photos.

"That's still like a needle in a hay stack, if the needle's even still there," Win mutters.

I flip to the pages with Olivie, or Olivia secretary, and 2nd floor, and take pictures of both.

"Now we know there may have been coins somewhere in Lambertville, New Jersey, with somebody's assistant, and on the second floor," Marilyn says. "Hey, it's a start."

I open to the page that has LPLDM written in pencil. "Maybe this will tell us, whatever LPLDM means." I snap the final pictures.

"This is just what I love, figuring out a puzzle." She drinks her coffee. "Win, do you remember if your father ever said much about this? He died such a long time ago."

He shrugs, sits back in his chair, and stares into his cup. "I thought it was more about his friendship with his war buddies than some old coins." There's something odd about his tone.

"The obvious question," I say, holding up the two books, "is where is the third part of this? And then, of course, the final question is who shot the old guy—that's for the police to investigate, of course. But is it tied to this book?"

Win has the last word. "And that's why I'd like to hire your private eye friend, the one who was here the other evening with the police. I want him to check out all of this."

"Well, as I said, the police are handling the investigation of the shooting," I say. "So that's already covered."

"Yeah, but I mean everything else, you know, my first edition and these ASE sections," he insists.

"Why not hire Ronnie?" Marilyn asks her husband. "She's a private investigator, too. And we know her."

Win doesn't look so sure. "Ronnie, aren't you still a rookie? I need someone experienced like...uh..." He struggles for the name.

A feeling of disappointment washes over me. For just a moment, I thought that I'd landed my first important case. Of course that would be difficult and unethical on my part, since Marilyn has also asked to hire me to look into Win. "Will," I answer. "Will Benson. He's the best."

"That's it. Will Benson." Win turns on the charm. "Ronnie, can you text me his contact info? And also give him a quick call and let him know I'll be in touch?"

"Absolutely. Happy to help." I text him Will's number, trying not to grimace. "Thanks, both of you, for the delicious supper and excellent company." I pick up the chunk of the paperback I found behind the bush and turn to leave.

"Now where do you think you're going with that?" Win asks.

"Tomorrow I'll drop it off with Detective Russo."

"Hold it," Win says. "That little book was found on our property, and it's staying right here."

"Win, it could be important to the investigation. So, technically this should go to the police. And if Will were here, he'd do the same." Truth be told, Detective Rossi is the last person I want to give this book to, and I'm certainly not going to be in a hurry to get it to her.

"I don't want this all over the press, the three parts of this paperback and everything we've discussed this evening about what it all means."

"I don't blame you, and I will not make a big deal out of this when I talk to Rossi. It's just something I found and thought she might want to see. End of story."

"We hate to let it go," Marilyn says, her voice uncertain.

"Which is why I've been taking pictures of the clue pages. I will print out a copy of both sections for you and one for Will and me. Win, may I also borrow your piece—"

"Hold it, hold it," he objects.

"Win, it's just to study," I insist. "Will and I do not plan to take your section to Detective Rossi. We'll keep it in a safe place. I promise."

"I vote for Ronnie taking it," Marilyn says. "We've already had one robbery in the house."

"Okay." Win hands me his piece of the ASE paperback.

"I'll see you at my lunch tomorrow," Marilyn says to me. I nod yes, give her a hug, and make a quick exit.

As I walk to the top of the stairs, I hear Marilyn chastise Win. "I hate to say it, but that was not nice, the way you dismissed Ronnie."

"This is important, Marilyn, and I want the best man for the job."

"That is such chauvinistic, good old boy talk," she answers. "Ronnie may be new at it, but you saw firsthand that she has good instincts and asks the right questions."

"Well, I'll think about it," Win answers. "Let's see what Will Benson says first."

I run down the steps and leave. I'm glad I can count on my friend to stick up for me.

~~~~~

As I drive home, my cell phone rings. It's Will, and I click the button on my steering wheel. "I was just going to call to let you know that Win Watson wants to hire you, and he'll be contacting you in the morning most likely."

"He's already gotten in touch. I'm too busy to take the case," he says over the speaker. "Ronnie, you should take the job. You're ready for this."

"I think he prefers working with a man."

"Oh, come on."

"I'm serious. Hey, it surprised me, too." I brake for a stop sign. "Anyway, Marilyn thinks she's hired me on a separate matter, but it's about her husband. I tried to talk her out of it, but she wouldn't listen."

"Now that presents a problem."

"I agree." A deer jumps out from the brush along the side of the road. "Oh no," I gasp, slamming the brakes hard, and I almost hit him. "That was close."

"What's going on?" Will asks. "Are you okay?"

"A deer dashed onto the road. A beautiful young buck. Thank god, I missed him." I start driving again, but much more slowly. "Hard to believe the police have a murder to solve out here in quiet, little Willowbrook. Nothing like that ever happens here."

"And you keep on remembering that, Ronnie. The *police* are working on the shooting—it's not yet officially a murder—and we're, I mean, you're working on finding the book. And that's my final point," Will says. "You're the best person for the Watson job since you live in that Willowbrook world of dinner parties and book collecting. You've already gathered a lot of info, and you haven't even officially started."

I turn onto the gravel road on my property. "That's nice of you to say, but—"

"I'll call Win Watson in the morning and work things out. If he still insists on hiring me, I'll tell him that you and I will work on it together with you as the lead investigator. He can pay my company, and I'll cut you a check for the full amount."

"Thanks, Will."

"You're also going to have to tell Win's wife that you can't officially work for her while you're on the payroll looking for her husband's missing book."

"I'll call her and let her know."

"Now, between you and me, it doesn't mean you can't keep your eyes open, and if something comes up regarding her concerns, well, come talk to me first."

"Okay." I pull up to my house and turn off the engine. "Got a moment?"

"Sure."

"Let me bring you up to speed on a new angle about a beat up old paperback I found this evening at the Watsons'…"

CHAPTER TWENTY

Water cascades from the fountains and sparkles like hard, white diamonds in the mid-morning sun of the next day. I guide my car past the long reflective pool in front of Sheffield Hall and drive about a quarter of a mile further down the gravel road.

A rambling stone barn with two vehicles parked out front appears. I pull up alongside a gleaming white Tesla. Off in the distance I hear the sound of a shotgun firing.

I look at my watch. I'm early, so I've got enough time to check out this beautiful automobile. I love the idea that you can plug the Tesla into a charger instead of gassing up. There are no protruding door handles, just the outlines of where they should be. I've read that when you approach with your key, the handles pop out. I glance inside the front and admire the tightly upholstered smooth black leather seats.

Enough of this elegant vehicle! I pop the trunk of my perky Mustang and prep for skeet shooting with Jamie Gordon. Opening a canvas-covered case, I assemble the pieces of my twelve-gauge Beretta shotgun. I can't help but smile, remembering all the lessons with my brothers Frank and Peter.

Next, I dump three boxes of shotgun shells into a leather pouch. The fourth box I empty into the right-hand pocket of my quilted shooting vest. I check my glove compartment up front to retrieve ear plugs and shooting glasses and put them in the vest's left pocket.

As I walk back to the Mustang's trunk to get my gun, I glance down inside the Tesla for another glimpse of those beautiful leather seats. I see a familiar red Birkin bag in the back driver's side foot well. I stop.

There's a small black leather notebook, maybe a diary, on the back seat above the purse. I look in the direction of the gunfire and think of my friend Marilyn and her suspicions of Katya. I wish I could get a look inside that diary.

The shooting has stopped. I move around to the rear of my car to reach for the shotgun. Even though I know it's empty, I break it, glance into the chambers one more time, then place it on my shoulder, draping my arm over the barrel that tips toward the ground. I grab the leather pouch and close the trunk.

I walk around to the back of the stone barn and head down a path to the skeet course. As I step out of a stand of trees and into the bright sunlight, I take in perhaps the most elegant skeet and trap course I have ever seen. Growing up, there was nothing fancy about learning to shoot skeet with Frank and Peter at Meadow Farm where we lived. My brothers would mark the different shooting stations with large rocks, then set up two portable machines that would spit out the round orange clays.

Sheffield Hall is the other end of the spectrum. The high house and the low house, which contain the clay throwing machines, are handsome stone towers with slate roofs. A golf course-quality lawn surrounds the entire area, and a perfectly edged arced gravel path cuts through the lawn to connect the towers. Stone pads along the path mark the shooting stations. The entire setup looks out over a beautiful vista of hills, valleys, woods, and fields.

Jamie lounges in one of several Adirondack chairs off to the side. He hasn't seen me appear from the woods behind him because he's busy watching a woman in a khaki shooting vest, her dark hair pulled into a pony tail that pops out the back of a cap. She stands midway along the skeet course at the top of the arc path.

I watch silently as the bright orange clays alternatingly burst from each tower and sail across a crystal clear blue sky.

"Pull," she calls again, and Jamie hits the button on the control. Katya hits every single target, and I can't help but admire her ability.

After she smashes the last two clays, Jamie claps and calls out, "Bravo! Very impressive, Katya. You're more than ready for England."

Katya sees me and I wave, calling out hello. Almost before she can respond, Jamie is by my side, taking me in his arms for a long hug. That's not an easy feat with a broken shotgun between the two of us, and we laugh at our clumsiness.

"Hey," he says for my ears only.

"Hey," I say back quietly, just for him.

"Perfect timing," Jamie says. "Katya's just finished her third time through the course."

"Did I get the meeting time wrong?" I ask.

"No. You're perfect," he says. "Katya showed up late."

I glance toward her and catch her surprised expression. I know it's childish, but I can't help but feel a momentary flicker of satisfaction before thinking to myself, *Grow up, Ronnie.*

As Jamie walks me over to her, he says, "I believe you two have met?"

Katya, still somewhat surprised by my presence, answers in a deep measured tone, "No, Jamie, darling, I don't believe I've had the pleasure." She reaches her hand out to shake mine.

"Ronnie Lake, Katya Alessandro," he says.

My hand meets hers half way as I say, "Nice to meet you." Her black eyes are appraising me, and I wonder if this is the same way she assesses the first editions that pass through her shops…or her next conquests.

"Katya Alessandro," I repeat, "What an unusual name. Isn't Katya Russian and Alessandro Italian?"

She looks at me suspiciously. "Yes, you're right. My parents came from Europe."

I wait a moment for her to say more, but that's all she offers, so I change the subject. "Did Jamie teach you to shoot?"

"My father first taught me to shoot when I was twelve," she says with a slight edge in her distinctively low voice. "One can never stop learning, and practicing here is glorious."

"That's a beautiful shotgun," I say, looking at it. "Holland & Holland?"

"Good eye," Jamie says before she can answer, and she looks momentarily annoyed.

"My father gave it to me as a gift on my twenty-first birthday." Katya slides her hand down the barrel the way I would stroke Warrior's soft coat on his back.

"My brother Peter shoots with our father's Holland & Holland," I say.

"We should visit their gun room in New York. You may want one of your own," Jamie says, much to Katya's and my surprise.

"Nice idea, Jamie, but I like my gun just fine." I hold it out in front of me. "This was a recent decade-birthday present to myself."

"Must have been for your thirtieth birthday," Jamie teases.

I look at him with an expression that I hope communicates *You've got to be kidding using that old line.*

"And on that note, I must leave." Katya air kisses Jamie on each cheek. "I should have news for you about that book later in the week, darling."

We say our goodbyes, and Katya walks up the path toward the barn. I think she may be leaving earlier than she planned.

"She's quite amazing," I say to no one in particular.

Jamie leans in, lifts my hair, and says quietly into my ear, "Not nearly as amazing as you." My stomach does a somersault. His voice grows husky as he says, "Time for us to shoot."

Before he can make the move, I make a grab for the push-button control that sends out the clays. "You first," I insist.

He's almost speechless. "Wait a minute—"

"Come on." I lean my gun against the chair, sit down with the control in my hand, and smile. "I'm a little rusty, and waiting to be inspired."

He chuckles and reaches for his shotgun. He walks up to the first station, drops two shells into the barrels of his 12-guage over-and-under, and snaps it shut. He pauses a moment and then calls, "Pull."

I hit the controls, and we begin. He hits the singles out of the high house and low house, and then the double. He breaks his gun before moving to the next station.

Jamie hits every clay target on the entire course. I marvel that he's as much of a dead-eye marksman as Katya.

I stand up and replay his perfect shooting as I stare out to where he pulverized the clays just moments ago. Behind me I hear the clicking sound of a shotgun barrel closing. Instinctively, I quickly turn and drop low.

Somehow, I know it's Jamie behind me, but that doesn't slow my racing heart. What am I doing out here by myself with an armed man I barely know? My mind races as I scramble to think of anyone I might have told I was coming here today, not that I could count on Katya to report that she'd seen me here if something happened. For a moment, pure fear courses through my body. Everything stops until I remember that Marilyn knows I'm here. I slow down my breathing.

I feel silly a moment later when I see him staring at me, the gun now broken and the barrel pointed towards the ground.

"Are you okay?" he asks, and I jump up from squatting next to the chair. I try to think of a good excuse that won't make me seem even crazier, but an understanding look crosses his face when he realizes he's scared me. He puts his gun down, and walks over to me.

"I apologize if I startled you. I heard some funny noises before when I closed my gun to shoot. I should have warned you I was checking it."

I try not to look sheepish...or that only a split second ago I was suspicious of him. "Not a problem. Now are you ready to pull? Because I'm ready to shoot!"

CHAPTER TWENTY-ONE

Detective Rossi sits in her glass-walled office with the door open, talking on the phone and flipping through a huge file. She looks very busy, but glances up and spots me. I can see the expression of annoyance—maybe even infuriation—on her face from all the way down the hall.

I knew I would regret this. I told myself on the way over that I had to do the right thing—even though I really didn't want to—and bring her this beat-up paperback. After all, it was probably in Casey Whitmore's possession right before he died. It was my civic duty and my obligation as a PI because it might be important to her case.

I match her scowl with my own look of irritation as I wait for the officer at the front desk to get off his phone. Tired of waiting, I wave a brown envelope at her. "Hey, there," I call out and march down the hall to drop it off.

She jumps up. "Can I get back to you in five?" she says to her caller. She hangs up and quickly walks to the door, blocking her office. "What are you doing here?"

God, this woman is irritating, but I respond as sweet

as honey and I throw in a tone of false flightiness for good measure.

"Hiiiii, Detective Rossi." I shoot her a huge smile. "How's the case? Do you have any solid suspects?"

She stares at me.

"I have some thoughts that I'd love to share with you—"

Behind me, I hear a commotion break out. We both glance toward the front desk where several officers are hustling in two drunk guys who are screaming at each other.

"Okaaay. Well." I start to pull the book in its clear evidence bag from the envelope. "I noticed this on the ground—"

"Isn't that peachy? Did you buy your little detective kit online?" she says, referring to the bag holding the book.

I'd like to wipe that smirk right off her face. "Hey if it's not important—"

And then all hell breaks loose out front when one of the guys throws up all over the two cops' shoes. The third officer slips and falls trying to jump back from the spray of vomit, and it just gets worse from there.

"Come back when you've been to the police academy." Detective Rossi rushes past me to help her fellow officers.

"Are you sure *you* even went to the academy?" I try not to smile triumphantly on my way out of the station. *It's not my job to do your job*, I think to myself.

I pull out of the police station just as Will calls, and I tell him what just happened.

"So what are you going to do now?" he asks.

"Solve the puzzle."

"Ronnie—"

"Hey, I tried to do the right thing," I snap.

"Whew! Don't mess with you, Ronnie Lake!"

"That's right. Sofia shut me down, so all bets are off."

~~~~~

I go from Detective Rossi's bitchiness to the welcome cushiness of being back at the Watsons' house, sitting among dozens of women scattered around their living room. We clap for the speaker, who's just finished her presentation about violence against Central American immigrant women trying to make their way to the US-Mexican border.

I have to admit that I sometimes begrudgingly attend these gatherings, but certainly not because I don't care about the issues. I just care more about supporting Marilyn when she opens her home to worthy causes for fund-raising events. I finish my tea and stand with the rest of the attendees.

As others depart and the catering team cleans up, I head for the powder room toward the back of the foyer, only to find it busy.

"Ronnie, honey, use one upstairs." Marilyn smiles at me as she continues thanking several of the attendees who are leaving.

I run up the main stairway to find an empty bathroom off a guest room, but stop immediately when I hear something fall in the master bedroom suite.

The door is open and I walk in, ready to help. But the room is empty. I hear more noise, and it sounds as though it's coming from further back, beyond Marilyn's dressing room.

Then I hear it—a woman's voice muttering quiet profanities. I tiptoe into my friend's dressing room, grateful for the soft carpet that muffles my footsteps. I hide behind the door leading to Win's little library.

I peek through the crack where the door is hinged to the frame. A redhead with a cloth hobo bag over her shoulder crouches to pick up a dozen books from the floor next to Win's favorite reading chair.

Sally Richards stands up and begins stacking the volumes on the table that I assume she knocked over when I heard the noise a moment ago. I pull out my phone and hold it up to the crack to take a video.

Sally fumbles around inside her bag and pulls out a small book and a folded piece of paper. She steps over to the desk and slowly opens the glass door to the cabinet on top. She carefully slides the book onto the shelf in the empty slot that Win showed me last night.

Rather than leave, Sally walks to one of the open bookcases and scans the shelves. She opens the paper, glances at it, then impatiently moves to the next one, mumbling, "Lee…Lee…Lee…where is it?" Finally, her hand stops and she pulls out a volume. She opens the book and spends some moments on one page. This is definitely weird.

Finally, she slips this book into her shoulder bag and quickly exits the room while I flatten myself against the wall behind the door, not making a sound. Once the young woman is gone, I head straight for the shelf in Win's glass-fronted cabinet to video the book that Sally put back.

There sits the missing first edition *Gatsby*. I pull the book out and see the bruised corner and the cut and scratch on the back of the dust jacket. I flip open the book and reread the handwritten note from the author inside. I snap several stills with my phone.

I dash out of the library and through the rest of the bedroom suite, down the stairs, through the dining room, and into the kitchen. Marilyn is giving clean-up instructions to the caterers, but I don't see Sally.

"Marilyn, may I speak to you for a moment?"

Marilyn walks over, and I ask her quietly,"Did you give anyone working today permission to be in Win's upstairs library?"

"Absolutely not. What on earth are you talking about?" she asks, glancing around the kitchen at the staff.

"Don't worry about it. Everything's okay—"

My attention is diverted to the big kitchen window. Sally is walking around the side of the house where the caterers have parked their cars. "I've got to hurry. Promise to tell you later."

I rush outside, doing my best to stroll toward my

Mustang as Sally drives by in her black VW Jetta. We see each other and wave. I start my car and leave the Watson property, too.

Doing my best to keep some distance between us, I call Will to give him all the details.

"Did she see you?" Will asks.

"No. I stumbled on her by accident after the tea. I hid behind the door and actually watched her put the book back. I still can't believe it. And then I watched her take another book from one of Win's shelves. I've got it all on video, by the way."

"Did you confront her?"

"No." I panic when I lose sight of the Jetta in the afternoon village traffic. "Hold on a sec." I scan both sides of the road and finally spot Sally pulling into the public library. I drive into a gas station as though I need to top off my tank. "She's at the library." I point the Mustang so that I have a clear view of Sally walking into the building.

"I'll go inside and watch her from a distance."

"Don't do anything before I get there," Will says. "When she sees two of us cornering her, she'll be less likely to run or cause a commotion."

"Text me when you get here, and I'll tell you where I am inside," I say.

"See you in ten."

CHAPTER TWENTY-TWO

Sally sits quietly in a small meeting room in the back of the library reading the book she just stole. Will and I walk in together, and she freezes when she sees us. I click on my phone's video camera.

"Um, Mrs. Lake! Wh-what are you doing here?" Sally's voice quivers, and she closes the book. I go in close with my phone to video the title of book, Harper Lee's *To Kill a Mockingbird.*

She pulls it away, glances toward Will, and jumps up with a classic deer caught in the headlights look, ready to bolt.

"Come on, Sally," I nod toward Will. "We just want to talk."

Will also moves toward the petite young woman, her face now almost as flushed as her flaming red hair. Her eyes look up at him and then dart around the room, desperate for an escape. We slowly approach from different sides of the table. Sally finally sits back down with a look of resignation.

"So what's going on?" I ask.

"I, I'm reading a favorite book that, uh, a friend lent to me," Sally finally answers, clutching the book close to her belly as if she were a caged animal protecting her young.

"Win Watson's first edition of *To Kill a Mockingbird*? Is it signed, too? Like his copy of *Gatsby*?"

She looks at me in surprise and then blurts out, "Well, he knows I study 20th century American lit and lets me borrow books."

"Really?" I ask.

The heavy tone of skepticism in my voice broadcasts to her that I'm not buying it. She says nothing as awareness washes over her face. She spotted me at the Watsons' a short while ago, and she comprehends there's also a good chance I know she was upstairs.

I nod. "That's right. I saw you put the *Gatsby* back on the shelf in the library, and that really surprised me."

She continues to say nothing, and the silence feels interminable. Will finally breaks it by asking, "Hey, Ronnie. What do you want to do?"

"By the way, young lady, meet Will Benson." I don't mean to sound like a scolding parent, but I think I probably do. "He's a first-rate private-eye, and we work together. I know you didn't borrow *Gatsby* because the Watsons hired us to find their missing book."

Shock registers on Sally's face. Her body caves in surrender, and she sinks back onto the chair. Tears begin to roll down her face.

I keep my voice soft and gentle. "How did you come

into possession of the Watson *Gatsby* in the first place?" Before I can ask her about the warehouse robbery, she jumps in.

"I borrowed it from Mr. Smithson." Sally's voice almost squeaks as she answers.

"Borrowed it?" Will's tone is one of incredulity. "Does he know that you borrowed it?"

"Not really," she mutters.

"Where was the book when you borrowed it?" Will's tone is sharp, and Sally flinches.

"Will, let's hear her out." I'm feeling slightly guilty for being in possession of Casey's paperback, probably also stolen property, and I attempt to ignore the strange feeling of guilt. I try to convince myself that there's stealing and then there's *really* stealing, but I don't do a good job.

"At his warehouse." Her voice cracks as she speaks, and she's so quiet that I find it hard to hear her clearly.

"Please speak up. Again, where did you get the book?" I hold the camera phone steady.

"At the warehouse, okay!" Sally blasts, startling both Will and me.

"And I suppose you thought it was alright," Will jumps in, "to knock him over the head on your way out as you borrowed the book?"

"What? Knock him over the head? I did not! I just borrowed it to read." She breaks down, sobbing.

"Calm down, Sally. Let's talk and get to the bottom of this." I sigh and turn off the video. Will looks at me and shrugs. He leaves the work area, and fifteen seconds later, he's back with a box of tissues that he places on the table. We give her a moment, and I turn on my video again. "Now where were we?"

"I w-w-went to the warehouse to borrow the book, and before I got to it, I must have made a noise because he came after me down a row of book cases," she says between sniffs and pulling tissues from the box. "I pushed a rolling ladder in his way. I guess it caused Mr. Smithson to fall, and I'm very sorry that happened." She blows her nose. "He must have hit his head when he fell. I didn't mean for him to get hurt." She sniffs some more and then blows her nose again.

"And you just left him there?" Will says, crossing his arms and looking at her skeptically.

"No!" Sally says, her tone emphatic. "When I didn't hear any noise behind me, you know, like him still coming after me, I stopped to listen. It was too quiet, so I tiptoed back to check. He was out cold, sprawled on the floor. I, I thought he was dead, that I had k-killed him."

Sally starts to cry again and covers her face with her hands. I sit on the corner of the table, pull a tissue out of the box, and reach it to her. She blows her nose again, and dabs at her red eyes.

"Go on," I say, using a calm voice that I hope will encourage her.

Sally inhales deeply and continues. "I felt his pulse, and it was beating fine from what I could tell, and then I checked his breathing. So I figured he'd come to pretty soon, and I'd hang out until he did and then sneak away, which is what I did." She looks down at her hands and twists her fingers and bites her lip like a penitent child.

"So when did you take the book?" Will asks.

"While I was waiting for him to come to, I went to his desk just to see if the book was there. You know, maybe I could read a few pages while I waited. He had taken it out of his safe—which was open, by the way, I swear—and there it was, sitting out on his desk—this beautiful, rare, first edition *Gatsby*. I couldn't believe my luck. He started to wake up, so I grabbed it and got outta there."

"Oooh-kaaay." I sigh.

"This is one of the weirdest stories I've heard," Will says.

She looks up at the two of us. "Look I'm not proud of what I did. But I swear it's the truth!"

"And how did you know about this book in the first place?" I ask.

"Well, first, I saw some papers on Ms. Alessandro's desk..." She looks down at her hands, almost embarrassed. "Honestly, I wasn't snooping, but I was looking for a book in her office, and these letters were right on top of her desk. I saw the title *Gatsby*, but the writing just looked like chicken scratch."

At the mention of the letters, my radar goes on high alert and she's got my attention. "What did you do with the letters?"

"Nothing. Ms. Alessandro walked in when I was

standing over her desk and snatched them away." She almost shivers. "God, she went ballistic, screaming at me, treating me like a criminal…whatever."

"What does that have to do with Mr. Watson's copy of the book?" Will asks.

"There was a lot of talk about it at the shop. Ms. Alessandro has been nagging Mr. Watson to let her sell it for him. It got me thinking it was all the same book—the one in the letters and Mr. Watson's."

"That's a very interesting theory," Will says.

"And everybody heard about it getting damaged during the robbery at his house and that it went to Mr. Smithson for repairs—" She freezes for a moment, and her eyes overflow with tears. She breaks down completely, this time her body shuddering as she weeps and sucks in air, trying to catch her breath.

"What is it?" I ask, hoping my voice sounds soothing as I push the Kleenex box closer to her.

"Ms. Alessandro told all of us this morning at the store that Casey died, that *he* was the man who fell off the roof at the party." Her voice catches on every few words as her tears continue. "I can't believe it. I just can't see him doing something like that, you know, scaling a roof while all those people were there, and that he was a thief."

"You're right, and the police are looking into it." I gently touch her arm. "I'm so sorry for your loss."

"Thank you. He was my friend, always looking out for me…" She stares off into nothing for a long moment.

"So, let's go back to where we were. What is all this talk about borrowing the book?"

Sally's blotchy face lights up slightly. "All I wanted to do was reread it, and it had to be an actual copy that the author had touched. Mr. Fitzgerald had even written a letter inside on one of the pages." She looks down. "It's like I could pretend he was sitting right there next to me last night while I enjoyed his masterpiece. I swear I could feel his presence with me."

Will and I glance at each other while Sally looks off into a corner of the room and quotes out loud from Fitzgerald's book. "*Gatsby believed in the green light...*" She continues quoting from memory, finally stops, and looks back at Will and me. "It's beautiful, an amazing story, isn't it? Anyway, it's a short book, and I finished reading it at three this morning. I knew I was working at Mrs. Watson's house today and I couldn't very well bring it back to the warehouse after what happened, so it was my chance to bring the book back to Mr. Watson."

"How did you know where to put it?" Will asks.

"I heard him talking with Ms. Alessandro in the shop about it belonging with his best books in the desk in his upstairs library, so I kinda knew where to put it."

"Back to those letters you saw on Ms. Alessandro's desk," I say, and Sally looks at me curiously. "When she snatched them off her desk, did you happen to notice what she did with them?"

"I think she stuffed them in a folder, and she definitely made a big point of putting the folder underneath her purse. The whole time she was yelling at me to get out—"

Will interrupts, "What book do you have with you now, Sally?"

Her body slouches, as if she's disappointed that we remember. "Just the next one I want to read." She opens the copy of *To Kill a Mockingbird* by Harper Lee, turning to the copyright page. "OK. Here—1960, first edition—"

"You expect us to believe this crazy story of yours?" Will interrupts. "That you were borrowing priceless, irreplaceable books because you just love to touch them? And you weren't stealing them?"

"But it's the truth!" Sally pleads. "I'm not a thief. It's what I'm studying for my degree. And I love to read books that were printed when the writers first published. I could never afford these books myself so I borrow them for a little while. And then I bring them right back. Most of the time, the owner never even knows it was gone!"

"Exactly how many books have you borrowed before?" Will asks.

She looks at the ceiling and then counts on her fingers, mouthing the titles. She reaches in her bag for a folded piece of paper and hands it to Will. "I guess eight times, if you count *Mockingbird*."

"Come to think of it," I say, looking at the list in Will's hands, "George Smithson told me that there have been some incidents out here of valuable books disappearing from different collectors and then mysteriously reappearing." I turn my full gaze on Sally, who looks away.

"From the looks of this," he gestures with the paper, "there would have been plenty more of these book disappearances." He looks at Sally. "Oh, and I'll take that." Sally reluctantly hands over *Mockingbird*.

"How do you find out who has the books you want to read?" I ask.

"I hear about the collectors at the bookstore, and I see things when I work for different caterers part-time."

We stare at Sally speechless for what feels like an eternity, but in reality is probably only a few seconds.

"I don't doubt you love to read these books," I say. "But come on. Katya Alessandro put you up to this, didn't she? To get her hands on this book? That's her real endgame here, isn't it?"

Sally's reaction is one of fright and panic. "Ms. Alessandro doesn't know I borrow books. Please don't tell her. She'll fire me, and I need this job to help pay for college. I'm one semester away from getting my degree, please don't take that away from me!"

"Honey, you're looking at jail time, not just losing your job in some book store!" Will says. "And it isn't up to us to decide what happens. My boss on this job is Win Watson, who hired us to find his *Great Gatsby*. You'll have to talk to him. He'll make the decision whether or not to bring the police into this." Sally's eyes register fear.

"And you'll have to talk to George Smithson, too. It was his warehouse you broke into, and chasing you caused him bodily injury," I say. "It'll be up to him whether or not to press charges for theft and assault."

Now she's trembling. Maybe it's finally dawning on her how serious a matter her book borrowing obsession really is.

"One more thing, Ms. Richards." Will doesn't take his eyes off her. "Where were you last week, Thursday evening around ten p.m.?"

Sally looks up at the ceiling as if she's trying to think. "G-g-give me a s-second to remember." Her teeth almost chatter from the trembling. She shifts her gaze to her shaking hands where she counts on her fingers. "Sunday at Mr. Gordon's in Willowbrook, Saturday at the McDowds' in Summit, Friday I was off, and Thursday I worked at a dinner for a foundation in Short Hills. I was there all evening, and we didn't leave until about eleven. You can check with my boss." She scribbles a phone number and name on a piece of paper from her bag and pushes it across the table.

Will does just that, reaching for his phone and calling to confirm her alibi. At least we'll be sure she didn't kill Whitmore, just in case she's making up this whole story about him being her friend.

CHAPTER TWENTY-THREE

At her request, we accompany Sally home in order to confirm her story when we report back to our clients. She wants to show us that she has nothing to hide and offers up this plan if it means she will not end up at the police.

We arrive in a sketchy neighborhood a half-hour from the bookstore. She uses her key to open an inner door to the building, and we pass by a bank of about fifty mailboxes, a dozen of which have blocked keyholes.

Several young children race their tricycles down the dirty first floor hallway, and most of the lights are off or broken, leaving the corridor dark. The elevators have an out-of-order sign, so Sally leads us to a stairwell where we hoof it up to the fifth floor.

Her apartment is right next to the elevator—the noise must keep her up at night. Sally uses three keys to unlock the door, and with fierce pride, she says, "Come on in, and feel free to look around."

It reminds me of my first place straight out of college, and I feel right at home. The apartment is tiny, clean, and everything in its place. It's a studio with a kitchenette on one side and on the other a door that must lead to the bathroom. Between the two, her double bed is pushed against a third wall and neatly made. Mounds of pillows on the bed and several overturned open books tell me this may be where she does her reading.

There is one unmistakable similarity to Casey's house in that are many tall stacks of books. Unlike Casey's piles which filled every available surface and looked ready to tip over, Sally's towers are straight and neatly lined up against the walls wherever there is space.

While Sally makes tea, Will and I look around. He idly browses her stacks of books starting at one end, and I begin at the other. I'm amazed to find a dozen or so copies of *The Great Gatsby*. A few minutes later, she hands us each a steaming mug.

As Will makes his way around the room, she follows and tidies up behind him. Finally they shift gears, and she shows him her school materials and coursework and ID, all of which confirm that she's a college student and making good grades.

Meanwhile, I look at several framed photographs on her desk. "Are these your family? Friends?"

"They're my best friends from school." Sally picks up one of the pictures that shows her with two boys and another girl, all close in age, sitting outside at a picnic table.

I pick up a small framed photograph of her with Casey in the book shop. She stands a little behind him with an arm over one of his shoulders and her chin resting on the other, looking at him as if he were an adored uncle or big brother. They both look happy and comfortable in each other's presence.

Sally takes it from me and sighs. "I'm going to really miss him." She puts the photograph back down and sees me eyeing some folders. "Feel free to look through them. I'm an open book."

I carefully go through her papers, trying to leave everything the way I found it. Nothing looks out of the ordinary, and I glance at a small two-drawer file cabinet next to it. Sally opens the file drawer. "Help yourself. Like I said, I have nothing to hide."

I hesitate when I see a folder labeled with last year's IRS return. She whips it out. "Look at all the people I've worked for...this is all to pay for school."

I haven't asked to see this folder, because tax returns are legally private, but she's already opened it and shows me the attached tax forms from a half-dozen different caterers for whom she'd worked throughout the last calendar year. She must not have much free time, what with school, the book shop and all these jobs.

Next, I find a folder with a dozen old photographs and I flip through them.

"Sally, are these of you as a baby and young child?"

"Yeah."

I hold up one. "And are these your parents? Where do they live? In the area?"

"No. They died when I was little," she answers. "I don't really remember them."

"What happened?"

She says nothing. I wait. Still nothing. It's clear she doesn't want to discuss it.

I figure it's better to keep her talking. "Well, who took care of you?"

"An aunt, but she and I had a fight. I don't want to talk about it."

Will and I look at each other. "How old are you?" he asks. "You look like you're still in high school."

She looks at him, her eyes very determined, and snaps, "Twenty-two."

"Will means that it's tough to make your way in the world all by yourself," I interject. "Is there anyone—"

"Just Casey, and now he's gone." Tears dribble down her cheeks and she wipes them quickly with the back of her hand.

I feel a large envelope in the back of the bottom drawer. "What do we have here? Something feels stuck."

"Oh! Geez, I forgot all about that. I taped it to the back of the drawer to keep it safe. Let me get it." Sally pulls loose a brown eight-by-eleven-inch envelope. The writing on it reads *To: Sally Richards, Open only in an emergency.* She tears it open."Casey asked me to keep this for him."

We all sit at the table by the kitchenette and she pulls out an eight-by-ten photograph of a painting of a big, old house, really almost a mansion.

Sally looks at it and then flips it over, surprised to see writing on the back and reads aloud.

Dear Sally,

If you're reading this, then I am probably no longer alive, and I bequeath to you all my worldly goods. It's not a lot, but there may be one thing that could do more than help with college... if you're able to figure it out.

Our friendship was the highlight of these last years for me.

Your devoted friend,
Casey

She turns back to the other side and places it on the table, so that Will and I can see it. It looks familiar.

"I think I know this painting," I say, snapping a couple of photos. "It's at Casey's house."

"Yeah, it is," Sally says. "Hanging on the wall in his living room."

She flips it back over, so that we can all read the letter. I take pictures of it, then click to the dog toy list. The handwriting looks like it matches, so Casey wrote it.

"Wonder how much the painting's worth?" Sally asks.

"Hard to know. I didn't spot an artist's name anywhere on the canvas," I say. "Maybe it's hidden under the frame."

"Maybe Casey wanted me to sell it to pay for school?" Sally looks at the letter side again. "He knew how much I wanted to finish college."

"If that's the case," Will says, "that's a thoughtful present." He looks closely at the photograph. "I had a client some years back, and he had a painting of his own house. And this one has a similar style. Can't remember the name of the artist off the top of my head, but it was someone here in New Jersey."

"Did your client sell his painting?" I ask.

"Yeah, he got about twenty-five-thousand for it."

"Wow," Sally says. "That would really help pay for school. I can't believe Casey would do something so nice for me."

"Slow down, kid," Will says, still peering at the photo. "I've learned the hard way and through a lot of experience not to go necessarily with the first assumption about evidence."

"Huh?" Sally asks.

"You think there's something else?" I ask Will.

"Maybe what's in the painting is more important than the painting itself. You never know."

"So, it has to do with this actual house in the picture?" I ask.

"Too early to say," he responds. "I just think it's smart to slow down."

"I'd be happy with the twenty-five thousand for school," Sally says, but her sad tone at the situation that led to an inheritance belies her words.

"Hold on," I caution her. "Let's follow Will's advice and first see if there's more to this than meets the eye."

We tell Sally that she should go about her different jobs as she normally would, and that we will be back in touch. The next order of business is one that I'm dreading: telling Win Watson that I know what happened to his book.

~~~~~

Will and I get out of our cars. "How can you be so naïve?" he asks.

"I realize the entire story is far-fetched, but I believe her," I counter. He looks at me. "Do not eye-roll me, Will Benson. You know how I hate that. Anyway, Sally had nothing to gain by putting the book back."

We approach the front door at the Watsons', and Will argues, "Maybe she heard the book was too hot—"

Before we can get there, the door swings open, and Win steps through. "You said you have some news?"

Will nods at me to tell him, and I do, grinning. "You got your book back."

"What? Who stole it?"

"It's a long story. Let's go upstairs."

Fifteen minutes later, we're upstairs in the small library. Marilyn joins us, and Win sits in his wing chair, astonished that his book was back on its shelf. He carefully examines his cherished first edition for any new flaws.

"Unlike that Whitmore thief, Sally seems to have taken good care of the book. I don't see any further damage." He takes his copy of *To Kill a Mockingbird* from the table and examines it, too. "And this was going to be her next read?"

"That's what she told us." Will shakes his head.

"I thought I'd heard everything in the book collecting world, but this is a first for me." Win puts the book down. "I know Sally from the shop. She's the last person I would have pegged for this..." Win stares at the two books, lost in his thoughts. Marilyn quietly watches him.

Finally he looks up and asks, "And you say she's done this at other people's houses?"

Will and I nod.

"I always thought she was a nice kid. You know, helpful," Win says. "Not weird like this."

"I think she is nice, but misguided," I pipe up.

"So what do you want to do about her?" Will asks. "You know, bring in the police? And Ronnie and I still need to check in with George."

I jump in. "Please consider the fact that she brought your book back—"

"But borrowed another," Will counters.

Marilyn's head turns back and forth, watching the two of us as if she's at a tennis match.

Win puts his hands up signaling us to halt. "I want some time to think about Sally and her borrowing habit. I'll let you know how I want to proceed."

Will gets up to leave at the same moment I plan to speak but stop myself.

Marilyn notices and nods at me to go on. "Ronnie, is there something else?"

"Well, the expensive book is back now. But the police are no closer to knowing who killed Casey Whitmore, so that investigation continues, of course." I pause to gather my thoughts. "I feel like your first edition was almost an accidental diversion from the real prize—the two pieces of that beat up paperback."

"Go on," Win says.

"I have a theory that the paperback with all those penciled-in clues was more important to Casey, and who even knows where the third piece is."

"If it hasn't been destroyed at some point, you mean," Will says. "And if not, it could be anywhere out there. That's a total crapshoot."

The room goes quiet for a long moment.

"Humor me," Win says. "Even though the book is back, I think I'd still like to keep you on the payroll. Ronnie, you brought up some excellent questions at dinner last night."

"I can see where this is going," Marilyn says, smiling. "The treasure hunt, darling. Nothing I like more."

"I want you two to figure out the puzzle scribbled in the pages," Win says. "And take a shot at finding the third piece of the book."

CHAPTER TWENTY-FOUR

The police are finished processing Whitmore's house, so I return for another visit the next day. Maybe looking around again with Peachie will shake loose some new ideas. After all, I'll be doing most of the work on this puzzle angle while Will attends to his other clients.

After parking on a side street, Peachie and I stroll up the walk and quickly move around behind the house. Before looking in the windows, I decide to try the back door, just in case. I carefully turn the knob and discover the door is already unlocked. I pause. I open it a crack and peek inside. The room looks disheveled, as if the police were here searching, but not ransacked as if someone had broken in.

Hmmm. I weigh my options about going in or not. The owner is dead, so the house should be uninhabited. The police have finished investigating, so I wouldn't be disturbing their work. The door is unlocked, so I'm not really breaking in. I may even learn something by looking around, and it's unlikely I'll get caught. This would seem to be one of those gray areas that Will and I have discussed where private eyes take a more flexible approach than the police.

As I open the door, Peachie bounces up and down with excitement and little yips. I try to quiet her, but the little dog knows that she's come home. We don't enter until she settles down.

We walk into the kitchen, and I'm immediately drawn to Casey's papers, books, and coffee cup on the table, all of which show the residue of fingerprint dust from the police investigation. I see an open notebook that has no residue sitting on top of the papers. Someone else has also paid a visit after the police left. I listen again for any noise as I pull out my camera phone and focus on the notebook.

There's a list of book titles encased in a plastic sleeve. I quickly shoot some pictures. The facing page to the book list is another plastic sleeve that contains a sheet of paper with some writing in blue ink. At first glance it's a threatening phrase with a smudge at the end that catches my eye.

Stay away, —

I look again.

Stay away, —

I must have all of the book to finish what our families started. It's my heritage, not yours.

My mind is swirling with thoughts, as I quickly shoot

more pictures. I observe from the notebook's edges that it's a black leather diary, and it looks similar to the one that sat on the back seat of Katya's car.

My thoughts are interrupted by the sound of a woman crying.

"Bianca…Bianca…" The keening voice continues repeating the name in between sobs. The hair stands up on the back of my neck because I know who it is. Even though I'm not in the same room, I feel as if I'm intruding in a deeply private moment.

I accidentally fumble the leash and drop it as I tuck my phone in my pocket. Peachie tears away, running through the house. A moment later, I hear Katya's voice directed toward the dog, perhaps coming from the living room.

"Where did you come from?" A scuffling sound, and then Katya calls out, "Who's there?" Peach growls from the other room.

"I'm in the kitchen," I call back, flipping to the next page in the diary but looking up at the sound of her heels clicking on the floor.

Katya walks into the room with that same expensive bag swinging from one arm, Peachie still barking at her heels. Seeing me standing by the table, her slightly red eyes look at me with suspicion. She quickly walks over and slams her diary shut but not before I get a glimpse of an old photograph.

"What are *you* doing here?" Her tone is not only unfriendly, but her deep voice is somewhat higher in pitch, sounding tense.

Thinking fast, I say, "I've come for some dog food for Peachie. She's staying with me during the police investigation, and I wanted to see what Mr. Whitmore fed her. You don't happen to know where he keeps her food, do you?" She doesn't respond as I move toward several cabinets to look around. "FYI, I'm also here working as a private investigator for a client. What are *you* doing here?"

Her eyes register surprise as she quickly picks up the diary and tucks it inside her purse.

But I direct my attention to the orange Hermès shopping bag among the book piles beneath the wall cabinets, the same one I saw through the window during my prior visit. "Whoa. This looks nice." I reach in and remove a brown leather Birkin bag. "Isn't it like yours?"

Katya approaches me cautiously. Half-way to the kitchen counter, she announces, "It's a knock-off."

"How do you know?"

"The stitching is a dead give-away." She stops next to me. "It's too perfect because it's done by machine instead of by hand." She points at the stamped-in logo on the leather. "And the stamping sits on top of the leather on the fake, rather than being part of the leather the way it is on mine." Even though her tone is haughty, she can't resist showing me her authentic bag side-by-side with the counterfeit brown purse.

"Wow, somebody gave you a very generous present," I look at her red purse but pick up the brown one to examine the stitching more closely. "I looked these up online for the latest prices."

"Mine was a gift." Her tone is patronizing.

"Someone must think really highly of you to give you a present like that."

She pauses for dramatic effect and then continues with that superior tone, "Darling, I'm exceptional company to deserve a present like that." Then Katya seems to remember herself and pulls back. "Who hired *you* as an investigator?" I can hear that slight nervousness back in her voice.

Peach scurries around Katya and dashes for the table, and I walk over to reach for the dragging leash. "That is confidential, but I can assure you I'm here on business." Then I stare at the small stack of books by the diary. They don't appear to be anything out of the ordinary, but wait a minute—they're children's books. How curious. I pick up a couple of them and flip through the pages. "Again Ms. Alessandro, what's your story? And how'd you get into the house?" One of the pages has a written dedication to Bianca, but before I can read it, Katya grabs the book from me.

"Since you've been so busy investigating, you must surely know that Casey Whitmore was my employee, and he had some books here from my store. I've come to retrieve them." She scoops up the rest of the books.

"Are you sure that's the only reason you're here?"

We stare at each other. If eyes could kill, we'd each be at opposing ends of a battlefield, ready to fire.

"So what are you trying to hide?" I ask.

"It's not important." Her tone is defensive.

"I was instructed not to tamper with the scene, and I'm sure the same applies to you," I say, feigning nonchalance, and her black eyes fill with rage.

Suddenly Katya heads for a broom closet and removes a shopping bag. She stuffs the books into the bag and then sweeps past me with her parting shot. "Don't be fooled by that Jamie Gordon. He's not everything you think he is," she hisses. And then she's gone.

The comment about Jamie certainly came out of nowhere. I guess she picked up on the chemistry between Jamie and me when we were all skeet shooting yesterday. Even though I consider the source, it still throws me off balance somewhat. I get to work quickly.

First I dash into Casey's bedroom where I see the empty frame that used to hold the picture of the four GIs. My heart drops. Katya got to it first. I scroll through my phone to look at the blurry stills of that photograph from my first visit.

"How could I have been so stupid?" I rake the fingers of both fists through my hair and feel my shoulders slump in disappointment. "That photo just walked out of here in that diary. Shit."

I return to the kitchen and pull on gloves. I start with the table in the center, carefully looking through all the papers and books. There's nothing here except for plenty of fingerprint dust. I move on to the kitchen cabinets, but don't find anything especially interesting in them either.

I walk into the living room. Even though Casey has given the painting of the big house in the village to Sally for some reason, I'm still not sure it's relevant. I carefully lift it off the hook, sit on the sofa, and examine it. Then I flip the picture over, but find nothing on the back side.

I search the rest of the house, but I return to the kitchen when nothing interesting turns up. Peachie whines, and I let her out the back to pee.

I need a break and walk back to the kitchen counter for another look at the designer knock-off purse. It's a pretty good fake, and the leather feels soft.

I look inside and in one pocket I find a birthday card. It's sealed, and I flip it over.

To Sally
Happy Birthday

The police must have missed this as they did their search. I speculate how many other people will come and go from Casey's house before the dust settles. This gift is too easy for someone to grab. I take it with me to give to Sally.

CHAPTER TWENTY-FIVE

I walk down the gravel road at dusk with Warrior and Peachie, and my head feels as if it could explode. I've learned a lot in the last few days, and it's hard keeping everything straight.

Even though I consider myself a newbie investigator, I feel more determined than ever to get to the bottom of things. There's no way I'm close to the skills of a pro like Will, what with his background in the military, a lot of years on a police force, and then some time as a detective before he became a private eye. Still, I've got a good head on my shoulders, and I can try to think things through.

I take the dogs inside then open up a package of poster boards. I decide on a mug of herbal tea instead of my usual treat of a glass of wine and grab a black marker to begin the initial steps of my brain-dump. The first board cuts to the chase, the reason Win still has me on the payroll.

> *#1 Casey Whitmore had 1/3 of ASE Gatsby*
> *Win has 1/3*
> *Where's the other 1/3?*

Whenever I think of the elderly Casey Whitmore, I imagine him as an old-fashioned cat burglar like Cary Grant in the 1950s flick, *To Catch a Thief*. While I write, two sets of canine eyes in the corner study me. Peach is tucked next to Warrior on his oversized dog nest.

There's a message from Will on my phone, but I'll return the call later after I've finished writing out what I know. I grab a second board and continue writing, although Win has *not* hired me to find out the following—

#2 Who Killed Casey? And why? Shooting connected to paperback?

Since the police investigation of Whitmore's shooting is ongoing, both Will and Detective Rossi would tell me to not even think about it. I'll try not to spend too much time on this board.

I move the boards upstairs and lean them against one wall of my bathroom underneath a large photograph of Sean Connery as Secret Agent 007. It's the iconic one of him as James Bond, wearing black tie and holding a gun. It's the only picture hanging on my bathroom walls because a chat with my favorite spy while soaking in the tub is one of my preferred ways to unwind.

I turn on the faucet of my deep white ceramic tub that stands in the center of the room and click on some music. The first cut is Lee Hazelwood and Nancy Sinatra singing the psychedelic "Some Velvet Morning." As Hazlewood's gravelly voice comes through the speakers,

I take off my clothes and lower myself into the warm water. It feels really good, and I sigh with pleasure. My phone vibrates, but I ignore it. This bath is heavenly. The dogs watch me by the door.

I take a sip of my tea, lean back in the tub, and look up at the photograph. "Well, James, anything to add that'll lead me to the final chunk of that paperback? And you never know, maybe it'll even help solve the shooting, which I am *not* investigating, by the way."

I hear a low growl from Warrior and notice that he's restless. Still, I let my mind wander and relax, and eventually his vocalizations fade into the background as Simon & Garfunkel's "The Sound of Silence" replaces Hazelwood and Sinatra.

After losing myself in the song for couple of minutes, I stand up dripping wet, and reach for the mug. I recall the two things I heard Whitmore say right before he died. He stared hard at Jamie Gordon when he said, "The book," although Jamie didn't seem to recognize him. And Whitmore's, "Last thing I do," dying words were directed to Win.

I step out of the tub and write on a new board as the first bars of "Outlaw Man" by the Eagles play through my sound system. It's a little chilly in here, and I feel goose bumps on my arms as I write. It would help to put some clothes on, but I can't stop. I have to get it all down.

#3 Casey Whitmore?
"The book..." to Jamie
"...if it's the last thing I do..." to Win

My damn phone vibrates to voicemail again, but I'm remembering Win's subtle flinch when Casey addressed him. The memory of that flinch is all it takes for me to write some more.

Does Win know Casey or not?

I'm surprised that this even crosses my mind. Is it possible the man who employs me on this case knows more than he's saying?

Warrior and Peachie's growls distract me for a moment, and the little dog nips at one of Warrior's heels. "Better watch it, girl. Don't push your luck with him." I sit against the edge of the tub.

My German shepherd barks, which startles me. "What is it, Warrior?" He ambles out of the room and seems very relaxed as I hear him go down the stairs, making whiny noises. The sound of his footfalls and voice recede as an old Tina Turner song starts playing, "River Deep, Mountain High."

I again look up at 007. "Anything else, James?" Warrior barks downstairs, but I ignore him.

"You're right," I say to the photograph, grabbing an empty board. "I may as well put it all where I can see it." I start a new one.

#4 Peach's toy with list

I click on my phone. There are three messages from Will—I'll get to those in a moment. Instead, I examine the photos I took of the list and copy the mysterious dates and initials.

The Great Gatsby (ASE)
1944 J.W., L.A., M.G.
W. 8/8
S.J. 10/12

As Tina Turner wails in the background, I hear footsteps racing up my stairs, and I freeze.

Will, Warrior, and Peachie burst through the open door of my bathroom. They bark while he yells over the music, "Ronnie, are you okay—" He freezes when he sees me standing there nude.

"Will!" I shriek, staring back at him and covering my body with my arms. "What are you doing here?"

"Sorry!" he shouts. He politely averts his gaze, reaches for a terry cloth robe hanging on the back of the door, and tosses it to me.

"Hey, can you turn down the music?" he hollers as he rubs his ears with his fingers, which I do quickly, and the dogs settle down, too. "I'm pretty sure I saw someone trying to look in your windows, but whoever it was took off when I drove up."

"Oh my god," I respond. "We never have any problems out here. Should I call the police?"

"Don't bother. I scared him off when I pulled in." He looks over at my phone. "Don't you answer your phone? I saw your car here, but you didn't respond to me calling out and knocking on the door. So I opened it, because I got worried that something had happened. Warrior knows me so he didn't growl, and I came in to check that you were okay."

"Well, I am. Thank you for making sure." I tie the belt of the robe securely. "I'm embarrassed to admit how often I sing along at the top of my lungs. I guess that's why I didn't hear you downstairs."

"You should keep your doors locked. Anybody could waltz in."

"You're right. Uh, what brought you out here?"

"I've got a last-minute surveillance assignment for tonight that I can't do, and I want you to handle it." His voice drifts off as he looks around and sees the boards. "What exactly are you up to?"

"What does it look like I'm doing? I've been working on the case." I gather up the boards. "Come on. Let's go downstairs. I'll pour you a glass of wine and show you what I've got."

He looks at his watch. "I've got ten minutes."

Leaving Will with the poster boards and a glass of wine, I quickly throw on jeans and a sweater for the surveillance job. When I come back downstairs, I find Peach and Warrior curled up by him and the poster boards leaning up against the back of my sofa. Will points at my second poster board with a scowl.

#2 Who Killed Casey? And why?
Shooting connected to paperback?

"Now, Will, don't get mad. I'm *not* working on this one, I promise, but humor me, because I have some thoughts on the murder." I write quickly and add—

Premeditated
Who was shooter? Hired gun?
Same guy at Casey's house shooting at me?
Who knocked me out? Shooter?
Somebody else?

"Think about it." I put the board face down on the kitchen counter. "Someone knew Casey Whitmore would be at the Watson party. That shooter was out there waiting for him."

"I agree, but the police are working on the murder. By the way, it's now officially a murder."

"I've always thought so." I hope I don't sound gloating.

"Again, Detective Rossi reminded me that she does not want you involved *at all* in her investigation." He takes a deep breath. "Here's a copy of the police reports so far. I had to pull strings to get them because this is an ongoing investigation. Remember, this information is not known to the public, and it has to stay that way right now. Take a look when you have a moment, but Ronnie, focus on what Win wants and not the murder.

"Okay, okay. Take a look at this other board."

He reads board #3 about Casey. "What do you mean, *Does Win know Casey or not?*"

"I know he's our client, but it's something that's nagging at me. I need to think about it more."

"Remember, you cannot talk about this to Marilyn," Will cautions me. "Right now, we work for her husband."

"I know, I know. I told her that. We're cool."

"So, you've got my attention. Go on about Win and whether he may or may not know Casey," Will says as he rubs the top of Warrior's head. Peachie nudges his arm for some head-rubbing, too.

"I don't know yet, but I'll find out. Now, tell me where you want me to go this evening and what I'm supposed to do."

CHAPTER TWENTY-SIX

"Ouch," I shriek after a sip of scalding coffee burns my tongue and my hand. I almost drop the cup while I drive on I-287 in my brother's Toyota. "Damn. That hurts." Warrior, who's strapped into the front seat, looks at me with his big brown eyes and whines in sympathy, I'm sure.

I maneuver the cup into the car holder as the Range Rover—maybe black but hard to tell in the dark—cuts into my lane two cars ahead. We both pulled off the highway five minutes ago for a bathroom and coffee break—she for the bathroom and me for the coffee, where I could discreetly keep an eye on the tall, lanky woman with chic short brown hair. (I'd love to know who did that haircut.)

Her husband, Will's client, thinks she's having an affair. The client wants Will to follow her tonight because of a supposed girls' night out that came up at the last minute. He thinks his wife is really going to meet her lover instead, and wants the pictures to prove it. As I've already learned from doing work for Will on other occasions, a lot of bread-and-butter P.I. work consists of spying on cheating spouses.

We drive another twenty minutes, and the Range Rover exits the highway and turns into the business district of a small community. After a few more turns, the SUV finally drives into the parking lot of the local library. I pull over to the sidewalk and turn off my lights. The woman goes inside, where I watch her through the windows as she takes a magazine from the rack and sits down to read. The scene doesn't look like any ladies night out that I've ever seen, but maybe it's a book club that meets at the library and she's the first one there.

A Porsche zips into the lot, and Warrior sits up in his seat. Illuminated by the library's lights as it parks close to the window, the vehicle looks like a silver bullet. The woman looks up from her magazine, sees the car, and a happy look of recognition comes over her face. She puts the magazine back in the rack and walks toward the door as I grab my camera.

The moment the woman walks out of the library, I snap pictures as she gets back into her Land Rover. Only when the Porsche pulls out and she follows does my camera stop clicking.

I tail them to a motel fifteen minutes away. I hear a couple of explosive noises nearby. Police sirens start up, and a cruiser races past. The neighborhood isn't great, and I'm glad I've got Warrior with me.

I click on Gordon Lightfoot singing "Sundown"—it seems appropriate somehow. I keep the volume low while I shoot more pictures as a man, dark-haired and probably in his mid-forties, gets out of the Porsche. I duck down and continue photographing as he loosely drapes his arm around Will's client's wife. These photos are time-stamped, and it's now almost eight at night.

They enter a room, and from the looks of the establishment, it's probably forty-dollars a night. Oh well, they're probably well past the romance stage, if they ever had one in the first place.

Waiting for something to happen is the tedious part of surveillance. I sit there with the dregs of my cold coffee and try to imagine being in a marriage where I don't trust my partner. Even though my husband and I were married for almost thirty years, I never suspected him of cheating on me. No, our marriage came apart for other reasons. I glance at my German shepherd, then affectionately rub the top of Warrior's head.

I try to put myself in Marilyn's shoes and imagine what it's like to be worried about whether or not my spouse is planning to dump me. I take my yellow pad from between the two front seats and pretend it's one of my poster boards from earlier this evening.

Marilyn pointed out on the phone just this morning that my cover while investigating Win is to help solve the ASE paperback puzzle. She wasn't thrilled when I reminded her that I can't work on her case while working for Win. I wish I could have told her that I'm discreetly looking out for her and reporting back to Will, but I can't.

This is a tough one. I like Marilyn, and she's a friend. She's an unlikely candidate for any kind of crime, but you know what they say about a woman scorned, so I start writing.

> Marilyn Watson
> Win's diary about lawyer meetings
> Thinks mystery note to Win is from Katya
> Upset over possible Win-Katya affair
> Repeat of Win's other affair when they lived in Summit?
> Worried about being traded-in
> What would she do to stop it?

I think back to our conversation the other evening about Sydney Ballantine, Win's former lover, a socialite who disappeared. It was still thought to be an unsolved murder.

I let my imagination run wild—is it possible that Marilyn got rid of her? She did admit to fantasies of Katya going *poof* and disappearing. Ascribing it to the realm of very slim possibility, I add—

> Hire Casey's shooter to set up Katya? Or to shoot Katya?

There, I've put it on paper, but I don't believe it for a second.

I'm feeling a little sleepy so I call my youngest daughter, Jess, the one in school over in Pennsylvania. My call goes straight to voice mail, and I text her.

r u ok?

yeah, why not?

u didn't answer your phone

I'm busy

everything ok at school? classes? boys?

you're being weird. what's up?

on a stakeout

words I never thought I'd hear. my friend's mom does zumba but then you've got aikido. why the stakeout?

love triangle

ok, be home Sunday. we'll eat at our fav diner & tell me about the love triangle?

just sunday? come friday or saturday?

got a paper to finish. can't come sooner

what time Sunday?

around ten at the diner

love you, Jess

love you, too, Mom

I almost doze off when Warrior whines softly at a squirrel, and I sit up quickly. I'm wide awake when the guilty couple leaves the room, so I grab my camera from my lap and start clicking. As she turns to walk toward her car, he grabs her arm and pulls her to him for one last passionate embrace and a long kiss. I click away. When will cheating spouses learn to never, ever show public displays of affection?

Once they're gone, I let Warrior out for a pee while I stretch. I pour water in a travel bowl, and he takes a drink. When he's finished, he does a big down-dog stretch and then hops back into the car where I click him into his seatbelt.

I email Will that I have the amorous pictures of his client's wife, and head home where I will download and send them to him. I turn on one of my favorite classics, Gerry Rafferty's "Baker Street," feeling the loneliness of the haunting saxophone and wailing guitar between the song's verses.

CHAPTER TWENTY-SEVEN

After emailing Will the photographs, I decide to forget about husband-clients who don't trust their wives.

My mind is back to searching for *Gatsby*.

I settle the dogs for the night, sit on top of my bed, then spread out the poster boards I worked on earlier. I read over the police reports that Will left with me and sip another hot cup of herbal tea. The police found a shell casing on the hillside where the shooter positioned himself to fire at the thief. From that casing, they've determined that he used a .308-caliber Remington rifle.

I grab my board about the dead guy who's the focus of the police reports.

> #3 Who is Casey Whitmore?
> "The book..." to Jamie
> "...if it's the last thing I do..." to Win
> Does Win know Casey or not?

...and add more to the list—

Took Marilyn's necklace
Worked at Alessandro Rare Books in
Summit
Behind-the-scenes at store
Gatsby his store pick-of-week
His house full of books
War-time photo of soldiers
Dropped 1/3 of paperback Gatsby during
fall at Win's house
Looking for Win's 1/3 paperback, that fits
with his
Handled Win's $500K Gatsby, but did not
steal it. Why?
Damaged $500K Gatsby?
Purse gift for Sally
Painting of house for Sally

I hear two sets of snores, one softer than the other, coming from Warrior's dog bed and Peachie's crate. I look down and laugh. It's little Peach who has the noisier snore. Another sip of tea. I tell myself to stay focused.

The players. The players. *Think of all the players related to this case.* I already wrote out my thoughts about Marilyn during the stakeout, and I transfer it to a poster board. Then I switch to my employer, start a new board with his name at the top, and scribble everything I can think of.

Win Watson
Collects 20th cen. 1st editions
Dying Casey seemed to know him
Nasty talk with Katya (affair?) at store
& his party
History of affair in Summit?
What am I missing?

I move on quickly. The next board is devoted to the *femme fatale*.

Katya Alessandro
Expensive taste (car & purse)
Affair with Win Watson?
Fight with Win at Watson dinner &
bookstore
History with Jamie Gordon?
Tears & Bianca?
Owns Alessandro Rare Books
Casey's boss
Casey's dog toy list on Alessandro memo
paper
'Stay away' note about the book & what
our families started

I consider that stay-away note and add one more to the Katya list.

Does Katya want the ASE? And why?

The one who's making me feel the most confused is Jamie Gordon. I can't shake that image of Jamie embracing Katya at his party. I continue to wonder if they've had a relationship that goes beyond book collecting.

Damn, I hate that he's gotten under my skin. And as much as I'm attracted to him, I have to assign Jamie a board, which I reluctantly write.

Jamie Gordon
Collects 20th cen. 1st editions & forgeries
Dying thief seemed to know him
Mob business rumors
Client of Alessandro
History with Katya?
Friend of Watsons
Dead wife and kids

Although I find this far-fetched, I remember that he disappeared for a while at the end of the Watson dinner party. What if it was Jamie who dropped the treasured first edition, not Whitmore? The possibility intrigues and disturbs me.

Did Jamie damage $500K Gatsby?
Opportunity at party

I pull out another board and list a few bullets about our friendly rare book expert.

George Smithson
Respected book dealer
Robbery of $500K Gatsby at his warehouse
Chased Sally, fell & knocked out

I think back to the visit Josh Brown and I paid to

George at the warehouse and that strange phone call. "Why are you calling me here…" It's probably nothing, but still—

Strange phone call at warehouse?

I sit back in my bed and slowly read through all my boards, sipping my tea. There's something missing, and it's tickling the edges of my memory, driving me crazy.

After a third attempt at slowly reading through all the poster boards to figure out what I've forgotten, I go downstairs for a late night snack. The dogs come, too.

I'm holding an overflowing scoop of strawberry ice cream mid-air when it hits me like a Mack truck, and the scooper tumbles to the floor. The dogs pounce on the ice cream, licking it up and smearing it all over the floor in the process, but I hardly notice. Really, I don't even see them as I mentally run through the clues, first chronologically and then in order of importance, and I realize the one I left out.

Even though I'm not supposed to pursue it, I'm pretty sure I know who killed the old cat burglar. Means and opportunity definitely fit—motive I'm still working on. I need to set a trap to make sure I'm right and encourage the killer to make his move, and it may even help me find the rest of the paperback.

I don't dare tell Will until I have all my ducks in a row. I clean up what's left of the ice cream that the dogs haven't already slurped up.

CHAPTER TWENTY-EIGHT

His deep steady voice cuts through me. "I never took you for a coward, Mrs. Lake."

We're upstairs at Sheffield Hall. "Cowardice has nothing to do with it, Mr. Gordon. Thank you for inviting me to your lovely party. Good night." I smile and turn to make my exit.

He grabs my arm. "Not so fast, Ronnie."

As I turn back, he pulls me close, embracing me. My breath catches. His deep brown eyes stare into mine longingly, and time stops. Slowly, ever so slowly, our lips move toward each other—

A shrill ringing sound invades the moment, and I shoot up in bed, startled. "Huh?" My eyes snap open to darkness.

More ringing. *Ugh.* The clock says 5:15 a.m. I hear the rustle of the dogs near my bed.

I click on my phone and croak, "Hello."

"Ronnie?"

"Damn. Timing is everything," I moan. "Will, you've interrupted a very nice dream." I rub my eyes. "What's up?"

"I just got a text from early bird Win Watson."

"Seriously?"

"He was involved in a hit-and-run late last night. Someone broadsided him on the driver's side and fled the scene."

"Oh my god, was he injured?"

"The air bags saved him, but he was knocked unconscious and didn't really see the car that hit him. He just got home from being checked at the hospital and talking to the police. He's still pretty shaken up and wants one of us at his house as soon as possible, before he heads into the city. I'm leaving in half an hour for a meeting in Philadelphia. How soon can you get there?"

"6:00? I need some coffee first. What's so urgent?"

"He's got it in his head that this is tied in with *Gatsby*."

"I'll get over there." I switch on a lamp.

"Text him back and let him know you're on your way. Thanks, Ronnie." He clicks off.

~~~~~

"Win, calm down—" I urge.

"I am positive there's a link," he insists.

"Did something happen last night to make you think this?"

"Call it a hunch, Ronnie." Win sits at his sprawling oval pedestal table in the kitchen, bleary-eyed from a lack of sleep and sipping a large mug of coffee. I sit with him.

"First, I drove home after supper with George Smithson. We stopped by his warehouse so he could pick up his car and show me a couple of books he thought I might like to see. Then he went his way, and I went mine." He massages his temples before he continues.

"Take your time." I keep my voice calm.

"I was on the back roads when this car comes out of nowhere and broadsides me. When I regained consciousness and dug my way out of the air bag, I saw the back passenger door to my car was open, and it looked as if someone might have gone through my things."

"Your belongings must have been tossed around in the crash, so how could you tell?" I ask.

"I had several books in a satchel on the back floor. When I looked, the satchel was still there but unbuckled. It was fastened when I put it in the car," he insists.

"That is curious," I agree. "Did you report this to the police?"

"No. I only just realized it when I got home."

Marilyn comes into the kitchen. "Darling, your driver's here to take you into the city. Can't you reschedule this meeting and rest?"

"I'd love to, but the guy flew in for less than twenty-four hours, and then he's got to go back to London." He finishes his coffee.

Marilyn leans against a kitchen counter, exasperated.

"Ronnie, can you talk some sense into him?"

But Win jumps in. "Look. First, Whitmore gets shot off our roof and dies. Then my damaged *Gatsby* is stolen, or borrowed by that girl. I'm still not sure if I buy her story, by the way. Then another of these ASE pieces of a paperback *Gatsby* turns up. Then someone crashes into me and digs around in my belongings in the car. It doesn't feel like a coincidence."

"I do see your point," I say.

"I think whoever crashed into me was looking for more pieces of the paperback." He almost slams his coffee mug onto the table to emphasize his point.

"Ronnie, I'm so relieved those books are not here," Marilyn says, "but safely with you."

"I only hope that whoever smashed into Win doesn't find out I have them." I shake my head with worry and a slight scowl, but then smile confidently. "I agree, these incidents are tied to the paperback and, hey, probably that supposed treasure. Listen, you two," and they both lean in. "There are enough clues to start searching for the missing coins with or without the third piece of the paperback…that is, if the coins are still in their original hiding place. It's definitely worth a shot."

Win leaves for the city, and I mentally shift gears back to the night of the dinner party, only now I look through a different lens of the thief searching for the paperback instead of the expensive first edition. I walk outside and circle the building, thoroughly examining my surroundings.

There's a trellis on a guest wing wall that would have been far enough from the party to not be noticed. I step back to see that the lower roof above the lattice leads to a couple of windows that access the massive center of the house.

I go back inside, and as I walk along an upstairs hall, I pass those same two windows. I discover one of the screens hasn't been reattached properly. There's even a trace of fingerprint dust from the police, so this could be where Casey entered.

Once I've moved through the master bedroom suite and to Win's small library, I sit in his big chair and look across at the cabinet with the glass doors above the desk. I glance down and a piece of furniture blocks my view of the bottom shelf in one corner, the one where Win kept his ASE *Gatsby*.

Maybe Whitmore took out the piece he brought with him as he tried to determine where Win stored his. If Whitmore hoped to find Win's piece, then something must have interrupted him and caused him to act quickly. He must have stuffed the piece he already had into his pocket and left in haste.

I keep in mind that Jamie Gordon disappeared after dinner for a long time. Had Jamie come upstairs, and was that what caused Whitmore to make a hasty exit?

I consider the small window where the police thought Whitmore escaped, the only window in this room. I look through it and am surprised to observe Marilyn kneeling down behind several large bushes, digging a hole. What on earth is she doing out there? She has a gardener who takes care of the grounds. Her body blocks my sight line, but it appears she's placing something in the hole, and then she fills it. Given all the weird goings-on lately, every strange occurrence feels suspicious.

My mind wanders to a sinister place: how well do we really know anyone? You can think you do, and still, sometimes the nicest people turn out to be sociopaths.

CHAPTER TWENTY-NINE

The small window creaks when I crank it open, and I find another loose screen. I scoot onto the ledge with my legs out, my shoes propped on the slate roof. I can feel that my sneakers have solid traction.

I imagine the gunshot, envisioning it hitting its target and the old burglar sliding down the slate shingles, his arms and legs flailing for anything to grab onto. During his slide to death, the paperback falls out of his pocket and drops to the ground. Staring down at the tree that broke his fall makes me dizzy.

I look out in the direction from which the gunfire had to come and scan the horizon, which is mostly woods. There is one hilly area that stands above the trees. It's not that far off, perhaps just beyond the deer fencing that surrounds the Watson garden.

A high-pitched scream behind me startles me. I defensively grab the sides of the window and brace myself in case someone wants to push me out.

"Ronnie, don't go out there!" Marilyn screams.

I relax, turn around, and grin at her. "I wasn't thinking of it."

"Well, what on earth are you doing?"

"Trying to get inside the intruder's head on his last evening."

"Enough of that. Get yourself inside, right this minute," she pleads.

"I've seen plenty. I want to get my binoculars."

~~~~~

I walk through the garden in the general direction of the large shrubs, passing by the hole that Marilyn filled with dirt. There's got to be something interesting in there, but now's not the time to find out what.

Or is it? I look up at the window. No Marilyn. As a matter of fact, I don't see anybody near any of the back windows or doors. The loose, soft earth covering the small hole looks tantalizing.

I pull latex gloves from my pocket, slide them on, kneel down on the grass, and scoop out the soil with my hands. I don't dig very long before touching something solid. It feels like a handle, and I exhume…what? A silver letter opener? With a penny taped to one side of the blade? What kind of voodoo is Marilyn into?

I flip it over, and the engraving on the other side of the blade reads *To my partner in life, Happy Anniversary on our 30th!*

"Man, with an inscription like that, this would be perfect sticking out of his back." I put a letter opener up there with a toaster or a bathroom scale as a dud of an anniversary present. But it's the coin taped to the blade that makes it intriguing. I quickly snap a picture, drop the knife back into the hole, and fill it with dirt.

I scoot behind a wall of larger bushes and look for the opening in the deer fence next to the area where I found Peach. I spot some left-over yellow crime tape across the snipped wire in the fence, and I slip through.

The person who knocked me out could have carried the gun that shot Casey Whitmore, or could have been another thief looking for pieces of the ASE paperback. Whichever way this shakes out, I need to pursue this in order to find the third piece of the paperback.

I brush the dirt from my gloves as I continue along the trail that turns into a deer path up a hill. At the top, more crime scene tape runs around the top of an outcropping of boulders. I climb the monstrous rocks, step inside the tape, and plant myself in the middle. There it is—the perfect view of the Watsons' roof.

Since the shooter didn't know where Casey Whitmore would exit, this higher position was necessary to get the full view of the house. The way the rocks are clustered, I could even conveniently rest my gun while waiting for the thief to make his move.

Looking through my binoculars, I study the house more closely, especially the area around Win's library window. This is not the side of the house where Whitmore made his original entry. He would have had to climb over the top of the roof in order to get himself back to the guest wing so he could climb down that metal trellis.

Meanwhile, the killer would have looked through the scope of the rifle, waiting for the best shot. As the burglar climbed close to the top of the roof, the shooter would have felt pressure to fire or lose the opportunity before Whitmore descended down the other side and got away.

Somewhere within this crime scene, the killer's Remington ejected a shell casing that got stuck down among these huge stones. He couldn't take the time to search for it and had to get out of there in a hurry, and so the police recovered it later on.

I turn to go and spot an easier way down, slightly less steep than the way up. As I scramble down from the boulders, I consider the shooter as a hired gun. If so, who was his boss, or his client?

When I get close to the bottom, I catch a streak of bright golden yellow between two jagged rocks. Crouching down, I try to see what the object is, but can't make it out. I reach into the crack to retrieve it, but the opening is much too narrow. I get a stick, ready to poke it free, but stop myself. What if this thing is tied to the shooting? It's probably not, but I'd better play it safe.

I pull out my phone and step back to take wider shots showing the area and the pile of boulders. As I move closer, I take more pictures, and finally move in for a close-up showing the faint outline of a shiny yellow rectangle. I do my best to zoom in, but I still don't know what it is.

Breaking a long stick, I try to unsuccessfully fish it out and then resort to pushing it downhill. It finally pops out from the boulders. I've already got gloves on, reach down, and pick up a yellow patent leather case. I'm careful to hold it by its edges—there may be prints. On one corner of the yellow leather is a stamped-in logo that I don't recognize. I flip it open to see a gray lining that is ink-stained at one end.

I carefully deposit the pen holder in a plastic baggie. It's clean enough of dirt and other outdoor debris to make me think that it fell through these boulders recently.

~~~~~

An hour after starting my Internet search by visiting different pen companies, I decide it's time to stop being distracted by the most beautiful, elegant, and outrageously expensive fountain pens I've ever seen. I bet they never skip, but if I owned one, I'd constantly be afraid of losing it.

I continue scrolling through images of pen holders and eventually locate the stylish leather case. I click open a link under the image that takes me to a website belonging to Pelikan, a German pen company, and I see the same Pelikan logo that is stamped into the yellow leather on this case. I speculate where the pen is that goes with it, and who the owner is.

There's really no proof that it's tied to the murder. It could have dropped between these boulders before the shooting. This pen holder definitely falls into one of those gray areas of what to report or not report to the police when investigating a crime.

First I need to find out more, but one thing's for sure: Detective Rossi has made it clear that I'm not to waste anymore of her time.

CHAPTER THIRTY

After my curious run-in with Katya at Casey's house, I decide this is an appropriate time for surveillance. Her presence has moved beyond that of a clichéd femme fatale who may be having an affair with my friend's husband to something more that ties in with *Gatsby*.

I switch my perky red Mustang for my brother's old Toyota again. The car isn't my only effort to fade into the background. I stay in the clothes I threw on early this morning—jeans and a barn jacket—and pull my hair back in a sloppy bun topped by a dark baseball cap, and finally add light-lensed sun glasses. It's not even close to a disguise, just an effort to go unnoticed.

I hit the road. Since I have no idea where Katya is, I start with a quick phone call to her book shop once I'm on the highway. A man answers, and I ask for Sally Richards.

It's not long before her cheery voice comes on the line. "May I help you?"

"It's Ronnie. Please don't be nervous that I'm calling you. How's everything going?"

"Fine, thank you. How are you?" Still, Sally's voice sounds a little wobbly.

"Everything is good. I'm calling on a different matter. Any sign of those Edith Wharton books I ordered?"

"I'll check. May I put you on hold for a moment?"

"Sounds good." Of course I know there are no Wharton books waiting for me, but I need to find out where the boss is without raising Sally's suspicions.

She's back on in a moment. "There's no sign of them." She sounds tense again. "If I can find the paperwork, I can make the calls."

"Take a deep breath. Is your boss nearby? Is that why you sound upset?"

"She's here in her office, but she's leaving us all alone."

"So no drama at work?" I ask. *Good. Katya is there.*

"She just told us not to disturb her. She's busy working on something important."

"Okay, keep me posted if those Wharton books come in."

"Yes, ma'am."

"Bye, Sally." We hang up.

~~~~~

Once there, I drive around the block and spot the white Tesla parked behind the store. I position the Toyota so that I can see if Katya leaves. I've come prepared with my cup of coffee.

Finally, an hour later, Katya comes through the back

door, carrying a couple of bulky shopping bags. Sally follows awkwardly, her vision obstructed by several cardboard boxes stacked high in her arms. She trips over a cement parking block and tries to catch herself. The highest box in her arms tumbles to the ground, landing sideways and opening, its contents scattering across the pavement.

Katya goes ballistic. She screams at her, telling her how worthless she is as Sally scurries on her hands and knees to retrieve the fallen books. *What is this woman's problem?* Alessandro could be the kind of boss who treats all her employees this way and not just Sally. Maybe she's extra-upset because of something that happened yesterday at Casey's house?

Sally finishes putting the books back in the box. As she places it in the Tesla's trunk, Katya dismisses her with a command of, "Get back to work." Her head hanging, Sally rushes inside as Katya drives away.

Keeping my distance, I follow the Tesla all the way to Somerville. Katya drives to a large shopping mall, parks near Lord & Taylor, but doesn't get out. I circle around and park where I have a good view of her car. I can see that she's still sitting inside it. She looks like she's busy writing.

A dark green Jeep Cherokee pulls in and also parks near L&T. Of all people, George Smithson gets out, glances toward Katya, nods at her, and walks inside. She waits a beat and follows.

Then it's my turn. I grab a shopping bag filled with

towels I've needed to exchange and quickly walk past her car. I glance inside the windows, and what I see is so odd, I stop. There are open books scattered across the front passenger seat and some more in the back. She's penned the name *Bianca* and some short messages on the title pages.

I don't have time to take a closer look. I hurry toward the mall entrance and push open the large glass door like any other shopper on an errand. I see George and Katya walking together through the food court.

As they swing left into Barnes & Noble, I think, *How weird that these two are meeting?* After all, they're competitors. And why drive all the way to Somerville to conduct business?

They walk into the fiction stacks inside the store, and I do the same but go the next aisle over. I pretend to peruse the titles as I listen.

"Did you bring it?" Katya asks.

"Yes," George answers. "Why all the secrecy?"

"It's time-sensitive, and I need to protect my client's privacy. I don't need the team at my store to know all the details. Or anyone else besides you and me."

"Understood," he says.

I hear some rustling of paper, and I dash further down the aisle so I can peek around the corner. I witness an exchange between the two.

He gives her a brown envelope that could contain, I'm guessing, a book, since they're both dealers. She gives him an envelope that's smaller but large enough to hold money. She opens hers and smiles. He opens his and flips through a wad of something, probably money.

"Looks good," he says.

"Okay. I appreciate the professional courtesy. Thank you, George."

I quickly cut over a couple of aisles and make my way between two shelves, hoping to time my chance at accidentally running into them. I burst into the open a moment after they pass by and feign surprise. "George! Katya!"

They swing around, both looking somewhat horrified to be caught together. "Uh, Ronnie—" George says.

"What are you two doing here?" I smile innocently. They both hold their packages a little more snugly.

"Oh, you know, professional colleagues talking business." George tries to change the subject. "How's the case coming along with the ASE *Gatsby*?"

"Oh, you know about that?"

"Come on, Ronnie. I talk to Win almost every day," he says. "There's not much that gets by me."

Katya seems restless, as if she would like to get out of here.

"May I steal George away?" I ask her. "I really must speak with him."

"It's fine with me," she answers. "I need to pick up something while I'm here." She turns down a nearby aisle, and we do the same down a different one. I hear her footsteps close by, so I keep my voice low, but not too low. I want her to be able to eavesdrop.

"What did Win tell you?" I ask him, glancing around as we walk.

"Well, that the paperback may lead to some valuable coins," he says. "And the coins, if they exist, may be in Lambertville."

"That's just one of the interesting clues we discovered," I throw in. We turn down another aisle.

"You mean there's more?" he asks.

"There's plenty more," I affirm.

"If there really are some coins and they're actually recovered, who would get them?" George guides us in the direction of the exit.

"We're still missing one piece of the book, and I think that section might lead us to the legal owner."

"The whole thing sounds far-fetched, if you ask me."

"Hey, crazier things have happened." I laugh.

We come out of the stacks and catch a glimpse of Katya looking through the shelves close by. George gives me a suspicious look and says, "Do you think she's been listening to our conversation the whole time?"

"I don't know." I look at my watch. "George, I'm running late. See you around." After a quick hug, I head out the door, make a right turn, and walk away.

In the reflection of a store window, I see George leave one way, and Katya rush off in the other direction.

CHAPTER THIRTY-ONE

A glass of wine in hand, I hunt around on the web: knife and coin. I'm bothered by the letter opener I found buried at Marilyn's, and phrases like burying the hatchet come to mind as I come across different superstitions. My online search turns up everything from putting the knife under the bed for cutting the pain of childbirth to placing a knife with a black handle under your pillow to keep away nightmares.

Then I stumble on the one that practically makes me spit my merlot. There's a Viking superstition that giving someone a knife means your relationship will be severed. To break the curse, you actually have to sell it for a copper coin or attach the coin to it. Between this gift and Katya's intrusion into her life, no wonder my friend is going crazy and burying a letter opener in her garden. I consider whether the copper penny taped to the blade has any special meaning beyond a Norse legend.

It's time to think about other things, like which shoes to wear tonight with a black-and-white knee-length flirty dress that I love. Jamie told me to put on my dancing shoes. What that has to do with him cooking me dinner, I don't know, but I'm ready to find out. And I love to dance.

Once again, I drive up the mountain to Sheffield Hall and this time sing along to Linda Ronstadt's "Just One Look." As she belts out, "Just one look, that's all it took, hah," I arrive at the house.

As I drive along the spotlighted, sparkling fountains in the long pool, the massive front doors open and Jamie stands there, leaning against the door frame. My heart beats faster.

Before I can turn off the ignition, he's opening my car door and sweeping me into his arms. He leans down and kisses me long and hard. I can't help but notice how good he smells, like the outdoors. Time stops for me. I want this moment to go on forever.

But then Jamie takes my hand, and we walk up the steps and go inside. I follow as we continue through the foyer, where he removes my shawl. I start to say something, but he gently puts his index finger against my lips, signaling me to not say a word.

He stands back and slowly takes in my appearance, from my lips that he's just kissed all the way down my body and my legs until he arrives at my shoes—my special red-soled Louboutins that Juliana gave me. Around the moment that I'm wondering if this man has a shoe fetish, he smiles.

"Beautiful, all of you, so beautiful." He takes my hand, turns, and continues leading me down the long hallway and through the large doors into the old ballroom.

The last time I saw this room, I was with Juliana and it was packed with partiers. This time it's empty, and its grand expanse takes my breath away.

A ballroom is certainly irrelevant in today's world except in fairy tales, but as I take in the soft ivory-gray walls decorated with tailored moldings in a slightly darker shade, I appreciate how peacefully beautiful the vast space is. There's nothing fussy about this room. The lighting from the chandeliers and wall sconces is turned down low, giving the room a magical glow that reflects off the numerous multi-paned French doors throughout the room.

The music plays quietly in the background as Jamie lifts two glasses of champagne from a small table at the top of the stairs.

"To us," he toasts, and we drink.

Then he takes a remote to turn up the volume of the music as a new piece starts. I hear "The Blue Danube," and I can't help but chuckle.

"What?" he asks.

"In less than five minutes, I've gone from Linda Ronstadt in my car to Johann Strauss in your ballroom." He laughs. The sound of it is wonderful, and I laugh with him.

Jamie guides me down the stairs and into the middle of the room. We look into each other's eyes as he puts his other hand around my waist. He gives me a hint of a smile, and I respond with the same.

On the count, we begin with the basic one-two-three and then add the turns. At Jamie's party, I imagined dancing a waltz here. Now here we are, just the two of us in this ballroom with its magic light, floating from one end to the other. Around and around the room we waltz, and we do it well, as if we've always danced together. For the second time tonight, I wish this moment would also never end.

Several waltzes later, we walk back upstairs, and Jamie shows me around Sheffield Hall. We quickly scoot through the more public rooms that were open to everyone the night of the party. It's easier to enjoy them now without the crowd scattered throughout the house, and it's fun. As we make the rounds, Jamie seems very detached from these professionally decorated rooms, as if he were walking through a hotel.

He even takes me upstairs to the top of the house through the unused servants' quarters, into the attic filled with ancient trunks and boxes.

"This was all left behind when I bought the place, and I haven't had the time to look through it to see if there's anything worth keeping."

"There are people who do this professionally— they'll unpack and organize your things. You could save yourself a lot of time," I say. "If you're interested, I can email you a name and number."

"I'll take you up on that," he says as we leave the attic.

We walk down the stairs and enter the second floor

hall where he catches me glancing at the large double doors to the master bedroom.

"Come on." He guides me toward them. "Admit it. You're curious to see what's behind those doors." He laughs as he opens them and waits for me to enter first.

I step into the most wonderfully masculine olive and khaki cocoon with rich, dark fabrics for the duvet, shams, curtains, and chairs sitting atop Persian rugs with darker browns and chestnut-colored designs. It's a large room with two halls leading to closets and a bathroom, and several shelved alcoves filled with books that are perfect for curling up and reading.

I walk to a set of glass-paned doors opposite the king-sized bed and look into the night. There's almost a full moon out, so I can see a lot of the property even though it's evening.

"There it is again, the moonlight in your hair." He comes up behind me and puts his arms around me. I relax into his body and he kisses my neck, which sends a delightful shiver down all of me.

Jamie turns me around and sees me glance toward his books. "If you want to know more about who I am, then feel free to take a look around—" A loud chime interrupts him. "That's the front door. I'll be right back."

He leaves, and I decide to do as he says. I find his bathroom, where I pick up a monstrous bar of soap and hold it up to my nose. It has a wonderful smell of pine, the same scent I noticed when I first arrived and he pulled me close and kissed me.

On my way back into the bedroom, I flip on the light to a spacious closet with everything perfectly organized, folded, and hung. I run my hand down the piles of soft cashmere sweaters in dreamy colors that must all look wonderful on him.

I head for one of the cozy alcoves with a huge chair and peruse the titles in this corner. There are many classic titles, but I also see that he enjoys bestsellers.

One corner of the room isn't a corner because the wall is rounded with an old curved window. Next to another comfortable chair in the center of that space is a telescope. Does Jamie like to gaze at the stars? Or the neighbors? I chuckle, because there aren't really many neighbors up here.

I look at the small built-in book case behind the chair, and my heart skips a beat. Among a handful of books is a silver-framed photograph of a woman sitting cross-legged in the grass with her arms around two children. I pick it up and look closely. It has to be his wife, son, and daughter—his family that died in a car accident. The kids look to be eight and ten and his wife in her early thirties. They're all beautiful, and I can only imagine his sadness over this huge loss, but I'm sure it's ongoing, as mine will always be over Tommy.

I glance around. This appears to be the only photograph in the room. I carefully put it back on the shelf. I glance at a couple of small stacks of books piled haphazardly on the bottom shelf, and something else catches my eye. An old black-and-white photograph sticks out of the side of one of the books, and something about the four sets of men's legs in loose pants looks familiar.

I remove the picture and my heart stops. No. It can't be. There are four World War II soldiers standing together. Doubt and wariness jolt through me, and I feel a curtain crash down on the happiness I've felt all evening.

It's the same photograph as the one in Casey's house. I'm sure of it. I drop into the chair and turn on a lamp for more light. There, staring me in the face, is proof of Jamie's link to Casey.

Four GIs stand in the sunshine, all looking into the camera, all wearing fatigues and friendly smiles. I flip the photo over and read the back.

Luca, Joe, Felix, Mike
Tirrenia July 1944

The year chokes my breath in my throat. I look towards the door to make sure I'm still alone and pull my phone from my pocket. I click over to my photos and find Casey's list of initials.

The Great Gatsby (ASE)
1944 J.W., L.A., M.G.
W. 8/8
S.,J. 10/12

I study the initials after 1944. Are they the men in the photo? But there are only three sets, and four guys in the picture.

I try out the name, Luca Alessandro, taking a random guess as I look at the initials L.A. and then the tall, olive-skinned GI on the left. *That's why Katya stole the picture*, I think to myself. *To get her hands on the names.*

I glance back and forth between the photograph and Casey's list, wondering how the ASE paperback fits.

The first one on the left is Luca…

J.W. The second one is Joe…Joe Watson, Win's father.

There are no initials for Felix on Casey's list. The man I see is small and wiry like Casey, so maybe Felix is Casey's father.

But who is the fourth man, Mike?

M.G. Mike…oh my god…Mike Gordon.

"Hey you, sorry about that. UPS dropping something off." Jamie says from the doorway. I look up at him and then back at the picture, studying the man on the right with one hand on his hip. And now I know why he looks so familiar.

"Is my bedroom that fascinating?" Jamie asks, smiling.

"You tell me, only if you're a vampire." I stand up and face him with the picture. "Because here you are in World War II."

Silence. He doesn't move.

"When were you planning to tell about this?"

More silence.

"One GI was Casey's father, Felix." I point to the shortest man in the group, second from the right in the picture. "And this man on the left with the cap may be

Katya Alessandro's father, more likely her grandfather. Luca, I think that's his name. And I'm pretty sure this one is Win Watson's father, Joe. But you already knew all of that, didn't you?"

Jamie just stands there, looking at me.

"And this one's Mike. I kept thinking he reminded me of someone, and now as I look at you and this picture, I can see there's no mistaking that he's probably your father. Otherwise, why would you even have this picture?"

"It's a long story—"

"Don't long story me. Casey had two parts of the ASE, and I believe he was looking for the third. I haven't figured out the exact connection between that book and these men yet. But you are tied in somehow, and you could have told me that when I spotted the piece behind the bush at the Watsons'."

"Please let me explain—"

I cut him off. "No need. Supper with Marilyn on Monday—that would have been the time to speak up." I put the picture down and walk toward the door. "If not, then certainly after our skeet shooting a couple of days ago. So, do you have it?" He looks at me quizzically, and I spell it out. "The third part of the book?"

Jamie remains silent and stands in the way of me going through the door. "I thought I could trust you," I say.

"You can," he protests.

"Hardly. Please move out of my way. I'm going home."

Jamie stares hard at me with those dark eyes. They look stormy, and he's blocking me from leaving. I have a moment of fear. I remember his temper and also what a great shot he is. What do I really know about this man?

Then the storminess in his eyes gives way to resignation, and he steps aside.

I sweep past him without a backward glance, and practically run down the stairs, grab my shawl, and dash out to my car. Adrenaline and shock carry me. I can't get away from Sheffield Hall fast enough.

CHAPTER THIRTY-TWO

I get in my car, collapse against the steering wheel, and several hoarse sobs come from somewhere very deep inside. I hunt for the one piece of music that perhaps can soothe my bruised soul. I find it—Joan Baez's achingly beautiful voice singing "Diamonds & Rust"—turn it on, and start down the steep road.

About the time she sings "...heading straight for a fall," the tears flow and blur my vision, but I manage to make it down in one piece, and my thumping heart slowly settles back to its normal rate. I still can't believe how deceived I feel, but the rational side of me is grateful that I found out before things moved forward between us.

Then I hear the sound and glance into my rearview mirror to see headlights come up behind me quickly. The vehicle is almost on my rear when it brakes a little. Then it speeds up again and taps my bumper. Son of a gun.

I try to pull away and put some space between us on this narrow twisty road. Feeling my tires lose the connection with the pavement on a couple of hairpin turns that I take too fast, I panic that I'll slide over the edge in a fatal crash.

As I pull out ahead, I wonder if Jamie's come after me and is trying to stop me. But that's a strange way to do it, and there's no way I'm halting for anybody on a dark and empty road.

Then the mystery car revs up, shoots toward me, and bashes into the back of my Mustang. As I grip the steering wheel to keep my car on the road, I hear several loud bangs, either gun shots or the engine backfiring.

I nearly freak out at the thought that it might be Casey's shooter, who came after me at Whitmore's house. I almost lose control when my phone rings suddenly, and that's when the driver veers off for a left turn and disappears into the night.

The phone rings again, and I answer. It's my brother, thank god, calling to change a lunch date we made for tomorrow because his late-morning meeting got pushed back. He hears the panic in my voice.

"Ronnie, are you okay?"

"I think so."

"Where are you?"

"Dri-driving home—" I can't get more out because I'm hyper-ventilating and crying from relief at the same time.

Then my brother does something that is pure Frank and one of the reasons I love him so much. He makes up a lame excuse to drop by at this late hour and hangs up before I can object.

~~~~~

Frank is already there when I pull into my driveway. I screech to a stop, jump out, and run into his arms for a consoling big-brother hug. Still shaky, I manage to explain what happened on the road, but I do not tell him that the tears streaming down my face have more to do with my disappointment over Jamie. I leave out any discussion about my date at Sheffield Hall.

We walk around my car to examine the back of my Mustang. After looking closely, Franks says, "I don't see any marks or residue that might lead to the person who hit you. Do you want to call the police?"

"Absolutely not. The guy drove off, and I didn't get a good look at the vehicle, so I can't identify anyone. Besides, Detective Rossi hates me and will be all over my case. I'll take the car to the shop in the morning. Right now I just need a good night's sleep."

I pull him toward my door. "But first, please come inside and keep me company while I settle down."

I let the dogs out into their pen and start the decaf. Frank perches on a stool, and I place his favorite oatmeal cookies on a plate and push it across the kitchen counter toward him.

My brother bites into one, and a look of pure bliss sweeps across his face. He drinks his steaming coffee and then takes another bite. He eases into the conversation by asking me for input on an upcoming birthday celebration for his son, my nephew Richard. We talk logistics, food, and the guest list. This takes all of five minutes, and then he cuts to the chase.

"How are you and Jamie doing? Are you two having fun?"

"Yep." My answer's true if I just focus on our waltz and not our conversation before I left.

"You spending a lot of time together?" he asks, trying to sound nonchalant and chatty. My brother is not the chatty type. He looks around uncomfortably. "Uh, do you have serious feelings for him?"

"Well, Frank, it's rather soon to be asking—we've barely met—and, by the way, that's a very personal question."

"Not unlike the questions you used to ask me about Jules."

I ignore the semi-goodhearted jab about my snooping into his wife's past when they were dating. "Anyway, whatever budding relationship we may or may not have, it's between Jamie and me."

"I only asked if you have serious feelings. I didn't ask for details." He takes another sip. "You sound a little defensive."

"I'm not defensive." I slam my mug with more force than I intended on the counter. The noise surprises both of us. "It's been a long time, and this is private. Why do you care anyway?"

"Let me remind you that it's exactly the same way you cared when Juliana and I got together," Frank answers in a calm tone.

"Point taken," I mutter. "What I'm not hearing is you sounding happy for me."

"That's your take, not mine—"

I interrupt. "But why do I feel like you don't approve of Jamie?"

Frank puts his hands up as if to ward off another aggressive kid-sister reaction and shakes his head. "I didn't say that. Of course, I'd like nothing more than to see you end up with a great guy." He tilts his head, and in a gentle tone, asks, "But in this case, are you sure you're thinking clearly?"

"What do you mean?"

"Well, we're coming up on Tommy's anniversary, which has to be emotional for you…maybe it makes you less rational?"

"When was I ever rational?" I feel a slight smile on my face.

"How well do you really know the guy?" Frank asks. He doesn't know it, but his question is a painful reminder of exactly why I've been chastising myself. I try to keep my slight smile frozen on my face.

My brother goes on. "I would caution you to go slowly because I'm hearing some sketchy reports. I have to wonder, what's the guy's real story, you know, his background?" If Frank only knew that I'm asking the same question, in light of the photograph I saw an hour ago…

At this point, instead of crying, I burst out laughing, which surprises even me.

"What's so funny?" Frank asks.

"You're right. You do sound just like me when you

and Jules first came back here from California." I refill Frank's mug. "It's like you're me now."

Frank looks horrified at the mere thought. "Well, now I know how it feels to be you." He grins.

I get up from my stool and let the dogs in. "Look, Frank, I've had a lot of time to think about my past behavior about Juliana. I know I made a lot of mistakes, and I pushed things too far. I stuck my nose in where I had no business." I stop and take a deep breath. "But the family knew nothing about her, and it was all so soon after Joanie's death. We were worried. Bottom line—I was terrified it would be a repetition of what happened to Peter when he married."

"I've said this many times, I'm not Peter," Frank interrupts. "And I'd never marry and cut myself off from my family the way he did. Ronnie, you know me better than that."

"Yes, but there were all these strange events when you came home…" I sip my coffee. "Hey, I developed tunnel vision when it came to protecting you. I know I interfered too much."

"It's in the past, Ronnie. I think some of that energy of yours at the time was channeled from your grief for Tommy." I feel a wave of emotion roll over me the way it did when I first got the news. I want to cry but I hold it back.

My brother goes on. "It was a blow to the entire family, but I can't even imagine what it was like for you to lose a child. Bottom line—you're my sister, and I love you."

I sigh. "You had a very happy thirty years with Joanie. I still miss her." Then I can't help but smile. "And I also know that you and Juliana are very happy, and that she's an incredible person."

"Thank you. Now, can we get back to the subject of Jamie Gordon?"

"I thought we were finished with that." I sigh. "Don't tell me you're paying any attention to the swirl of rumors around him. It's because he's fabulously rich, and he gives big parties at Sheffield Hall. So, who cares that his family hasn't been around here for generations?"

"Don't for one moment think I buy into that old family nonsense!" Frank's tone reveals his indignation. "You know I'm the last person who cares about that. Take a look at the Watsons. Win and Marilyn have been out here all of three years, and Juliana and I see them a lot. They're simply good people."

"Okay, okay. Calm down, Frank. I like them, too. I get a kick out of Win." But I have to wonder, *How much do we really know about the Watsons, either?*

"Jamie's a different matter." Frank's tone is firm but gentle.

"How so?"

"There are stories floating around…"

"About what?" I demand.

"About his business dealings with some unsavory guys," he answers.

"What are you talking about?"

"I'm not going to add to the rumor mill, and I don't

know what's true and what isn't. But the stories concern me. He may be involved with some bad people." He pauses. "I know you think I'm being nosy, but I care about you."

"I am a big girl. I can take care of myself. I'll be careful…" I roll my eyes. "…with my heart."

A slow smiles plays across Frank's face. He takes his coffee mug, and I take mine. We clink mugs and laugh.

~~~~~

Frank has gone home, and I'm upstairs. The hot water runs over my hand as the faucet fills the tub in my bathroom. What started out as a magical evening has taken some interesting turns. Still feeling ridiculously hasty for having fallen for Jamie, I shake my head in disbelief. After all, I'm an adult with a few miles on me, not some naïve twenty-something.

I turn off the faucet, step in, and sink into the steaming water. I look up at the photo of my favorite spy and sigh.

"It's my own fault. Frank is right. I hardly know Jamie…" I stop myself.

Thoughts of other duplicitous behavior stops me. I reach for my phone and flip through my pictures to find the note that Marilyn showed me, the one she found among Win's papers.

Dear Win,   *August 8*
You've got what I want, and I'm coming to get it. Nothing can stop me. I've waited so long…

I look back and forth between Casey's dog toy list and that note. I check the date and look at the list again—*W. 8/8*. There it is. 8/8 and August 8—they match.

Marilyn was sure that note came from Katya, but now I'm sure it didn't. Win and Katya may be having an affair, but this note was written by Casey to Win about the ASE *Gatsby*.

I swipe to the photo of the note from Katya's diary. I'm sure it was also written by Casey.

Stay away, —
I must have all of the book to finish what our families started.
It's my heritage, not yours.

I pinch the screen to zoom in to study the smudge after *Stay away*. It could be a *K* as in Katya. And *all of the book* has got be the ASE *Gatsby*. Casey had one piece of it, and he was looking for Win's section. And for some reason, he was telling Katya to back off. This is all getting too complicated.

I lean my head against the back of the tub and drift off.

Later, I awaken in the cold water of the tub with Warrior nudging at my arm. Shivering, I grab a towel and dry off quickly, slide into bed, and fall fast asleep.

CHAPTER THIRTY-THREE

Three women in their mid-to-late thirties clink their glasses filled with pink Cosmopolitans.

"Here's to marrying the big bucks!" the tall, leggy blonde says. She looks familiar.

"You know what they say, the good ones are always married," a petite, brown-haired beauty says in a sparkly voice. Wait a minute, I know her.

"So, keep that in mind and forget Jamie Gordon," blondie long-legs says. "He made mincemeat out of the last woman who fell for him."

"Who was it?" a third friend asks, leaning in.

"Somebody named Ronnie Lake," she answers.

Oh no, it's the three gossips from Jamie's buffet table at his party. Do they know I'm listening? I feel myself go still as a statue.

"Do we know her?" number three asks,

ready for some juicy gossip.
"Nah, she's old," the leggy blonde says.
"What did he ever want with her—"

Bam! Bam! Bam! Warrior and Peachie go ballistic with barking, and my German shepherd dashes out of my room and down the steps to the front door. Great—now I have barking in stereo, growling and snarling coming from both downstairs and the small khaki crate on the other side of my bed.

I squint at my clock. It's 6 a.m. Who in the world…

Bam! Bam! Bam! The canine racket goes up in volume. After a night of more bizarre dreams and fitful sleep, this is no way to start the morning.

I stumble over to the window and peek out. Jamie Gordon stands on the stoop, looking around for signs of life.

Bleary-eyed, I open the window a crack. "Go away."

"Ronnie—"

"Go away, Jamie. Do you know what time it is?"

"If you want to know the story behind that photograph and get a look at the third piece of that paperback *Gatsby*, then you'd better let me in." He taps on a brown accordion folder tucked under his arm. "I've got everything you want to know right here, and I'm ready to talk."

My eyes pop open, and I stare at the folder. "I'll be down in a moment," I mumble.

I throw on some jeans, a tee-shirt, and a sweater,

splash water on my face, brush my teeth, and let the dogs out in their pen. I open the door to let him in and put on the coffee.

I'm still waking up and not very talkative. I more or less grunt and wave to him to help himself to the coffee while I get breakfast ready for Warrior and Peachie. They come back inside, look back and forth between Jamie and their food bowls, dismiss him with a few quiet growls, and head for their kibble.

I open the refrigerator. "I can offer you yogurt?" I reach for a wooden bowl. "Also a banana or a muffin?" I pull out a box of blueberry muffins from my favorite bakery.

"Thanks, but I ate before I drove here."

I feel tense, so I heat up a muffin. I don't trust this man standing in my kitchen and therefore feel the need for some comfort food.

He sips his coffee while I pour myself a cup, and the pleasant aroma cuts through my grogginess. I break open the muffin and take a bite. "So, what gives?"

He pulls out the picture of the four GIs. "First, you're right." He points to the fourth soldier. "Mike Gordon was my father."

"So, as I said last night," and I point to each figure in the picture, "Joe Watson, Luca Alessandro, Felix Whitmore, and your father."

"Yes," Jamie says, looking closely at the picture with me.

I open the photo of Casey's list on my phone screen.

The Great Gatsby (ASE)
1944 J.W., L.A., M.G.
W. 8/8
S.,J. 10/12

"I believe this list of Casey's also includes the dates of a couple of notes he wrote to the offspring of these men," I say. "So, have you received any notes similar to this one?" I show him the note to Win.

"No," Jamie says. I look at him suspiciously. Do I believe him or not? He shakes his head. "I swear, I never got a note from Casey."

"Maybe it's because you're not listed. Look at this. Who in the world is S.J.?" I click back to the list.

"It's not S.J." He zooms in on the last line. "See. There's a comma between the *S* and the *J*. *S* is Steven, my brother, who died several years ago, and I'm the *J*."

"I didn't know you had a brother—"

"There's a lot you don't know about me," he snaps before he can stop himself. I don't respond, and the sudden anger on his face dissipates, so he continues, "Also, the date reads 10/12, and we're not there yet. So he probably hadn't written my note yet."

I take a bite of my blueberry muffin and wash it down with coffee while I process what Jamie tells me.

"So, if Casey had this picture, and you have this picture, I'm curious if Win also has a copy?"

"I have no idea. I've never discussed this with either of them."

"Why not?"

"Ronnie, I'm very private, to the extreme, in case you haven't noticed. To me, this was just a photograph of four war buddies who read *The Great Gatsby* when they had some down time during the war...anyway, that's what I remember my father telling me."

"Okay, fine. So, it appears that Casey was after Win's ASE paperback *Gatsby* and not his five-hundred-thousand-dollar first edition. And I've now seen two-thirds of this specific ASE." I take a deep breath. "Jamie?"

He opens the brown accordion folder, withdraws the final third of the little book, and pushes it across the counter toward me.

I pick it up and flip it over to see the beat-up back cover. "Does this have clues written in pencil in the margins?"

"I don't know. I never paid much attention," he says, as I flip through the pages and come to the first penciled phrase five pages in.

Loose panel

I grab a pen and pad, start back at the beginning and write the list of clues from my photos of Win's part-one-section of the book.

Liberty Head Nickel
Twenty-dollar Double Eagle
Wheat Penny
Lambert —

Then I switch to the pictures of the pages from Casey's middle section and continue writing.

—ville, NJ
LPLDM
Olivia secretary
2ⁿᵈ floor

Then I start slowly paging through the back, the third section of the book from Jamie, and add those notes.

Loose panel
Third from right, bottom row
Press button —
Jiggle drawer

"This is amazing." I look up and see Jamie staring at the photograph with his father and the other three soldiers. He looks lost in his thoughts.

Since I'm hoping for an honest answer, I use a gentle tone and ask, "Why didn't you tell me any of this when we first found the mid-section? Why didn't you tell me that you had another piece of the book?"

"I already told you, I'm obsessively private," he says. "I had just met you. I wasn't going to bore you with my life story." He takes a slow sip of coffee and looks at me with those deep, dark eyes, but they are unfathomable to me.

I shake my head in resignation.

"Look, I wasn't intentionally hiding this. I just wasn't ready to share with you all sorts of details about my life. And lately, being with you, well to be honest, this book was the last thing on my mind." He smiles at me almost shyly. "But I'm here now, and I'm talking."

"That you are." I can't help myself and smile back. I sip my coffee.

Jamie looks off as if he's revisiting the past. "My father died a long time ago, and I tossed the book in a drawer. I never figured it had any value. I can't remember the last time I even thought about any of this until it came up when you found that section the other night. And the photograph? I found it in my dad's papers some time ago. I thought it was a cool war picture that had my father in it. It's as simple as that."

I finish my muffin and coffee, and Jamie empties his mug. I put everything in the dishwasher and clean up.

"So Ronnie, are we alright?"

I take a moment to let the dogs out and think about it. Finally, I answer, "For the moment, I think we're good." As I walk back to the island, I realize I have already scratched him from my list of candidates who tried to chase me off the road last night. His hands go around my waist as we kiss slowly and gently.

The kiss ends, but he keeps me close. "I don't know if this works with your schedule, but I had already decided when I got up this morning to play hooky with the hope of spending the day with you."

"You did?"

"Yes, and it's your choice how we spend it."

"Give me a sec, and you stay here." I disengage from his embrace and walk over to a kitchen cabinet. I root around the back for a tea canister and take out a little key. Then I head for a small closet under my stairway.

Inside, I unlock a fireproof file cabinet and remove the other two pieces of the ASE Gatsby—Win's and Casey's. I come back to the island and pick up his portion of the ASE *Gatsby* and hold the three pieces together. They fit perfectly as the one book it originally was.

"After I drop my car at the shop, let's go on a treasure hunt in Lambertville!"

CHAPTER THIRTY-FOUR

"Okay, where would you like to start?" Jamie asks as he parks the car near the bridge on the Lambertville side of the Delaware River. It's taken us less than two hours to get here.

"Fortunately, the clue says Lambertville..." I answer as we get out of the car. "...or we'd have to walk over the bridge and check things out in New Hope, too." We stare across at the town on the other side in Pennsylvania.

"And that would create an even larger haystack..." he mumbles, "...you know, to find the needle in a haystack."

"Hey, it's a small town, only several thousand people, so it's not that large a haystack. Come on, humor me. We may finally get some answers, or at the very least, have fun on this treasure hunt." I look up and smile at him. "We need to be on the alert for something that can help us figure out the next clue in the book after Lambert and ville—we're looking for LPLDM or something that's similar to that."

"Casey's father couldn't have created a more

indecipherable clue." Jamie links his arm through mine.

"But we're going to figure it out," I say with determination as we start out.

We walk along Bridge Street and make our first left. We're not sure where to begin and find ourselves easily distracted by the charming shops and galleries that line the streets in this historic community.

"Even if we figure out what this means, and that's a huge if," Jamie says, "how much do you want to bet that the coins aren't there anymore, that someone else found them years ago?" He glances around. "Shouldn't we stop for a coffee and a mid-morning snack? I'm hungry."

I burst out laughing. "Wow. I don't believe it. Jamie Gordon, we just got here, and all you can think about is filling your stomach."

He embraces me for a long kiss, and it's then that I sense a vehicle driving by us very slowly and stopping sporadically. Since my back is to the road, I open my eyes during the kiss and watch the reflection in the café window while a small, dark SUV drives by. As Jamie practically waltzes me into an adorable café, the car quickly drives away, leaving me unsettled.

~~~~~

Half an hour later, we're back outside, continuing our walk. We cover the center of town, quickly moving past more shops and art galleries, antiques stores, the library, restaurants, a bed-and-breakfast, and a couple of inns.

Several times I notice a small, navy blue SUV with

dark tinted windows. It sounds like the same vehicle that passed us earlier. I can't see inside the vehicle, but I memorize the number on the rear New Jersey license plate. Maybe Will can have a buddy run the plates for him.

I don't say anything to Jamie because we're having fun, and I don't want to alarm him. He probably already thinks I have an overactive imagination about finding these coins, and I don't need to add fuel to the fire by announcing that I think someone may be following us.

Then a different thought stops me. What if that car has nothing to do with these coins? Recalling the active rumor mill surrounding Jamie, I wonder if this vehicle concerns his supposed shady business dealings. Have I fallen for a man of questionable character?

Fortunately, he interrupts my runaway thoughts. "Well, we've combed through this town, and so far we haven't come up with anything. What should we do next?"

"LPLDM. LPLDM," I repeat, more to myself than Jamie. "There are two Ls. It's probably a good guess that one of them stands for Lambertville."

Jamie looks at me and shakes his head with a smile. "I agree, probably a good guess. But what do you make of the rest of the letters?"

"I don't know. I need to think about it." I reach up and kiss him despite his possible outlaw status. "Come on. It's been at least a couple of hours since we had anything to eat," I tease. "Let's take a break." He gives me a huge grin. I think he's had enough of our treasure hunt.

~~~~~

We walk out of the train station restaurant after lunch, and Jamie heads in the direction of the car.

"Where are you going?" I ask.

"Home? Aren't we ready to leave?"

"That was just a break. Let's give it one more shot and slowly retrace our steps. This time let's pretend we're Casey's father as we look around."

"You're kidding?" There's that slight smile again. "I mean about pretending to be Casey's father?"

"No," I answer. "Try to imagine what he was thinking when he was looking for the perfect place to hide the coins."

"Okay." Jamie laughs. "Let's go." He walks briskly down the street.

"I said slooowly." I run after him. "Slowly retrace where Casey's dad might have gone."

Hearing a car behind us pick up speed, I glance back. Sure enough, it's the navy blue SUV, but it makes a fast right turn and I lose sight of it. It's spooky. I'm pretty sure no one even knows we're here.

We meander along the charming streets all over again, but come at them from the opposite direction in order to get a different view of the buildings. This time we also stop to read every sign and historical marker. It's like a local history lesson, but nothing triggers LPLDM.

We do take our eye off the ball for a moment as we hold hands like school kids enjoying each other's company and almost walk by an old nineteenth century mansion.

"Wait."

"What?"

"Come on. Let's check this out." I take his hand and backtrack. "First, I need the right angle."

"What are you talking about?"

"I think I've seen that mansion in a painting at Casey's house." I stop on what I believe to be the exact spot, pull out my phone, and find the pictures. "This is it."

"You're right. It's the same place," Jamie says, as he looks at my phone and then at the building. "That's bizarre. We walked by this one before."

"Yep, and missed it." We study the photo of the painting and agree it's the same house. I snap a couple shots of the exterior from the same angle as the painting.

We walk up the steps and stop to read the handsome dark green plaque to the right of the door.

Lambertville Public Library
Established 1932
Dunbar Mansion
Constructed 1870
Residence of Dr. John Dunbar
Prominent Lambertville Citizen

"Lambertville Public Library, Dunbar Mansion," I say. "L-P-L-D-M. It works for me, what do you think?"

Jamie looks surprised and impressed at the same time. "I agree. We're at the right place."

The sign on the door lists the days and hours of operation, and we enter a cozy, old-fashioned library with lots of nooks to settle in with a good book. I glance into a room on the right—perhaps the old dining room—and see a half dozen computer stations for patrons who wish to access the library's twenty-first century resources.

A librarian is on the phone in a small room behind the check-out desk. We pass by the wide staircase and a sign that says non-fiction is downstairs and fiction upstairs.

We go through what was once perhaps a front parlor on the left and is now a whimsical children's book room, where the furniture is scaled to these young readers. I have to smile, as I remember taking my own kids to story-time with Ms. Fairchild at our local library.

Jamie and I continue searching, and everywhere there are rows of book shelves artfully positioned to not make the spaces feel cramped. The overstuffed chairs arranged around the fireplaces in each room beckon readers to relax with whatever book they've just found in the stacks, so I sit down.

"What are you doing?" Jamie stares at me sitting in an especially large overstuffed chair.

"I want to check something." I pat the space next to me and he sits down.

I pull out the three pieces of *Gatsby* and with Jamie's help fan out the edges of book's pages. There are several marks that matchup between the three sections.

"See this?" I say to Jamie. "It's nothing like the beautiful book George Smithson showed me, but I've been thinking this is a sort of crude fore-edged drawing. It's not perfect, but doesn't it look like someone drew a rectangle with a line in the middle?"

He studies it for a moment. "Well, sure. But it's not the greatest rectangle. Look the top isn't very straight."

"Or maybe a curve on purpose?"

"What do you mean?"

"Like a piece of furniture?" I offer.

"So far, I haven't seen much furniture except for these large chairs," he points out.

"There's still more on the fiction floor." I get up and take his hand to follow. "Remember, the next clue was second floor."

We find similar rooms upstairs—each with a reading area close to an old fireplace. The difference on this floor is that a number of antique side tables, bureaus, and highboys add more richness and warmth to the rooms.

I notice that Jamie, ever the dedicated book collector, has now become distracted from our mission, no longer in such a hurry as he looks through the fiction stacks. We slow down and wander around the second floor. I walk through the right side and he heads left.

"Is anyone upstairs?" the voice that was on the phone when we first came in calls out.

"Yes," I call back and go to the top of the stairs. Jamie looks out from one of the doors. "My friend and I've been transferred to Philadelphia with our jobs, and we think we may want to live in Lambertville." Jamie raises his eyebrows, while I continue, "We've been walking around since early this morning. There's so much to see. It's such a charming community."

A woman, perhaps in her mid-seventies, comes into view downstairs. "You're right about that, and welcome to our town, by the way." She peers up at me over reading glasses that rest on the tip of her nose."Would you like to fill out the form to get a library card?"

"May we pick that up on our way out?" I ask. "We are so enjoying our break and browsing upstairs."

"Take your time," the librarian says. "I've lived in town for fifty years, so please let me know if I can answer any questions."

"Thank you," I respond.

Jamie and I arrive at the back room, where there are no shelves filled with books. This one feels more like an elegant old reading room. Magazine-filled tables sit among comfortable old chairs. Beautiful paintings hang on the walls, each with a discreet sign displaying the name of the donor and giving some background on the artist.

Almost simultaneously, we glance at the wall to the left of the fireplace, and there it stands. It's beautiful, and we can't take our eyes off of it.

CHAPTER THIRTY-FIVE

The tall desk with an attached bookcase above it gleams in the sunlight from a nearby window.

"Is this a stretch?" I ask, quickly fanning the page edges again to reveal the crude, curve-topped rectangle with a line halfway through it. "This piece roughly matches the drawing. The line through the middle could represent the top of the desk and the bottom of the bookcase. What do you think?"

Jamie looks down at the fanned pages and breaks into his wonderful laugh. "Yeah, I think you're right, Sherlock."

The light also twinkles off a number of green glass ovals inlaid in the panels surrounding the cubby holes of the desk. I quickly snap some pictures with my phone.

"Somebody has polished this secretary with tender-loving care," Jamie says as we walk over to it.

"Don't you mean desk? Olivia's the secretary," I say. "Well, she was somebody's secretary."

"I think in this case, the word secretary is being used as a piece of furniture." Jamie's eyes crinkle with interest, and

I grin back. "And where'd you come up with Olivia?"

I click through my pictures of paperback pages with the clues. "See? Olivie secretary? I figured it was a mistake, and that maybe the writer meant Olivia-comma-secretary. What do you think?"

"That makes sense, except these green ovals inlaid in the desk take me in a different direction. They could be olivine, or glass copies of—"

"Olivine?"

"Sometimes it's called peridot," Jamie says. "So I'm thinking Olivie secretary is really Olivine secretary. And whoever wrote this down left out the *n*—you know, a hand-written typo." He smiles. "It would be unusual and an easy way to describe it."

I put my hands on my hips and look at him, astonished. "How do you know all of that?"

"It's simple. I like old American desks." Jamie laughs. "So, it's something I know a little about."

"That I buy, but how do you know about olivine?"

"I'm a science geek, too." He grins. "That started in second grade."

"You were reading about rocks when you were seven? Unbelievable." My hand lightly sweeps over the doors as I admire the clean lines of the storage cabinet above the desk. "I love that you can put stuff away."

"Are you telling me that you're a clean fiend?"

"My kids never described it that way, but yes, I guess it's true," I say, laughing at myself.

"Well, to further appeal to that neatnik in you..."

Jamie lifts the writing table up to its tipped-in position, where we're surprised to see the same green stones inlaid on the underside of the writing table that now faces out. The stones glimmer in the sunlight.

"The slant-top desk could also stay shut to hide clutter." He turns the key in the lock, and the desk is now closed. "These types of secretaries combined writing space and storage."

"Well, it's a beauty." I read a small inscription on the wall next to it. "Donated in 1935 by Rebecca Dunbar, daughter of Dr. John Dunbar."

"It's nice that the family left it with the house, so that it's part of the public library."

"Where do we start?" I ask. I take a large picture book from one of the tables. It's about historic Lambertville and New Hope, and filled with photographs. I open it to the middle and put it on a coffee table in front of a sofa near the secretary.

"What are you doing?" Jamie asks.

"If someone comes up here, we need to be doing something else, like looking through this book together." I smile.

He grins and shakes his head. "Okay, read to me from your list, the part that comes after the secretary and second floor clues." He unlocks the slant top and carefully lowers it, which reveals empty pigeon holes, slots, and shelving.

"Okay." I pull out my paper. "It says loose panel…next comes third from right, bottom row, then press button, and finally jiggle drawer."

He stares at all the slots. "Third from right, bottom row sounds like a good place to begin."

Below the open storage compartments runs a row of small drawers. Jamie reaches for the little knob on the third one from the right. It opens smoothly, and we look inside the empty drawer. He jiggles it several times, but nothing happens. He pulls it, but it doesn't come out.

"I guess this is a false clue—"

"Not so fast. Have a little more faith." Jamie pulls out the drawer as far as it will go. He also opens the drawers on both sides, which come out further, and their interiors are much longer than the middle one. He removes those two drawers and tries to slide his hand inside their empty slots, but his knuckles jam up against the openings.

"Come on, you give it a try," he says.

I slide my smaller hand into the opening to the right of the original drawer.

"I can touch the back." I wiggle my fingers around. "What am I looking for?"

"Do you feel any kind of depression in the wood?"

"Nothing," I say. "It's all very smooth."

"Try the other side," he urges.

I take off my rings and slide my left hand into the opening on the other side. "There's a little dent toward the back next to this shorter drawer."

"Good. Press it. It should release a slot or spring."

I try my best with the tip of my finger and finally feel something release. "I think I got it."

The drawer pulls out further and reveals several tiny

compartments, all of them empty except for one. We peer inside. On the bottom of the drawer is what looks like a plain, old penny. I take some pictures, which could be important should I need to prove where this coin was found.

I pick it up and hold it up to the light from the window. "Let's see. It's dated 1943." I flip it around in my fingers. "Well, this penny hardly looks important." Still, I snap close-up shots of both sides of it.

"Don't be so quick to judge," Jamie says. "I don't know anything about coins, but we can do the research later. Put it some place safe."

I tuck it deep into my front right hip jeans pocket, and he laughs. "Well, that took care of third from right, bottom row. What's next?"

I look back at my notes. "Let's see. Loose panel. That was the first one."

Jamie moves around the desk examining its walls and paneling. I walk to the door and listen for any noise coming from downstairs that might tell me the librarian is busy putting books back on the shelves, talking on the phone, or coming upstairs to see what's taking us so long. It's quiet.

Jamie tilts up the writing table for a better view of the three large lower drawers in the desk. He opens them one by one and looks inside. When he gets to the bottom drawer, he stops. "This front piece looks thicker than the other two."

He uses the brass pulls to try to move the front of the

drawer slightly to the left, right, up and down, and it finally loosens. Jamie carefully jiggles it up three inches, revealing a secret drawer.

While he holds up the panel, I pull out the drawer and find a yellowed old envelope in one corner. I take some more photos with my phone and then remove it. Other than that, the little drawer is empty, so I push it in. Jamie lowers the panel while I carefully tear open the envelope.

I hold up a gold coin and Lady Liberty is on one side with a torch in one hand and a branch in the other. I turn it, and the flip side says twenty dollars above an eagle, and the date is 1933.

"The twenty-dollar Double Eagle. I think this looks more promising." I take pictures of both sides of the coin and then slip it into my jeans pocket along with the penny. "According to the book, there's one more coin to find." I stick the envelope in my purse.

"The Liberty Head nickel," Jamie answers after looking at my list.

Footsteps on the stairs startle us, and Jamie quickly closes the big drawer and lowers the slant-top writing table. We hurriedly sit on the sofa. Jamie puts the large book in his lap, and we flip through its pages.

The librarian walks into one of the other rooms with a patron. We sit quietly and can hear them talking about a specific book they're trying to find.

Finally, they retrace their steps toward the stairway. The librarian pops her head into our door. "Everything alright here?" she asks in a friendly tone. "Anything I can help you with?"

"We're learning a little more about Lambertville and New Hope." I flip to the next page in the book. "These are fabulous old photographs of the area." Jamie holds it up so the librarian can see the cover.

"Yes, it's a wonderful book. The author is local." She smiles and heads for the steps. "I'll be at the check-out desk if you need anything."

We wait until we're sure she's back downstairs and then put the book aside.

"The final search clues are press button and jiggle drawer," I say, looking nervously toward the stairs. "They may go together, because there's a dash after press button."

We study the pigeon holes, slots, and shelving area of the desk. In the middle are two wooden pilasters, one to each side of the center drawers, which are blocked from opening by those columns. A little further to the left and right are small carved circles in the different corners. They're about as large as a medium-sized button, and I press them one at a time on the left side.

The top circle near the left side pilaster pushes in, and we hear a clicking noise as the pilaster drops slightly. It's just enough for me to remove the column. Jamie repeats the same steps on the right side.

We quickly check the drawers, but they're all empty. Jamie keeps the bottom one open and uses it as leverage to slide out the entire box containing the four small drawers. Pressing all the surfaces inside the opening that held the box of drawers, he discovers a false bottom that snaps up enough to remove.

Underneath it on the right side is a miniscule drawer with a tiny pull. I jiggle it open and feel disappointed when all I see is a nickel in the drawer. Still, I grab some shots before I remove it.

As Jamie rapidly reassembles the parts of this center section of the desk, I examine the coin closely and then take close-ups with my phone. "It's from 1913, and it has the profile of a woman on one side."

"Tuck it in that pocket of yours, and let's get out of here."

"Wait." I tug on his arm. "Don't you think we should tell the librarian that we've found these coins?"

"You can do that later, once you figure out who else is after these coins and what they're worth." He nudges me toward the stairs. "Someone's been following us all day, and I think the money be why."

"You noticed that?" I ask, cringing a little. I noticed because I'm on a case, but what reason would Jamie Gordon have to look over his shoulder, unless it was something he's used to?

"Yes, I just didn't want to scare you off your case when you were so close. Besides, we can do a better job protecting these coins than that nice librarian downstairs. Let's go."

I remember the painting of this house, and Will's cautionary words. *Maybe what's in the painting is more important than the painting itself.*

This house was already a library when Casey's father hid the coins in the secretary before going off to war. But Casey didn't know any of that, which is why he needed the three parts of the book.

While he searched for the pieces of the book that would lead him to the coins, he probably looked at the painting almost every day, but had no idea that the location of the treasure was right under his nose inside that frame.

I stop to thank the librarian and politely take a library card form before Jamie can whisk me out the front door.

CHAPTER THIRTY-SIX

"I find it hard to believe that nobody ever checked out—"

"Shhh." He hurries me down the outside steps.

I throw in quickly, "...all the hiding places in that desk—"

"Don't say a word," Jamie instructs, as he marches me down the street and into a sprawling diner.

We sit side-by-side in a high-backed booth next to the window and order coffee. I spot the navy blue SUV parked further down the block. Glancing around the restaurant, I consider whether the driver is sitting in here among the many patrons. On our way to the table, I had observed a lot of people coming and going through a couple of front entrances plus a door out back.

Now my back is to the doors for the most part, which puts me at a disadvantage when someone slides into the booth behind us. Of course, it doesn't help that Jamie chooses that exact moment to lean over and kiss me. Anyway, there's a continuous flow of tables turning over to new customers. As the waitress brings our coffee, I finally give up watching for the mysterious driver.

"I feel like a thief with these coins in my pocket," I say in a stage whisper.

"There is no reason to feel that way, Ronnie. Think of yourself as a treasure hunter who's finally succeeded. Casey most likely died trying to find these coins, and there are others who want to find them, too—the first one at the top of the list would probably be the person who shot him."

"You're right."

"I like it when you're so agreeable." His fingers tenderly stroke the top of my hand, and we look into each other's eyes and smile. He picks up his coffee, and I do, too.

"So, first things first." He toasts against my mug as if we were holding wine glasses. "Congratulations on finding the coins. It's amazing, and you owe it to yourself to see this to the very end. To start with, research their value."

"Okay."

"Then decide on the right thing to do with them."

"Fine." I pull the coins from my pocket. "Let's get to work. I'll take the penny, and you start with this one."

He takes the nickel. "Let's save the gold coin for last—"

"—and research it together." I stop myself before I continue. Embarrassed, I quickly pull my mini-notepad out of my bag.

"Hey, you." His voice in my ear is quiet and warm.

"Hey." I glance up at his handsome face.

A smile plays around the corners of his mouth. "Are you always this bossy, Mrs. Lake?"

I sigh. "I'll try harder not to be so—"

"No, don't change a thing." He leans over and kisses my hair affectionately.

I connect online and dig into the available research, while Jamie does the same on his phone. After ten minutes, we pause when the waitress freshens up our coffee.

"It says here that in 1943 the U.S. Mint struck pennies out of steel, because copper was rationed for the military." I show him the website. "But the Mint made a mistake, and a few Lincoln pennies were struck from bronze."

I flip the penny over to the side that shows the stalks of wheat and give it to Jamie. "So, if it turns out that this is one of those rare 1943 bronze wheat pennies, it could be worth a lot. Some of them have sold at auction for $100,000."

"We'll have to find you a reputable coin expert to check this out." He hands the penny back to me.

I tuck it in my pocket. "Is there anything interesting about the nickel?"

"Actually, the year on this one is what's critical." He quickly reads the screen on his phone and then holds up the face side of the coin. "This appears to be a 1913 Liberty Head nickel, the same year the Mint introduced the Indian Head, or Buffalo nickel, to replace the Liberty Head."

He gives me the nickel and scrolls through a web page. "The Mint's records don't list production of any Liberty Head nickels in 1913. By 1920, word spread that there were five 1913 Liberty Head nickels owned by one collector. That collector had been a Mint employee in 1913, and may have fraudulently struck the coins and pocketed them. That's one theory anyway."

I turn the coin over and over in my hand. "There are really only five of these? That must make them pretty valuable."

"You're not kidding. It says here that a collector bought one at auction for five-million in 2007. And in 2010, another one sold at auction for more than three-point-seven-million." He scrolls down further on his phone. "And in 2013, another sold for almost three-point-two."

"Wow." I insert the nickel way deep in my jeans pocket. "If this should turn out to be one of the original five and not a fake, we're really talking seven figures? Unbelievable." I dig around in my pocket for the gold coin.

The waitress appears with menus. "More coffee? Something to eat?"

A man in a hurry passes by and thuds into her. She knocks into Jamie, who in turn bumps into me just as I pull all the coins out of my pocket.

I watch in horror—I swear it feels like slow motion—as the coins fall out of my hand and bounce on the linoleum floor. "Oh, no!" I dive under the table and slam my hand over one that's spinning. The waitress stomps her foot over another one, while I watch the third gold one roll under a heater, hit the wall, and stop.

I pick up the nickel, stuff it back in my jeans, and look at the waitress's sneaker-clad foot standing on my coin. "Thank you for stopping my lucky penny," I say from under the table, looking up at her, my voice dripping with gratitude that she can't help but get the message that there's a big tip if she moves her foot. She does move it, and I snatch up the penny.

"Jamie, please hand me my phone." I turn on its flashlight and recoil slightly. It's filthy under the heater, and the gold coin sits back in the corner beyond the dust bunnies and dead bugs. I reach up to the table, take my fork, and maneuver the double eagle coin through the mine field of grime. I fumble for a paper napkin and use it to pick up the coin.

"Disaster averted," Jamie says as he helps me climb back onto the banquette while I brush myself off. He asks, "How about a bite to eat before we hit the road?"

"Sounds perfect." I'm hungry but not famished. "Want to split a sandwich?"

Jamie says to the waitress, but looks at me. "We'll have a grilled cheese and tomato on whole wheat, two plates?" I nod. "And we'll also split a piece of that apple-crumb pie I saw on the way in. Please bring us our check, too."

She goes off with our order, and I get up to go to the restroom to thoroughly wash the coins and my hands.

When I've finished, I scan the crowd for the possible driver as I walk back through the spacious restaurant, but no one seems to fit the job description. I do notice that the booth behind us is now empty, and when I look out on the street, I see the SUV is gone.

"Did you get a look at the guy sitting behind us before he left?"

"No. Hey, are you okay?" Jamie asks as I sit down.

"I'm fine. Let's get to work on the last coin." I tap *1933 double eagle gold coin* into my phone. We skim through the articles and learn that even though almost a half-million were minted, they weren't circulated but melted down instead. From what we can tell, twenty-two of them were rescued, avoiding the melt-down, and most of the surviving coins were stolen.

"It looks like the Secret Service recovered and destroyed nine of them," Jamie says.

"That makes the few that are left pretty rare." I turn the twenty-dollar coin over in my hand.

"And that affects the price. It says here that one sold at auction a few years back for seven-and-a-half-million dollars."

"Oh my god." I jam the coin back in my pocket, as deep as I can push it down. "If these are for real, I've got maybe ten-million dollars here," I whisper. "I've got to get them out of my blue jeans and authenticated ASAP."

The waitress shows up with our food and check. Jamie gives her a generous tip, and she leaves with an appreciative smile.

CHAPTER THIRTY-SEVEN

Jamie drives me to Meadow Farm so that I can pick up the old Toyota, my usual surveillance vehicle. Frank said I could use it until my car is ready at the shop.

While I put my things in the back seat, we talk about making plans for the next day. Jamie grabs my hand as I step toward the driver's door and pulls me toward him. He sweeps me into an all-enveloping embrace, and I willingly melt into him.

"I really don't want to let you go." His dark eyes cut right through me. He lifts me up onto the hood of the car and my legs circle around his hips. He buries his face in my neck, his lips travelling softly up to my mouth. I don't even perceive the evening chill as our kiss builds from gentle to hungry and deep.

Then his mouth travels to my ear and electricity shoots through my body. Just when I expect him to say "Your place or mine," he surprises me by pulling apart.

His eyes continue to hold my gaze, and I feel as if he's coming to some kind of decision.

Then he grins and his dark eyes crinkle at the corners. "Even though every part of me wants to do the opposite, I'm sending you home. You and I…we've got lots of time to be together…" He beams his glorious smile. "All the time in the world ahead of us." He nibbles at my ear. "And going slow is tantalizing and…" He searches for another word.

"Tormenting." I laugh and softly bite his lower lip.

We kiss one last time and reluctantly part, each going our separate ways.

~~~~~

When I arrive home, I only find Warrior in his crate. There's no sign of Peachie, and I am in a panic as I search the house calling her name. Once I'm satisfied that she's nowhere inside, I head out with my German shepherd and continue the search.

"Peachie," I call out repeatedly, walking the circumference of my house. Warrior stays by my side in the low light of early evening.

Then I hear barking way, way off, in the direction of the stream. I short-cut through the woods with Warrior at heel next to me. This feels a little like a repeat of the first time I heard the little terrier barking and searched for her at the Watsons' a week-and-a-half ago, but without Warrior. "Peachie," I continue to call out.

The sound of a noise on my right makes me turn quickly, the same way I did that night of the party, right before someone knocked me out. Later, I'd felt sure I'd seen a face before everything went black but I couldn't remember who. Once again a feeling of déjà vu comes over me like it did during Aikido class with Will. This time though, I see the face and know who it is.

More barking interrupts my thoughts, and I hurry in the direction of the noise. Then I simultaneously hear and see Peach in the brush up ahead, and I hurry over. Relieved to discover her collar stuck on a broken branch, I crouch down and release her.

"Peachie!" She practically jumps into my arms, but is quickly sidetracked by the sight of Warrior, and happily licks his face as he lowers his head to sniff her.

Unnerved, I wonder how the terrier got loose in the first place. The three of us walk home, and I pause before we walk through the door. Is my house even safe? I glance around, but Warrior is calm and quiet at my side, so we go in.

I lock up and fix a cup of tea. While I wait for the water to boil, I take another look at the Casey's fake brown Birkin bag for Sally. I unzip a large inside pocket, expecting it to be empty. But I pull out an old yellowed envelope. There's nothing written on the outside and the flap is tucked in. So I open it and carefully pull out a piece of paper folded into thirds.

The kettle whistles, and I pour hot water into my cup. As the tea bag steeps, I read:

Dear Casey,   June 10, 2005

I served with your father during World War II, and I thought you might like to have this. Before you throw it away, read this letter.

Four of us from New Jersey fought together during the last years of the war. We shipped out to Italy in 1944, and then Felix got a letter from home, and Janice tells him he's going to be a father. Well, he wanted to make sure it was really his son. Bottom line is your dad had hidden away some valuable coins before the war and didn't want to give them to Janice if the kid wasn't his.

We were all supposed to meet up after the war if Felix didn't make it, and if the kid was his, we were supposed to put these three pieces of the books together, go after the coins, and sell them. He wanted each of us to keep a little for ourselves and then give the rest to Janice to raise you.

We never met up after the war was over, and Felix was the only one of us who didn't make it back. I really did try over the years to find our buddies and get the whole book to you. I even got my granddaughter out there looking. Anyhow, I think you should have my part of the book.

Maybe you can find the other two guys from our group, if they're still alive. Last I heard, they were both somewhere in New Jersey, Joe Watson and Mike Gordon.

I hope you find what is rightfully yours.

Sincerely,
Luca Alessandro

My mind reels with the idea that Casey's whole life could have been different if these men had followed through with their agreement. No wonder he took to climbing into windows to steal a beat-up book.

I reread this mind-blowing letter a half dozen times before I head upstairs for bed. I'm exhausted and need to get some sleep in order to process what all of this means.

I make my way to the bathroom. I don't even flip on the light, but turn on the water and start brushing my teeth in the half-dark.

I finally glance up and notice a paper stuck to the mirror. I flip on the light, and what I see wakes me up fast. I accidentally swallow before I remember I'm brushing and then cough up the toothpaste.

There, stuck to the mirror, is a smeared message in black ink.

Bring the coins to Sally's. No police if you want her alive.

I reflexively reach into my pocket and feel for the coins. All three are still there. I spit out the rest of the toothpaste and quickly rinse my mouth, leaving the note on the mirror.

I move through my house in shock, my adrenaline shooting through my body at both the threat to Sally and the home invasion. I leave Peachie in her crate in the kitchen and rush out, taking Warrior with me.

~~~~~

We arrive at Sally's apartment twenty minutes later. I've already texted Will with an update but I don't wait for a response. There's not a moment to spare. I want to leave my dog in the car, but Warrior's nervous, nudging at my arm and barking. It's as if he knows there's danger inside the building and doesn't want me to go alone.

"Okay, boy. I could probably use some protection." I head toward the building with my German shepherd.

I rush to catch up to a couple of people entering the building. Warrior and I slip inside right behind them.

The guys go one way, and we turn the other and head for the elevators. This time the doors open and Warrior and I step inside. A sign written with a marker taped to the mirror greets me.

Laundry Room out of order tonite.

Once we reach Sally's floor, I peek out the elevator door to an empty hallway and cautiously approach her front door. Using a hand signal, I instruct Warrior to sit to the side of the door, safely out of the way because I don't know what's on the other side.

The door is slightly ajar, and I knock. "Hello?"

Nothing. Not a sound.

Another knock. "Hello? Anybody there?" I keep my voice low.

I also stay to the side and push the door open. Nothing. So I enter slowly. The apartment looks the same as the first time Will and I came here with Sally except there's another smudged black ink message, this time stuck to the refrigerator door.

Laundry room. No police. Just coins.

Warrior and I descend the stairs quickly, trying to stay as silent as possible. I can't help but notice noise from some sort of commotion downstairs, maybe in the basement.

When we get to the first floor, I see another sign like the one in the elevator that the laundry room is out of order. I thought that handwriting looked familiar. It's similar to the one in the note stuck to the fridge in Sally's apartment, as well as the one stuck to my bathroom mirror at home.

Just then someone throws open the door to the basement, and it makes a loud, banging sound as it slams against the wall. The commotion, including voices, gets momentarily louder. Warrior emits a low growl as we hear heavy footfalls clomping up the steps.

An out-of-breath, mousy, fortyish woman jumps back in fright at the sight of Warrior for just a moment and then flies by, warning us, "There's a crazy bitch down there screaming at some girl. Like the sign says, don't do your laundry tonight."

"Call the police," I say to her back as she continues up the steps.

"Nooooo. One thing you learn here is to stay out of other people's bizness. I can get my things tomorrow."

I take a deep breath. Warrior and I slowly and silently descend to the basement.

As we get closer, I make out Katya's and Sally's voices arguing over the sounds of a vibrating washing machine and a whirling, thumping dryer. In the basement hallway, we stop near the door to the laundry room, and I signal Warrior to sit and wait.

"You just had to put yourself in the middle of this," Katya snarls.

"I don't know what you're talking about," Sally responds, obviously frightened.

I peek through the slightly open door. Sally sits at a table with her back to me, her hands tied behind her. "One minute I'm doing homework, and the next you barge into my apartment with a gun, and then haul me down here," she says. "Why?"

Katya stands over her gesturing wildly with a hand gun. "As if you don't know."

I observe the room full of washing machines and dryers. There's even an unplugged iron sitting on top of a small padded tabletop board. Thank god, there only appears to have been one tenant doing her wash, and she's probably not coming back until the morning.

I'm surprised to see a stain on the front pocket area of Katya's faded jeans. I wouldn't have been so quick to notice with anyone else, but she's always perfectly groomed and dressed.

The fury is building in Katya's voice. "Don't you pretend with me."

"I'm not pretending," Sally screams back over the sound of the machines. "I really don't know what's going on."

I also note a pen sticking out of the top of Katya's ink-stained pocket. It's probably the pen she used to write the two smudgy notes.

Katya raises her weapon as if she plans to strike Sally across the face with it, and I dash into the noisy washroom.

"Your Pelikan is leaking all over your jeans," I shout over the noise, hoping that my voice sounds calm.

She freezes, and instead of pistol-whipping Sally, looks down at the stain. "Damn pen." She pulls it out of her pocket, one end already wrapped in a black ink-stained handkerchief. "It's given me nothing but trouble."

Katya catches me inching toward her on her other side and waves the gun at me. "That's far enough, Mrs. Lake."

"Now that I'm here, you can let Sally go." I walk toward Sally, as if to do so. I want to keep Katya off-balance.

"Not so fast," she roars. Sally and I are both stunned by her ferociousness. "Nothing happens until I have the coins. And then we're going to walk out of here together, so that I can make sure you didn't bring the police."

"I didn't bring any police." Nobody said anything about a private eye, I think to myself, hoping Will got my text and that he'll arrive soon. "And I don't know about any coins." I walk toward a huge wash basin, the kind with a roller coaster of drain pipes underneath. I want Katya to focus her gun on me instead of Sally.

"Don't insult me." Katya's tone is haughty. "I was at the restaurant. I saw you drop the coins on the floor. My grandfather was always after me to find those coins, and I spent years searching for them, trying to be a good girl and make him happy." Her voice turns shrill. "And then I find out that Nonno Luca sent *my* part of the book to Casey." She waves the gun wildly, practically screaming, "After all the years I spent looking…those coins are mine."

"What coins?" Sally is bewildered.

"Oh, shut up." Katya swings her gun back to Sally.

"Hold it. Don't point that gun at her," I interject. "Leave her alone. She doesn't know anything about the coins." Pulling them out of my pocket, I display them in my hand. "You mean these?"

She surprises me with her swiftness as she lunges toward me, so I toss them down the drain in the basin. I'm counting on the curved elbow pipe beneath the sink to trap them.

Katya tries to grab the coins, but they're gone. She shrieks like a fatally wounded animal. Her howl shocks both Sally and me, and I jerk away from the sink as quickly as I can and dart over toward a line of washing machines across from Sally. I wish Katya would stop waving that gun around.

"I wouldn't turn the water on, or they'll be lost in the town sewage." I hope my tone doesn't sound glib.

Katya bellows, "You don't know what you've done!"

Her behavior becomes histrionic with dramatic weeping and arm waving straight out of a Greek tragedy. I just wish she'd put the gun down.

"All I know is those coins belonged to Casey," I insist, "and I'm pretty sure he wanted Sally to have them. Not you!"

Katya snaps out of it, and slowly points the gun toward Sally. I realize I shouldn't have said that. In desperation, I take my last shot.

"Bianca!" I cry out. Katya jolts as if she's touched a live wire. "Think about Bianca!"

And now everything feels like slow motion. The gun moves away from Sally and toward me as I dive for the iron on the tabletop ironing board. She fires at me, but I'm moving and she misses. I hear the bullet splatter the plaster on the wall behind me. Out of the corner of my eye, I see Sally tip her chair over and flatten herself as much as possible on the ground.

As Katya lunges toward me, I grab the iron in my right hand and bash it against the revolver in her left before she can aim and shoot again. She misfires and the bullet ricochets off a metal dryer. The gun flies out of her hand and lands between two dryers, but her momentum hurls her toward me. By the time she's almost on top of me, years of Aikido kick in.

I use the heel of my palm and punch upward toward Katya's chin. She's not expecting it, and my blow causes her head to snap back. The force throws her against the washing machines and she crashes to the cement floor, her head bouncing hard on it.

Katya's in a daze and moaning as I handcuff and drag her over to the wash basin. "What a lovely name." I dig out more plastic ties from my pocket to cuff her to the pipes beneath the sink. "Did you choose the name Bianca?"

"Don't you dare say her name," she snarls, pulling on the restraints like a rabid dog. "Ouch! Those are tight." She glares at me with a look that could kill. "How'd you know about her?" she hisses at me.

"I saw all the kids' books in your car that you signed to Bianca," I respond, as I check the ties. "She's your daughter, isn't she?" Katya doesn't answer. "I predict a lengthy prison sentence for you, so I don't think you'll be seeing Bianca for a long time—"

She dives toward my left arm to bite me and misses because of the restraints. I hear the clicking sound of her upper and lower teeth colliding as they bite down on nothing.

"Bitch!" she screams.

I take my right fist and sock her in the jaw as hard as I can. She grunts, her head wobbling on its neck, and then she moans and slumps down heavily.

"That's for killing Casey—"

A screeching wail cuts me off. It's Katya and the sound is feral, until she switches to grunts as she bangs her wrists against the pipes under the basin, trying to snap the ties. It doesn't work. Then just as quickly she goes quiet, as if she's resigned to her fate.

Meanwhile, Sally tries to right herself in the tipped chair, her arms tugging to free herself. I rush over to untie her wrists, and that's when I barely hear it over the washer and dryer. A whimpering sound. An *animal* whimpering.

CHAPTER THIRTY-EIGHT

"Warrior," I cry out. The whimpering turns into a feeble bark somewhere out by the elevator.

I dash into the hallway to find my dog sprawled on his side, his leg twitching in a pool of blood. His eyes are open and show fear and anxiety.

"Oh my god." At first glance, I panic that he's been mortally wounded. I get down on all fours and head toward him slowly. It looks like he's been shot in his left front leg, below his shoulder and above his elbow.

Blood pours from his the wound, and I worry that the bullet may have hit an artery. I stay low and speak quietly, using soothing tones even though my heart is pounding. "Warrior, you're such a good boy." I need to get close in order to help him.

Sally pops through the door, and at the sight of my injured German shepherd, she exclaims, "Oh no, he's hurt—"

She steps forward, and Warrior growls. My arm shoots out for her to stop. "Shhh," I caution in a gentle tone. "We both need to speak quietly."

"Where'd he come from?" Sally's voice is a whisper.

"He's my dog," I answer. "Sally, Warrior and I need your help."

"Sure. What should I do?"

"Please see if you can find any towels in that dryer that I can use to stop the bleeding, and keep a lot of distance between you and Katya while you do so. Also, please call Will Benson on my phone and tell him what's happened. Tell him I need help getting Warrior to an animal ER. Here." I toss her my phone. "Look up Will's number in my contacts. Oh, if you see it, don't go anywhere near Katya's gun. That's for the police to handle."

"Got it." She's gone.

I continue approaching Warrior, always remaining in his field of vision so that he's not surprised. I speak to him the entire time.

All this blood has me worried. I need him to relax while I try to stop the bleeding. Generally, it's not a smart idea to handle an injured dog that hasn't been muzzled. To do so is to risk being bitten. But Warrior trusts me, and I'm going to take my chances.

He continues whimpering. When I reach him, I start with an area that I'm pretty sure doesn't hurt by softly stroking his neck. As expected, there are no twinges or verbal responses indicating pain. He doesn't growl, so at the moment he's cooperating.

In the background, I hear Sally talking on the phone as she opens and shuts the one dryer, looking for towels.

I scratch between Warrior's ears. I never stop talking

to him. "You are my good boy. You are going to be fine." I stroke his good leg.

"Oh my dear, dear Warrior." His dark eyes stay locked on my face. I carefully move my hand to his wounded leg, and he tries to pull away.

Sally appears with several towels draped over her arms.

"Walk slowly toward me and stay low," I instruct.

She does so and hands me a towel that I use to carefully dab up some of the blood around the bullet entry point on his leg. As I work my way closer to the wound, pressing softly, he flinches.

Sally folds the remaining towels, which I very cautiously press against the wound to staunch the bleeding. Warrior whines repeatedly in pain, and it breaks my heart. But I am relieved that he stays docile, because many dogs become aggressive when injured.

"What can I do to help?" Sally asks.

"See if you can find something small to elevate his leg above his heart. A small box, maybe."

She returns to the laundry room while I keep pressure on the wound. In less than thirty seconds she's back with a couple of large cardboard boxes of detergents.

"Let's try that big one of *Tide*," I direct. "I'll lift his leg and you slide it under." Warrior groans as I slowly lift his limb, and Sally successfully pushes the box underneath. My precious dog is not happy, but we've got his leg elevated and that may also slow the bleeding.

It feels like an hour, but it's probably only five

minutes later when I hear an elevator descending. The doors open, and Will and two volunteers from the rescue squad enter the basement with a stretcher.

"We've been on standby, waiting for the police to clear us to go in," Will says, "but Sally called with the update so we decided to go ahead. FYI, Detective Rossi's on her way over here."

My buddy's face shows compassion and worry as he looks at Warrior, but he says to Sally, "I know you said you're alright, but Billy and Joe need to see you first before they get to Warrior." The two EMTs look surprised at Will's reference to the dog, but say nothing and go into the laundry room with Sally. Will follows them and returns two minutes later.

"They'll be right back to help Warrior once they check Sally and the suspect," he says to me in a reassuring tone. "How's he doing?"

"He's hanging in—" I try to stifle a sob, but the tears stream down my face.

"How'd this happen?"

"I'm pretty sure it's a ricochet from Katya's second shot at me."

"Where's her weapon?"

"I knocked it out of her hand with the iron, and I think it landed between two dryers. I think it's a Smith & Wesson."

There's a very long pause as he stares at me. This has to be one of the rare occasions when Will is speechless. Maybe he's trying to imagine the scene I've just described. If I weren't so upset over my dog, I could better savor the moment.

The two rescue squad members come out of the laundry room. "She's fine. No injuries," Billy says, referring to Sally.

"How about the suspect?" Will asks.

"She's fine from what we can see," Joe says, "without removing the restraints.

"This is more important," Will says, nodding at Warrior. "Can you transport this dog to the nearby animal hospital? I think it's called *24-Hr Pet ER*, something like that. It's about ten minutes from here."

"We don't normally do this kind of call." Joe hesitates. "I don't know…"

"Look guys, this is Warrior," Will says. "He's a war veteran, a bomb sniffing dog. He saved a lot of our soldiers' lives in Afghanistan."

"Say no more." Billy nods at Joe, who nods back. "As a favor to you, buddy."

I'm not sure if they're talking to Will or to Warrior. "I'll go, too…to help keep him calm. He won't need a muzzle if I come along."

The men push the stretcher alongside my dog. I talk to Warrior as they move him onto it.

As the elevator opens, Sofia Rossi dashes through the basement door with several fellow officers. She sees me about to go and yells, "Wait!"

"No offense, Detective, but I've got to leave *now* with Warrior. The hostage can fill you in. The suspect's handcuffed to the basin pipes. Oh, and don't turn on the water in that basin."

"Why?"

"I threw the coins down the drain and they're trapped there."

"The coins?"

"Yeah, keep them safe. And don't forget the Pelikan pen in Katya's jeans pocket. Take pictures. It's evidence."

"Huh?"

"It ties her to the Whitmore shooting."

"Come on, lady," Billy says, as I continue pressing the *Open* button in the elevator. I jump in.

"Hold it," Rossi calls out, reaching her arm out to keep the elevator from closing.

"Detective, let her go," Will says.

The last thing I hear as the doors close is Rossi asking, "What is it with that woman and her dog?"

~~~~~

Several hours later, I sit in an exam room, so relieved that Warrior has successfully come through the surgery to remove the bullet. He's fortunate, because there are no broken bones from the gunshot.

Will and Detective Rossi open the door to the room just as the vet tech wheels in a stretcher carrying my groggy German shepherd. I wave them in.

Warrior has a serious bandage wrapped around the wound. The enormous cone-like collar around his neck to prevent him from licking or chewing the bandage is a big part of why he looks like such a sad-sack.

"Oh, Warrior, my sweet Warrior." I sniffle and bury my face in the soft furry coat on his back.

I glance at Will and then at Rossi, who's looking down at her feet uncomfortably. She looks up at me. Before I can say anything, she jumps in. "Will told me about Warrior and your son. I lost my brother in Afghanistan, so I… I get it about your dog. I'm glad he's okay."

"Thank you. I couldn't be with my son at the end, but Warrior was. And for that I'll always be grateful. He means the world to me, and I'd do anything for him." I give him a kiss between his ears.

Will comes close and carefully rubs Warrior's head. "Hey boy, you gave us all a scare." He shifts his gaze to me. "Everything's under control back at Sally's."

"We've placed Alessandro under arrest, and Sally's filled in a lot of details," Rossi says. "Still, I'm going to need to talk to you. Why is that leaky pen so important? I got the pictures of it in her jeans and I took it into evidence, but how does it fit in?"

"I think I have the ink-stained Pelikan case that goes with it. I found it among the boulders where she took the shot that knocked Casey off the Watsons' roof. I saw her at Jamie Gordon's skeet course, and she's an expert marksman. In any case, I'm betting the Pelikan case has her prints and ties her to the scene."

Rossi defaults to her predictable expression of

annoyance at me, and I quickly add, "I have pictures, and I have the case in a safe place at home in an evidence bag."

She nods but doesn't say anything as I continue stroking Warrior's back. But it's just a moment. "Where do those coins fit in?"

"It's a long story, and I'll fill you in tomorrow at my house, since I'm on Warrior-recovery-duty all day." I nod at my dog, then remember something and say in a panic, "Will, don't let anybody turn on the wash basin in the laundry room at Sally's until you've removed—"

"I've already taken care of that," he says.

Rossi jumps in. "And they're temporarily in police custody."

"But they belonged to Casey," I say. "He wanted Sally to have them."

"I said temporarily." She shakes her head. "Do you always interrupt so much?"

We look at each other for a long moment, and then I glance at Will. "Ask him."

I carefully circle my arms around Warrior and kiss his forehead.

EPILOGUE

It's been several days since Jamie and I returned from Lambertville. The recent events have shocked the community.

Katya's fingerprints were identified on both the leaky Pelikan pen and its ink-stained holder. The police located the murder weapon, that Remington rifle, with more of her prints, hidden away in her New York apartment. They also confirmed that she used that same rifle to shoot at me when I went to Casey's house the first time.

Katya, who was teetering on the edge of a nervous breakdown, has pretty much confessed everything. Her lawyer is negotiating a deal, although she's probably going away for a very long time.

Still, her desperation was painful to witness. She grew up obsessed with finding the coins and even ended up in the book business in her quest to find the pieces of the ASE. But in this case, the stakes were high. The police are now looking for her ex-husband, believed to be hiding out in Cuba with their daughter until he gets the pay-off that Katya promised him.

Last night, Marilyn came over to my house and we shared a bottle of wine by the fireplace. She looked more relaxed than I've seen her since this mess all started. She even tried to pay me for my investigative work regarding her husband.

"No way will I accept money from you. I was officially Win's client anyway, and he's already cut a check for Will and me." I sipped my wine. "Besides, I didn't really prove that your husband was faithful or unfaithful, even though I would swear nothing was going on there. Marilyn, Win's crazy about you."

"It's still hard to trust again when you've been hurt." Marilyn drank from her glass. "Win and I did sit down for a heart-to-heart, and it turns out Katya was pressuring him with some hair-brained business scheme."

"Really?"

"Yes, really. It involved priceless first editions. Her demands and expectations had escalated to the ridiculous, and when Win saw Casey Whitmore on the ground dying, he thought Katya may have sent him. It was all part of why he had been meeting with his lawyer...he wanted guidance. Win didn't tell me about it, because he was worried about upsetting me."

"I had a feeling there was perfectly good reason."

"Oh, before I forget," Marilyn said as she pulled out her phone, "I'm texting you the name and number of a highly regarded coin expert from Win. He'll do a great job for that girl. He already took a quick preliminary look, and the coins appear to be genuine."

"That's great of you to help Sally," I said.

"Yeah, well, I think she's misguided, but basically harmless. Win and George have agreed not to press charges against her, and she's promised to not borrow any more valuable books. George even offered her a job at his warehouse, now that Alessandro's is no longer in business."

~~~~~

This morning, when I took Sally out for breakfast and told her the good news, her response wasn't what I quite expected.

"I can't take those coins," she insisted as she pushed her wild hair out of her face.

"It's not the coins, it's the money from selling the coins," I clarified. "Just think, you can finish school and go to grad school if you want."

"Casey was my friend, but he was a thief, and I can't take the money," she said, digging into her pancakes.

"Stop a minute. These coins were not stolen. They were his inheritance from his father, and now they belong to you." I drank my coffee and took a bite of toast. "That's what Casey wanted."

"But he broke into the Watsons' house. And when you think about it, I kind of broke in, too. It doesn't feel right."

"He has no police record as a thief, so we don't really know about his past. Sure, he broke into their house and slipped Marilyn's necklace into his pocket, but it never left their property, because…well, he fell off the roof and died."

Sally gave me a look and took another bite of her pancakes.

"Sure, sure…it's pushing it, I know. But in this instance we know that Casey was not the one who did anything wrong." I broke off a piece of bacon. "He never even found the coins, much less touched them. And if something happened to him, he definitely wanted you to have them. End of story."

Sally crinkled her brow. "But how did his father get the coins?"

"That we'll never know—"

"Do you think his father stole them?" She put her hand up to stop me from answering as she gathered her thoughts. "How did Casey's dad end up with three such valuable coins? Not a single one is a dud. I mean, come on, how'd he get so lucky?"

"Sally, we'll never know if they were a gift from a friend who was maybe a coin collector, or if they were simply an innocent family heirloom, or if they were ill-gotten gains from a theft. And it's unlikely we'll ever know who owned them before Casey's dad…anybody who knows the truth about those coins is long gone." I finished the piece of bacon and took another sip of coffee. "Look, the proceeds from the sale of the coins are yours. If you don't want to spend it on yourself or your education, then go out and do something else good with the money, something that benefits others."

There followed a long silence at the table, until Sally said, "Well, when you put it that way—"

"Here's an idea. How about an anonymous donation to the public library where Jamie Gordon and I found the coins, where Casey's father hid them decades ago? It's a miracle that they were there. I still can't believe it. Anyway, a library's a good place to start, and you'll come up with other ideas, too."

"That's sounds like a good donation," she agreed. "Okay, I'll think about it." She quickly twisted her hair up into a sloppy knot.

I pulled a large orange Hermès shopping bag from under the table. "Here, I found this at Casey's house, and he wanted you to have it."

Her eyes grew huge at the sight of the paper bag. She pulled on the leather handles sticking out the top and removed the handbag. "Wow, he said he was going to do this. I didn't believe him, but he did it. My very own fake Birkin bag." Sally beamed from ear to ear.

"He told you it would be a fake?"

"Of course. Who can pay full price? But these aren't cheap either." She raised it to her face and inhaled deeply, and a small tear rolled down her cheek. "I love the smell of the leather. And I love even more that Casey picked it out for me."

I waved to the waitress for a check. "I think it's time we drive to my house and have a visit with Peachie. I feel confident that Casey would want you to look after her."

Sally said nothing. Now her eyes overflowed with

tears, and she put her head down on her arms and began to cry for her lost friend Casey.

I placed my hand on her arm. "There's no hurry, but whatever you decide, please promise me that Peachie and Warrior can plan some play dates."

She rubbed her eyes and laughed.

~~~~~

It's afternoon, and I find it odd that I still haven't heard from Jamie after several days. I finally dialed moments ago to learn Jamie's cell phone has been disconnected.

This doesn't make sense. Something strange is going on, and I deserve to know what it is. I drive up to Sheffield Hall, while Warrior, his leg still bandaged, sits in the front, staring at me nervously.

And now the radio just has to play another old Gerry Rafferty song, "Right down the Line," and my heart feels ready to break.

Get a hold of yourself, Ronnie.

I climb the hill and pull over a couple of times, as two large trucks pass me coming down the winding, narrow road. One is a moving van, and my heart skips a beat. I continue driving, and it feels like it takes an eternity to get to Jamie's house.

As I exit the woods and come into the open, I see more huge vans parked around the big house. I also see crews of men carrying wrapped furniture and large boxes to the trucks. Now my heart races, as well as my breathing. I pull over as another truck approaches to exit the property.

I drive up, park, and jump out. Running up the stairs and into the huge formal foyer, I'm shocked to see it now stripped of its massive pieces of furniture, ancient tapestries, and enormous paintings. I look into several of the rooms and they, too, are bare.

"Jamie," I call out. My voice echoes off the walls. There's no answer, except the pounding of my heart.

In a panic, I run up the stairs to find several movers packing books in Jamie's small library. I move quickly to the end of the hall and throw open the doors to his vacant master bedroom.

"Jamie?" I call out again, feeling a slight tremor in my throat as I look around the emptiness of the space.

"May I help you?" The female voice startles me.

I turn and stare at a young woman in black horn-rimmed glasses, who barely looks out of college. I ask her, "Is Mr. Gordon here?"

"No."

"When will he be back?"

"Uh, never, I think," she says. The shock on my face must alarm her, because she steps back.

I try to calm myself and then ask, "Where did he go, why are they packing up his house?"

"I, I don't know," she answers. "Mr. Westerly gives me my instructions. He's Mr. Gordon's lawyer." She rummages in her tote bag and extends a business card. "I can give you his card, if you would like to speak with him."

I stand there dumbfounded in the doorway to Jamie's

bedroom. I feel like I'm in an episode of "The Twilight Zone."

The silence is deafening, and then the young woman registers a look of recognition. "Are you, by any chance, Mrs. Veronica Rutherfurd Lake?"

"Yes," I respond. "Why?"

"Please follow me." She walks past me into the bedroom to the one remaining table and chair by a window. There's a package on top of the small table. She picks up the parcel and reads, "Mrs. Veronica Rutherford Lake," and looks up at me. "Mr. Gordon left instructions to give you this." She gestures toward the chair. "Please. Take your time."

I continue to stand in the doorway, and the young woman senses something is off. She comes over to me and says in a gentle tone, "I'm Sarah, and I'll be downstairs if you need anything." She goes into the hallway and disappears.

I walk over to the table, pick up the package, and sit in the chair. Tearing off the brown paper, I uncover a book encased in bubble wrap. I carefully remove the plastic and the tissue paper to find a hardcover of *The Great Gatsby*, protected by a clear archival cover over its dust jacket.

"It can't be," I say to myself. I turn to the copyright page to confirm that it's a true first edition, and I discover a folded sheet of ivory stationary. I feel a lump in my throat as I open it.

Dear Ronnie,

If you're reading this, you're most likely sitting in my empty house, wondering what-the-hell is going on. Where to start...

Meeting you has been the best thing that has happened to me since Diana and the children died. But I need to put my house in order to be worthy of you, and I need to do it by myself where no one knows me. I'm leaving for a while and haven't decided where I will land. My lawyer, Jack Weatherly, is handling the sale of Sheffield Hall. Even if I stayed, it's too big, too many rooms, and too empty.

This first edition may not be as valuable as Win's, but it's close, because Fitzgerald wrote an inscription to his editor, Max Perkins, on the title page. I've treasured this book for many years, and I want you to have it. Think of us every time you look at it.

I don't know how long my soul-searching will take, and I do not want you to wait for *me. I want you to live life to the fullest and be open to all the good that comes your way.*

I love you.

Jamie

A tear falls on the clear cover protecting the book, and I quickly wipe it away and dab my eyes. I cover the volume loosely in the plastic and paper and put it in my bag, give the empty room one last look, and leave quickly.

I open the door to my Mustang, and my beloved Warrior sits there obediently and quietly, his brown eyes staring into mine. He gives me a low whine, he knows something's up. I get in and lean over to put the bag in the back foot well. Warrior nuzzles my neck and whines again. I bury my face in his soft, furry neck for a moment and take a few deeps breaths, tears still pricking behind my eyelids. My phone beeps with a text from Will.

How bad is it? Ice cream or wine?

I smile as his message swims in front of my eyes, I don't even need to ask how he knows. I tap out the letters on my screen.

This one's going to take wine

I'll be right over

I start the car and head down the drive, leaving Sheffield Hall behind.

ACKNOWLEDGEMENTS

Without the kindness, support and expertise of the following people, *Searching for Gatsby: A Ronnie Lake Murder Mystery* would still be a work in progress:

First, Jim Cummins, of James Cummins Bookseller, and Harry O'Mealia, collector of first edition 20th century American and English fiction, who introduced me to the world of rare book collecting. A conversation with them about books at a wedding provided the inspiration that would develop into this novel;

My fabulous editor, Mercy Pilkington, who challenges and pushes me in my growth as a writer, as well as working with me to deliver the best book I can;

Lt. Vito Abrusci (Retired), Mendham Township Police Department, New Jersey, who is my go-to resource when it comes to his invaluable input on correct law enforcement procedures in the Ronnie Lake mystery series;

Walter Sutton, senior training manager for The Seeing Eye, Inc., who continues to share his extensive knowledge of the German shepherd breed, so critical to writing the character of Warrior, Ronnie's trusted four-legged companion;

Karen De Paola, 6th Dan, SkylandsAikikai.com, consultant for Aikido and fight scenes, who helps me keep it real;

Other wonderful colleagues, friends, and family, especially Jane Balaguero, who have served as an informal focus group and have read my advance review copies for final input.

Words cannot fully express the gratitude I feel for all their help.

N.D. November 2016

A NOTE FROM THE AUTHOR

Thank you very much for taking the time to read *Searching for Gatsby: A Ronnie Murder Mystery*. If you have a moment to spare, please consider writing a short, honest review on the page or site where you bought the book. Your help in spreading the word is greatly appreciated. Reviews from readers like you make a huge difference in helping others find stories such as *Searching for Gatsby*. Thank you.

I can't even count the number of times that my work has been read and reread, but please email mc at nikidanforth5@gmail.com should you spot a typo!

To be notified of future Niki Danforth books, please sign up at http://nikidanforth.com/ for an occasional email.

If you purchased this paperback on Amazon, remember you can receive a free eBook of *Searching for Gatsby: A Ronnie Lake Murder Mystery #3*, which contains bonus material from *Stunner: A Ronnie Lake Mystery #1* and the short story *Delilah: A Ronnie Lake Cold Case #2*. Look for the **Matchbook Price** below the book description on the Amazon sales page of *Searching for Gatsby*. Put your curser over *What's this?* and click the Learn more about Kindle MatchBook link to get access to your eBook.

Thanks,
Niki Danforth

ABOUT THE AUTHOR

Niki Danforth, daughter of a Cold War covert intelligence officer, has the thriller/adventure gene in her DNA. After a career in New York television, including as a director on *Lifestyles of the Rich & Famous*, this empty-nester has recreated herself as an author of suspenseful mysteries. And like her character Ronnie Lake, she studied Japanese Aikido, earning a black belt in time for a decade birthday. Danforth lives in the New Jersey countryside with her husband and two drama-queen dogs. She's busy at work on her next book.